CHASING THE BROWN MOUNTAIN LIGHTS

BROWN MOUNTAIN LIGHTS BOOK 4

CC TILLERY

SPRING CREEK PRESS

This novel is a work of fiction. Though it contains incidental references to actual events and places, those references are merely to lend the fiction a realistic setting. All other names, places, and incidents are the products of the authors' imagination. Any resemblance to actual persons, living or dead, events or locales is entirely coincidental.

First Edition

ISBN 9780989464185

Published by **Spring Creek Press**

Cover Photography and Design 2019 by Kimberly Maxwell

Dedication

Although the writing process can be exhaustive and arduous, it is, nonetheless, an exciting journey. And as we have traveled this journey, two special men have been by our sides, hauling us and our books (as well as the various and sundry items that go along with them) around the Southeast, performing the physical labor of setting up and taking down booths at numerous festivals, presentations and events, taking over for us when we need a break, and actually selling books to those interested. So this book is dedicated with love to our husbands, Mike Hodges and Steve French. We definitely could not have done this without them.

Chapter One

August 1864 → August 2054

Hopelessly Hoping

I lay on the forest floor, my body tingling, feeling like I'd been torn apart and put back together again—poorly. Realizing I had my eyes squeezed shut, I opened them and glanced around with a sense of trepidation. How long had I been out, I wondered vaguely. It had been dark when we went into the light but now I could see the first tendrils of sunlight stealing over the forest, slowly eating away the night, casting the world around me in varying shades of gray. I spied Abbie lying next to me, her fingers digging into the ground as if afraid she would be launched into the air if she let go. Her face was turned away so I couldn't tell if she was conscious or not. Feeling too weak to stand, I sat up, looking for Josh, but he wasn't in sight. Did he go through, I wondered with a sense of panic. Oh, please, God, let him have come with us.

When I reached out and touched Abbie on the shoulder, she jumped as if an electric shock had gone through her body.

"Abbie, it's all right. It's me, Lizzie," I said, my voice shaking. I wasn't sure if it was from fright or shock.

She turned to me with a panicked look. "Did we go through the light?" she said, her tone rising with each word, as she rose to a sitting position.

I looked around, a sense of dread stealing over me. This was not the Brown Mountain I remembered, either from 1864 or 1969. Whereas before, the forest was verdant, filled with plants, trees and brush, most of it now lay bare. The trees were spindly, sickly looking, what few leaves they bore shriveled and dead or dying. Sparse areas of grass interspersed in the packed dirt, usually coated with layers of spongy leaves and pine needles, looked dead and brittle and I spied no wildflowers growing anywhere. The air, which had always seemed fresh and clear, had a strange odor to it, as if it were stale and musty with a slight taste of ... was that ash?

Oh, God, I thought to myself, remembering Pokni's warning and Amanda May's grandmother's comments. Had we gone forward, to the time of war they talked about?

I rose to my feet, turning in a full circle, and when I spied Table Rock knew we were still on the mountain. I looked at Abbie, panic crawling up my spine like a cluster of spiders. Tears sprang to my eyes as I said, "I'm so sorry, Abbie. I shouldn't have pushed you toward the light."

Her expression changed from one filled with fear to rage as she jumped to her feet. "I told you no, Lizzie," she screamed at me. "I told you I didn't want to go."

I glanced around, wanting to warn her to be quiet, there was no telling who was nearby or what they would do to us, but knew it would only be a waste of breath. Abbie was as angry as I'd ever seen her. Instead, I whispered, "I know. I'm so sorry."

She glared at me. "We got to find that light. We got to go back. Sarie and Amanda May are in danger, we got to help them."

"Yes, of course, you're right. But first, Abbie, have you seen Josh? Did he come through with us?"

She shook her head, giving me a belligerent look. "I hope he stayed behind. If'n he had any sense, he did."

Shoving my previous warning aside, I turned from her, yelling, "Josh! Are you here, Josh?"

Abbie made a disgusted sound behind me.

I reached out to touch her arm but she backed away. "I thought it was my light, I thought it was the right one until I realized the orange was wrong." Unable to stand her withering glare, I looked away. "Josh," I shouted, "can you hear me?"

"He ain't here," Abbie said, her voice bitter. "Looks like you're on your own, Lizzie." She stomped off toward the east, where the sun was just beginning to clear the mountain.

I ran to catch up with her. "Where are you going?"

"To Sarie's cabin. Maybe we didn't go too far forward or too far back. Maybe she's here, still."

I turned in a full circle, searching for Josh.

"Like I said, he ain't here," Abbie sneered. "Serves you right."

I clutched her arm. "Abbie, please forgive me. I thought I was getting us to safety, I didn't think—"

She jerked her arm out of my grasp. "No." She gave me a look I had never seen on her face before, one filled with intense loathing and fury. "You didn't. You didn't think about nobody but yourself. And now look where it's got us."

I nodded. "You're right. I was being selfish. I should have thought it through."

She ignored me as she trudged on through the forest. Well, it wouldn't be considered a forest now, I thought to myself, staring at the barren land as I hurried to catch up with her. What had happened here?

Walking beside Abbie, I occasionally called out for Josh, knowing it was ridiculous, but I couldn't help hoping he was here, somewhere. I kept stealing surreptitious looks at my friend. She rarely got mad and never stayed angry long and wasn't one to hold grudges, but what I had done was unforgiveable. I couldn't blame her if she never found it in her to absolve me for what I'd done to her.

When we stepped into the clearing where Sarie's cabin sat, Abbie and I stopped, staring ahead, then turned and smiled at one another.

"It looks the same," Abbie said.

"Maybe we didn't go too far in the future or past," I replied as we broke into a run. But growing closer, I could see vast differences. The cabin appeared much older, the logs more weathered, some covered with moss, others sporting small saplings struggling to survive. The roofline seemed to sag on one end while vines more gray than green in color grew up the side of the cabin and crawled over the front porch. But worst of all, it looked vacant, as if it hadn't been lived in for decades.

Abbie jumped onto the front porch and threw the door open. When she hesitated, I bumped into her back in my haste to go inside. "What?" I asked, peering over her shoulder. She stepped aside, her shoulders sagging with defeat.

Sarie had by no means been rich but she had a knack for decorating and had created a comfortable, homey cabin with handmade furniture and bright furnishings, cut flowers everywhere during the blooming season. This cabin smelled musty, of dead ash and mold. The windows were caked with grime, casting a frail, milky light into the room, dimming it considerably. The stone fireplace stood empty, a heavy coating of ash spilling out onto the hearth. I walked around, noting the footprint hadn't changed much since I'd seen it last other than a small bathroom now stood in the far corner and a metal sink and faucet had been added in the kitchen area surrounded by some sort of smooth stone countertop. What furniture there was appeared to be from an era much older than the 19th century, most of it having fallen into disrepair.

Abbie crossed the room and kicked at what must have been some sort of chair, made of a material I didn't recognize. The chair toppled over, crumbling into bits and pieces. She raised her head and looked at me, her eyes filled with anguish. "Sarie ain't here. We've gone too far one way or another. She's probably dead or not even born yet."

"Oh, Abbie," I said, my own eyes filling with tears. "Oh, no." I had read passages in books where agitated women pulled their hair out and never, up to that moment, thought I would do such a thing but that's exactly what I wanted to do. Scream and scream while I yanked it out strand by strand. "Oh, God."

Abbie stomped past me, into the yard. I followed her, terrified of being alone, fearful that in her anger she would simply leave me behind. She stood facing the forest, her back turned to me. I didn't know if she was thinking or crying and didn't want to interrupt, knowing how upset she was with me.

Instead, I found myself wringing my hands together, praying frantically that we would find our light soon and go back, away from this strange place. Abbie raised her head, her posture tensing.

"What is it?" I said, my voice low, as I joined her.

"Somebody's comin."

"Should we hide?"

She gave me a scathing look. I inwardly sighed, wondering if she would ever forgive me. Can you blame her if she doesn't, my inner voice whispered.

We waited for whoever was coming toward us to reveal themselves. In a few moments, a small group of people dressed in camouflage stepped out of the tree line and into the yard. They stopped when they spied us. Several had weaponry of some kind strapped to their bodies, either knives or guns, while others had what looked to be rifles slung over their shoulders. A tall man I surmised must be their leader moved in front of them, making a gesture with his hand, and they immediately stilled, watching us as he approached. When he left the shadows of the trees, I gasped. "Josh."

"It ain't him," Abbie said.

I never thought to question how Josh came to be with these people, much less what he was wearing. My only thought was getting to him, touching him, being with him. Ignoring her, I ran toward him, saying, "Josh, oh, God, I thought you got left behind. We've been looking everywhere for you."

He stopped as I plowed into him. I put my hands around his neck, my lips on his. He resisted at first but after a second or two returned the kiss and I knew instantly with a sense of shock that Abbie was right.

When I drew back from him, he held onto me. I wrenched out of his grasp, saying, "You're not Josh."

He gave me a wicked smile, drawling, "That's right, darlin, but I reckon I could be if you wanted."

I studied him for a moment. He could be Josh's twin from a distance. But up close, the differences were too great. Although his dark-green eyes were the same color as Josh's, his were hard and wary, whereas Josh's had always been warm and caring. His sandy-blond hair, also the same color, was cut shorter, in what looked to be some sort of military haircut. His face, which resembled Josh's so much, had deep grooves from his nose to the corners of his lips, and his forehead was furrowed as if he worried a lot. His tall, lean build was exactly the same, yet I had noticed when I placed my body against his that my body didn't conform to his as it did to Josh's.

I looked at Abbie, who shrugged and turned to walk away. I made to follow her but the man grabbed me back, saying to Abbie, "Hold it right there." I struggled to get out of his grasp but he was too strong for me. His fingers dug into my upper arm, and I knew I'd have a nasty bruise there later.

Abbie stopped and slowly pivoted back in his direction. I'd never seen her look so defiant as she said, "Mister, I don't reckon you got the right to tell me what to do."

This shocked me. Our Abbie, usually so passive and amiable, had turned into a spitfire, it seemed. I wildly wondered if the light had altered her personality in some way.

He smiled at her. "Oh, but I do," he said softly. As if signaled, his team raised their weapons in a menacing manner.

Abbie tilted her head at him. "You think that scares me? Shoot, you'd be doin me a favor if you shot me right here and now." She turned her eyes on me, her look scathing. "I'd rather be dead than be here."

"I'm so sorry, Abbie," I said, for what seemed the hundredth time.

The man raised his gun and put it to my head. "You may want to be dead but what about your friend here? You want her dead?"

Abbie smirked, her eyes never leaving his. "Well, Lizzie, he for sure ain't our Josh, is he?"

"No," I answered, "nowhere near." I once more tried to jerk out of his grasp but he was too strong for me. I turned frantic eyes on Abbie. "Run!" I said, kicking behind me, aiming for his knee but connecting with his shin.

He cursed as he cocked the gun, grinding it into my temple. Abbie drew up at that. "Run, Abbie," I shouted at her. "Don't worry about me."

She shook her head with a resigned look. "I may be mad at you, Lizzie, but not mad enough to risk him killin you."

The man holding me must have given another signal because two of his companions, both heavily muscled men, walked over and grabbed Abbie's arms, holding her in place. "Pat her down," he said, and I felt his own hands running over my body, checking for weapons. I jerked away, feeling violated, only to be shoved back in his direction by one of his men.

"Inside." He pushed against my arm, guiding me in the direction of the cabin. Once inside, he let go, waving his hand toward a small faux wooden table flanked by four plastic chairs in the kitchen area of the cabin. "Sit," he said.

Instead, I turned toward the door, waiting for Abbie.

When Abbie joined me, the man gave me a look, as if I were a great bother, saying, "Sit," again. The two men escorting her released her and at a signal from their leader went back outside, closing the door behind them.

I waited for Abbie's cue, expecting her to continue standing, but she walked over to a crooked wooden table near the fireplace, pulled out a matching chair and sat, giving him a belligerent look. "I ain't got no idea why you're so interested in us. We ain't done nothin but check out my sister's cabin."

Interest flared in his eyes as he looked at her. "Sister?"

"Sarie Collins. You any idea where she might be?"

"Sarie …" his voice trailed off. "You're a Collins?"

"Abbie." She tilted her head in my direction. "This here's Lizzie Baker. Our cabin's about a quarter-mile from here."

"Your cabin?" He seemed flabbergasted as he slid out a chair and settled in it. "We've been all over this mountain, hell, I've lived here all my life, and I've never seen you or her."

I leaned toward him. "What year is it?"

He gave me a bemused look. "I reckon you'd know that as well as me."

I ground my teeth, wondering how in the world I'd mistaken him for my beloved Josh. "What year is it?"

He tilted his head, watching me curiously, but didn't reply.

"Well?" I demanded, losing my patience.

He shrugged. "All right. I'll play along. It's 2054."

I gasped, looking at Abbie. "190 years."

Her eyes grew round with shock.

His own narrowed as he stared at us. "Where'd you come from?"

Feeling sick to my stomach, I said, "Not where, *when*. We came from here, 190 years in the past." I sat back, watching the expressions on his face, doubt changing to a mixture of horror warring with the thought that I might be crazy or delusional. "Actually, I came from 1969 originally but went back to 1859 and stayed there until 1864."

His eyes shifted back and forth from me to Abbie several times before he settled on me. "So you expect me to believe that you were on this mountain 190 years ago, during the Civil War?"

"Yes."

He contemplated this for a moment then shook his head with disbelief. "I've heard some wild excuses for being on the mountain but that beats them all. I'll give you credit for creativity but that won't save your butts."

I frowned at him. "From what?"

"From me. I don't know you, have never seen you. And that tells me you're up to no good here, which means you're an enemy."

"Enemy? What the heck? We don't even know you." I gestured toward Abbie. "We're time travelers, if you can understand that. We traveled through time." Saying this slowly as if he were a dullard.

Abbie leaned forward. "Listen, I wouldn't believe it either if I hadn't seen it for myself, then come through the light with her last night.

His gaze darted from Abbie to me. "So y'all are telling me you two traveled through time?"

I nodded.

He leaned back, folding his arms, and when he spoke his voice was filled with derision. "And just how did you manage to time travel, twice?"

"Ain't you heard about the lights?" Abbie said.

His eyebrows lifted. "The lights?"

"The Brown Mountain lights," I answered. "Surely you've heard the legends, people go looking for them and end up missing. Well, guess what happens to them?"

He shook his head. "I don't know what you're talking about. I've never heard of the Brown Mountain lights."

Abbie gave him her own disbelieving look. "You mean you've lived on this mountain all your life and ain't never seen the lights?"

He frowned at her. "All I've seen for most of my life are brown skies and enemies. I've never seen any lights much less heard about them. Hell, we're lucky if the sky clears enough to see the stars at night."

Abbie and I exchanged a glance. "You keep saying enemies. What enemies?" I asked.

He leaned back in his chair, studying me. "You tell me. For all I know, you're one of them."

"One of who?"

We stared at one another.

He didn't elucidate any further, saying, "Why don't you tell me who this Josh is and where he is on the mountain?"

"He's my ... someone we knew, who was going to come with us, I mean me." I glanced at Abbie. "Apparently he didn't go through the light like we did." Tears sprang to my eyes. "You've got to let us go so we can find that light and go back."

He ignored this as he said, "Or he's on the mountain somewhere doing recon for whatever group y'all are with."

"Group? We're not with a group. How many times do I have to tell you we're not your enemy? What's it going to take for you to believe us?"

"More than what you're telling me."

Abbie sighed. "We ain't got no reason to lie to you but you can believe this. We want out of this time and we can't do that lessen you let us go so we can find that light."

"That's not going to happen until I know you're who you say you are, and I got to tell you, you being time travelers is not something I'm inclined to believe."

Seeing this was going nowhere, I said, "Do you see any weapons on us? Do we look like we're on a recon mission to you or like we're from another time? Look at the way we're dressed, for Pete's sake."

He tilted his head, staring at our clothes, tattered pants that had belonged to a miner on the mountain who died of lung cancer, homemade flannel shirts and old boots, all obviously from another century.

I gestured at his camouflaged clothing. "I would think anyone on a recon mission would be wearing something similar to what you're wearing, along with some kind of weapon which we don't have."

I could see that, although he didn't believe me, he obviously agreed with my claim that we didn't look like the average enemy he encountered, whoever they may be. "That doesn't necessarily mean anything."

"Oh but I think it does." I leaned toward him. "Listen, for now, accept our story or don't accept it, but could you just explain to us what's happened to Brown Mountain? When we left last night, the forest was green and full of life, and we came through to this, dirty skies and dead vegetation. This isn't the Brown Mountain we left."

He drummed his fingers on the table before answering. "So you're telling me you don't know what's happened?"

"All I know is this is not the Brown Mountain we left. I told you that."

He thought for a long moment as he eyed us skeptically. "Okay, assuming you're telling the truth, which I'm disinclined to, this country is not the America you claim to be from. It's engaged in a war within itself, has been for well over 20 years now because of—"

"Wait, what? A war within itself? Like the Civil War?"

"Sort of. A war of factions, I call it. Between people, communities."

My mind turned to the 1960s, that time of great turmoil and revolt. "You mean like a race war?"

"No race to it."

"Over what, then?"

"Water, for one."

"Water?"

"It's a precious commodity now."

Abbie and I looked at one another. "But how did that come to be?" I asked, turning to him.

"Pollution, global warming were the start. Then the perfect storm happened when a small asteroid hit the Midwest, wiping out most of it. The fallout put an end to clean air and clean water save for underground springs and water in inaccessible areas, like mountains." He gestured toward the door. "Like here. We have to fight to keep our water from falling into the hands of people who would kill us or run us off the mountain then take it for themselves or sell it at high prices."

"We? You and who else?" I asked, curiosity overriding my horror.

"People who live on the mountain." He glanced out the window. "It's getting better, America is slowly coming back. It's not as bad as it was but we've got a long ways to go."

I turned to Abbie. "Abbie, Amanda May told me her grandmother was a time traveler who had come from over 200 years in the future. She said there was a war on when she went into the light, but if I remember right, she said something about America being invaded by another country." I looked at him. "Has that happened?"

"No, not that I know of. Of course, with the internet down, we don't know what's going on outside this mountain other than what we hear from people we meet occasionally who aren't trying to kill us for our water." He gave me a suspicious look.

I wondered briefly what he meant by internet but didn't ask as he continued, with a shrug. "Wouldn't surprise me if it does happen, though. We're in a weakened state, there's no doubt about that, but I would say due to our size and lack of sustainability, it wouldn't be worth the effort." He glanced out the window again. "I mean, who would want this? No clean water, low food supplies, millions of starving, dying people ..."

Abbie and I exchanged glances and I knew her look of dread mirrored my own. Maybe America hadn't been invaded now but it would be in the near future. What had I gotten us into? I wondered wildly, watching as she rose to her feet.

"Don't see no way we can help you out, so I think we best be on our way."

"I don't think so," he said, his voice hard and full of command.

I pushed my chair back and joined Abbie. "I don't see why you want to keep us, Mr. ..." I gave him a look. "I don't think you ever told us your name."

"Hampton. Jonah Hampton."

Feeling faint, I put my hand on the chair. "Hampton?"

He nodded, watching me with curiosity. I looked at Abbie.

"Just 'cause he's got the same last name don't mean nothin," she said.

"Since you think I resemble this Josh so much, I am thinking he must be an ancestor of mine." His eyes narrowed. "That is, if you're actually from almost 200 years in the past."

I sat down abruptly. If so, that meant Josh had married, had children. Had never followed me but instead had remained on this mountain in his own time. I swiped at the tears gathering in my eyes, glancing at Abbie who was watching me with concern.

She leaned close, whispering, "It don't matter, Lizzie. If we can get back, we can change that."

I stood up, taking her hand. "Let's go."

Jonah shoved his chair back as he rose. "You're not going anywhere. Not until we have some sort of proof you're who you say you are and not raiders here on a recon mission."

"Raiders?" I cried, gesturing at our clothing. "Like I said before, does this look like what people wear in this century? Do we look like we came from this century?"

His gaze roamed over my body, making me feel violated. When our eyes met, his were wary, filled with distrust. "Seems I remember reading that women of the 19th century wore long skirts, not pants."

"Well if we'd come from one of the plantations, I assure you we'd be dressed like a couple of Southern Belles, hoops and all," I said, my voice acerbic. "But we live ... lived on the mountain, our life was rougher, more primitive. Wearing pants was easier."

He shrugged as if it didn't matter one way or the other to him. "You could have dressed this way deliberately to throw us off. There's no way I'm going to release you until I know who you are, so you'll be coming with me until I decide what to do with you."

"Like hell." Still holding Abbie's hand, I made for the door. When we stepped onto the porch, the two sentries were there, waiting. Each grabbed us before we could take another step.

"Tie em up," Jonah said, behind us.

I struggled with my captor but he was too strong for me. He grabbed my arms and yanked them behind my back, holding them there while Jonah bound my wrists with some sort of smooth plastic tie which made a zipping sound as he tightened it. I watched as they did the same to Abbie, frustration pawing away at my brain like a dog with a bone.

My guard roughly pushed me off the porch and into the middle of the group waiting for us. I kicked at his feet, which caused me to lose my balance and fall to the ground.

Jonah yanked me up. "It won't do you any good to fight. There's no way you can get away from us. We're not going to hurt you unless you force us."

"Then why do you feel the need to tie us up?" I yelled at him, jerking out of his grasp. "We haven't done anything, we aren't of any importance to you or them. You don't have the right to do this to us."

"Shut up," Abbie said, her voice low.

I looked at her, stunned. She'd never talked to me like that.

"Won't do no good, Lizzie," she hissed. "He's gonna do what he's gonna do and all we can do is wait him out."

I glared at Jonah, saying, almost in a whisper, "I pray we go back and find Josh, because if we do, he won't marry whomever he did to produce the likes of you, and that means you won't exist. You'll just vanish, poof, into thin air." I opened my eyes wide.

His own flared with alarm for a moment before his face hardened. He pushed past me and walked away, into the forest.

Chapter Two

August 2054

It's a Boy

We traveled for an hour at least before he called a halt to rest. The day was hot and humid and sweat poured down my face, rippling down my sides and spine and between my breasts. Without the use of my hands to blot my face, I was forced to use my shoulders, which was inadequate. Abbie and I sat on the ground next to each other, under a large, dying pine tree, watching as the group took sips from canteens, wiped perspiration off their faces, and conversed with one another in low voices, occasionally giving us curious, sometimes hostile glances. Jonah eventually came over and offered us a large water bottle. I glared at him, lifting my shoulders up, as if to say, how do you expect us to drink without hands? With a sigh, he drew out a lethal-looking knife and cut the ties binding our hands behind our backs, then re-secured them in front with fresh ones.

"What happened to handcuffs?" I asked sardonically. He glared at me as he handed me the bottle but didn't respond. After we drank, he took back the bottle and walked a short distance away, where he sat on a rock, watching us.

I wiped my face with the tail of my shirt, then leaned close to Abbie and whispered, "Can you see anything about what's going to happen to us?"

She gave me a wary look. "I done told you a hundred times, if I'm too close to the person, I don't see it."

"What about them?" I nodded in the direction of our captors.

Abbie studied them for a long moment. She finally shook her head. "It's right strange. I can't see nothin at all."

"Do you think the light affected your ability?"

She shook her head. "Don't rightly know. I guess time will tell."

"Do you think our cabin is still here?"

She shrugged as she gave me a questioning look.

"Do you know where we are on the mountain?"

Abbie looked around. "Ever'thing's so different, Lizzie. I can't really tell. We been climbin, I know that, but I ain't seen any cabins I recognize. If I was to gander a guess, I'd say we're gettin close to where them Waverly bothers lived, the ones what ..." When she hesitated, I nodded my head.

"I remember them, redheads the both of them, and idiots to boot." I tried not to let my mind dwell on what Brett and his Home Guard had done to those two boys, telling myself, as I always did, they deserved it for standing by while their leader raped our friend Connie. I looked around, trying to find something familiar that would tell me where we were. I knew the vicinity where the Waverlys had lived but had never been there, although I had traipsed over most of this mountain during my five years here.

Abbie leaned against me, whispering, "Why do you want to know about our cabin?"

"Because when we escape, I figured we'd go there. There's a cave between our cabin and Pokni's place, remember?"

She nodded.

"We can hide there till we figure out how to get back."

Her face clouded and I could see the anger returning.

"I'll make it up to you," I said as our sentries approached, each grabbing an elbow and helping us to our feet. "I'll get you back, I swear it on my life."

We walked for another hour or so in a zigzag pattern, which I assumed was Jonah's way of making sure we weren't being followed. And since he viewed us as enemies, I was quite certain he didn't want us to know the way to wherever he was taking us. I came close to telling him not to bother, Abbie knew exactly where we were, but chose to remain silent. Near the top of the mountain, he led us to an encampment consisting of tents of varying colors and sizes scattered over the ground, centered around a huge fire pit. Above, some sort of camouflage webbing had been draped over the clearing, stretching from tree to tree. At the edge of the forest, a tall, weird-looking windmill stood next to a large two-story cabin that appeared to be several hundred years old.

"Is that the Waverlys' cabin?" I whispered to Abbie.

She studied it for a moment. "Kinda looks like it but I don't remember it bein but one story. I reckon somebody's added on to it."

Jonah gestured for us to follow as he strode to the cabin and walked up the wide front steps. He opened then held the wooden front door, waiting for us to precede him inside. Without a word, the two sentries escorting us turned around and stepped off the porch once we passed through the doorway. The interior was dim but light enough to see the cabin consisted of a roomy main room with a bathroom and large kitchen shooting off it on the far side and stairs leading up to the second floor against the opposite wall. A young woman dressed in a pale-yellow sundress sat in what looked to be a very old recliner near a large picture window overlooking the forest, her hands resting on top of her very swollen belly. Her eyes lit when she turned her head and spied Jonah.

He leaned down and kissed her on the forehead. "How are you feeling?" he said in a kind tone, reminding me of Josh's voice. Tears filled my eyes and I brushed them away with the back of my hand.

"Like I'm gonna burst open any minute now," she said, with a wry smile. She looked around him at Abbie and me and her eyebrows went up. She turned a questioning gaze on Jonah.

"We found em down the mountain. Don't know who they are or what they're doing here, although they claim they're from almost 200 years in the past and got here through what they call the Brown Mountain lights."

Her eyes widened as she stared at us. "Did you come through the lights?" she asked in a quiet voice.

"Yes'm, we did," Abbie said, stepping forward.

Jonah ignored Abbie as he asked Andrea, "You know about the lights?"

She smiled at him. "You'd be amazed what you can learn from reading."

"Fat lot of good it'll do me," he said in a grudging tone. "Besides, I don't have time for it and you know I don't believe in any of that nonsense. That's for scaring kids into behaving themselves." He strode over to a large, rectangular table near the door, placed his rifle on top and began removing belts containing ammunition he wore around his shoulder.

The young woman shook her head at him in a dismissive gesture, her attention diverted when Abbie reached out as if to put her hands on the woman's belly then hesitated. "When are you due?"

She rubbed her bulge affectionately. "Could be any day now, according to my very rudimentary calculation."

Abbie ran her hands down the length of her extended belly, lightly touching with her fingers. The woman didn't seem to be bothered by Abbie's touch, but when Jonah noticed, he grabbed Abbie back, saying, "What the hell do you think you're doing?"

Abbie jerked out of his grasp. "I'm checkin the position of the baby, and don't you ever touch me like that again."

He stepped back, exchanging a look with the young woman.

"Are you a doctor?" she asked, her voice filled with hope.

Abbie shook her head. "I'm a healer and a Bloodstopper." She tilted her head at me. "Lizzie's a doctor."

Jonah and the young woman stared at me, identical hopeful expressions on their faces.

"Can you help her?" Jonah said, his voice cracking, the hardness gone from his tone.

"I won't know until we examine her," I answered in a sarcastic tone, raising my bound hands in front of me. "And I can't do that tied up like a damn pig."

The young woman gave Jonah an angry look. "What the hell, Jonah?"

He shrugged with a sheepish expression. "They could be raiders, Andrea. I didn't want to take a chance."

Abbie snorted. "We was only tryin to get back to where we came from, mister, weren't no need for you to tie us up and drag us with you. You could have just let us be and we might be back home by now."

"I'm glad now I didn't," he said, his gaze darting to me. He approached me, pulling out the knife he wore clasped to his belt. Without saying anything, he sawed through my ties then stepped away to free Abbie. I immediately went to the young woman. When she smiled at me, I hesitated, finding her similarity to Sarie startling when she did. She had the same blond hair, although her eyes weren't blue but brown, and her face wasn't as narrow, but when she smiled, she could have been Sarie's twin. I glanced at Abbie, noting the expression on her face. She saw it too.

"My name's Andrea Hampton," the young woman said, holding out her hand. "And you're Lizzie?"

"Yes, Lizzie Baker." I nodded toward Abbie. "This is Abbie Collins."

"Right nice to meet you," Abbie said.

I knelt by Andrea. "May I?" I said, before putting my hands on her belly.

"Please do."

As I ran my hands over her abdomen, feeling for the position of the baby, she said, "I'm sorry Jonah treated you so poorly but I am glad he brought you with him. We don't have a doctor, not even a nurse or medic here, and I've been terrified of giving birth on my own." She gestured at a tattered book on the table by the recliner. "I've been reading up on what to do but it's all so overwhelming and the book is so old."

I smiled at her. "You needn't worry. Abbie's sister Maggie's the best midwife I've ever known and Abbie's learned a lot from her. You're in good hands with her."

I looked at Abbie, who was watching me. She raised her eyebrows slightly. I nodded surreptitiously before turning back to Andrea. "You're close. Looks like the baby's dropped, so it won't be long before you go into labor."

She leaned back against the chair, her face pale. "I'm terrified," she whispered.

Abbie patted her hand. "Long as we're here, we'll take right good care of you, Andrea, don't you worry."

"Wait," I said.

Abbie and Andrea looked at me. I turned to Jonah. "If you want us to help her, we'll examine her, make sure everything's as it should be, and give y'all instructions on what to do when the time comes. In return, I demand our freedom and no later than tonight. We need to find that light and get back to where we came from. Sarie, Abbie's sister, is in danger and needs us."

"Oh, I'm so sorry," Andrea said. "If you need to leave now, go, please, I don't want to make things worse for anyone."

"No," Jonah said, his voice harsh. "They help you first, then they can go."

I turned to Abbie, hoping she'd back me up. I wanted desperately to get out of there, find the light, and go back to Josh.

"She needs us, Lizzie," she said.

"After the baby's born," Jonah said, "no sooner."

I looked at Abbie.

She sighed. "It's only right. As you always tell me, Lizzie, it's our duty."

Nodding with reluctance, I rose to my feet and approached Jonah, holding out my hand. "Deal."

He shook it, obviously irritated at the bargain he'd made. "Deal." Someone knocked on the door and he answered it, speaking in low volumes to whoever was outside, then opened it wider for a young woman wearing camouflage and carrying a rifle to step through. After closing the door, he looked at Andrea.

As if reading his thoughts, she said, "I'll be fine, Jonah. I trust them."

He nodded. "I need to check on something, I'll be back soon." He glared at me. "We don't have weapons in the house so no use trying to find any. Andrea has a way to alert us if anything goes wrong. If so ..." he pointed his finger at the young woman "... she'll be right outside the door, guarding this place. You try anything, she has my permission to shoot you." He gestured at Andrea, saying, "Take care of her," before leaving, the young woman following in his wake.

I joined Abbie who was patting Andrea's hand in a reassuring manner.

Andrea shifted her weight, obviously uncomfortable. "Don't let him get to you," she said, "he gets edgy at times. It's only because he has so much on him." She waved at her stomach. "And with me pregnant ..."

"I reckon he's worried like all expectant fathers," I said.

She smiled, shaking her head. "Jonah's not my husband. He's my brother."

"Where's your husband?" Abbie asked.

Andrea's smile faded as tears filled her eyes. "He died. We were raided and he got shot. We don't have a doctor. We couldn't help him."

"I'm sorry," I said.

Abbie rose to her feet. "We're here now, we'll help you."

Telling myself I needed to distract Andrea, knowing that wasn't true, and trying not to show how much it meant to me, I said, "Do you have anything showing your ancestors, like a family Bible or genealogical chart?"

She gave me a curious look. "We do have a family Bible. Not sure where it's at now. Last time I saw it, it was in that bookcase over there. Is there a reason you want to know?"

"It's just, Jonah looks so much like a man I used to know and you favor Abbie's sister Sarie considerably."

Andrea turned her gaze on Abbie. "Your last name's Collins?"

Abbie nodded.

"I do know one of our ancestors married a Collins a long time back."

My eyes met Abbie's. No, I thought, it couldn't be. But what could be more telling than the resemblance Jonah and Andrea had to Josh and Sarie?

Abbie shook her head, giving me a warning look. "I reckon a cup of tea would do us all some good. Do you have tea, Andrea?"

Andrea tilted her head toward the kitchen. "It's old but still tastes pretty good. It's in the cupboard." She moved to get up. "I'll make some."

"No, no, you stay there," I said. "We'll get it."

I followed Abbie into the kitchen. Stealing a glance at Andrea, sitting back in the recliner, her eyes closed, I whispered, "Do you think there's a chance, Abbie?"

She gave me a questioning look, although I was fairly certain she knew what I meant.

"She resembles Sarie a lot and he looks like Josh. That could only mean one thing."

Abbie shook her head, but her eyes told the truth. "Could be someone else, Lizzie."

"That's impossible and you know it," I practically spat at her. "Sarie told me y'all were the last of the Collins. You have no brothers and Maggie's married already. That only leaves Sarie. And all you have to do is look at the two of them to know who she married."

She considered it for a moment, and when her gaze met mine, I knew she thought the same thing. "I reckon it's possible. Don't see how, not with the way Sarie feels about men and the way Josh loves you but ..." She glanced toward the living room then back to me. "I'm sorry, Lizzie."

I grasped the edge of the counter, feeling sick to my stomach. Why hadn't he come after me, I wondered. What had happened to make him stay?

Abbie put her hand on my arm. "There's a reason, Lizzie, we just don't know why yet. But we will. We'll go back and—"

"But if we do, we could possibly kill them," I hissed at her, waving my hand in the general direction of the living room.

Abbie shook her head. "Let's not worry about that now. We got other things to think about." She glanced toward Andrea. "It won't be long and she looks awful small."

"I know. But the sooner she has the baby, the sooner we can leave this miserable place and find our light."

Abbie shrugged. "I guess we'll just do what we have to and hope for the best." She began rummaging in the cupboard for the tea. I watched her for a long moment then with a sigh of resignation began to search for mugs.

Abbie was fascinated by the gas stove when I set the kettle on to boil. She glanced at the ceiling fan slowly revolving in the living room. "Is this that 'lectricity you told me about, Lizzie?"

I nodded as I turned on the water faucet. When it grew warm, I grabbed Abbie's hand and placed it under the water. "Feel that?"

She gasped with surprise. "It's so warm."

I nodded. "I'm surprised they have it, but yes, this is electricity. Wait until you take a hot shower, Abbie. You'll love it."

"I reckon I do already." She smiled at me for the first time.

As we drank our tea, I could hear the soft purr of a generator through the outer walls of the cabin and asked Andrea if this was how the cabin came to have electricity.

She nodded. "After the asteroid strike, all the power grids went down so we had to resort to a more primitive method. Thank goodness we've been able to find enough hemp oil to power the generators on the mountain."

"Hemp oil? Not gasoline?"

She waved a hand in the air. "Fossil fuels haven't been used for years, not since drilling and fracking, along with global warming, caused so much damage to the earth. There's an abundance of hemp oil since so many have died and so many communities have been abandoned, so for now we aren't too worried about it." She shrugged. "Of course, we supplement with power from wind turbines if it's windy enough and solar panels on days there's enough sunlight." When my stomach growled, she smiled at me, then Abbie. "Y'all must be starving. Let's have lunch."

Even though I wanted desperately to go back for Josh, I couldn't help but enjoy the comforts of this time. With Andrea's help, we made grilled cheese sandwiches and tomato soup for lunch, which tasted better to me than anything I'd ever had. I took a hot shower using soft soap and a scented shampoo, taking time to shave my legs and under my arms. For the first time since I went through the lights to the 19th century, where baths were quick dips in a freezing creek or whore's baths performed with a pitcher and ewer, I felt completely fresh and clean. I smiled when Abbie emerged from the shower sighing with pleasure. Andrea brought up laundered clothes from the basement, where she said Jonah stored those he found while scavenging. I ran my hands over the soft cotton sweater and drawstring pants I pulled on, thinking they were so much more comfortable than clothes of the 1800s. Although the jeans she found for Abbie were too long, she made do by rolling up the legs, commenting on how they didn't feel as stiff and coarse as the ones we had altered for our own use. Andrea found shoes made out of a material I didn't recognize, but they were soft and comfortable, much more so than the old leather boots I'd worn back in the 1800s. She also provided Abbie and me with new toothbrushes and a tube of toothpaste, and after I showed Abbie how to use them, we both agreed toothbrushes were a necessity to be taken back through the lights with us. On the mountain, all we had were feathery twigs which I felt were never good enough at cleaning teeth, tooth decay being a constant worry.

Although the cabin wasn't air-conditioned, it stood in the shadows of the trees at the edge of the forest, so ceiling fans in every room kept it comfortable enough. As the afternoon wore on, I enjoyed myself by showing Abbie how lights turned on and off, how to work the stove and oven, turn on the hot and cold water. She seemed to lose her anger at me as we both marveled at these luxuries, while Andrea watched us with a smile on her face.

Andrea told us about the camp in bits and spurts. "We have close to a hundred people on the mountain," she said. "Some choose to live here near us, in tents during warm weather or while they're on sentry duty. Others are scattered all over the mountain in cabins and houses." She gestured around her. "Jonah and Zachary and I stay here. This cabin's been in our family for over a hundred years now."

"Zachary?" I asked.

"He's our little brother. He's doing sentry duty on the mountain. You'll meet him later today."

Abbie looked around the cabin. "I reckon when we were here, this place belonged to the Waverly family though it wasn't near as pretty."

Andrea perked up. "I've always loved history. Tell me about our house and the time you came from."

And so we talked about our lives on Brown Mountain until it grew dark. I got up and turned on a lamp by the couch, frowning when Jonah walked through the door shortly afterward, the angles of his face hardened by anger. "Turn off the light," he hissed.

I did so without hesitation, giving him a questioning look.

"Raiders have been spotted on the mountain," he said to Andrea. "You know what to do. I've got guards posted outside, they'll make sure they don't get in here if they get this far." Glaring at me as if he felt I was responsible for their presence, he pointed his finger at me then Abbie. "If you two brought them here, you'll pay the price."

"We didn't," I said, "I told you who we are."

"Don't even think about leaving, because if you do, I'll track you down." He picked up the ammunition belts he had placed on the table beside the door, turned on his heel and went back outside.

Andrea rose to her feet, a panicked look on her face. "Follow me," she said, walking in an unsteady gait, due more to her size, I thought, than alarm, toward the kitchen. Abbie and I watched as she opened the pantry door, slid aside the back panel and gestured us to precede her down a flight of stairs.

Abbie went first and I followed close behind. When we were halfway down the stairs, Andrea closed the pantry door, slid the panel into place and we were swallowed by darkness. I stopped, waiting, afraid to go forward, afraid of stumbling. When a light flickered on, I glanced behind me at Andrea, bending over and holding her stomach, her face bright red. I ran up to her. "What's wrong?"

"I think it's just a cramp," she gasped.

I put my arm around her, waiting for it to pass. When she straightened, I noted sweat beading on her forehead and upper lip. "We need to get you downstairs quick."

Abbie stood at the bottom, waiting on us. After taking one look at Andrea, she immediately took her arm and guided her to a cot in the far corner of the room. I glanced around as I followed them, thinking this was obviously their hidey-hole. The room smelled musty and little-used. The walls looked to be concrete blocks. There were no windows at all, the only light coming from those overhead that looked to be recessed into the ceiling, which I surmised must have come on when Andrea flicked the switch above. Four cots were lined up against one wall, each with a pillow and blanket piled neatly on top. Boxes of what appeared to be packaged and canned goods had been tidily stacked against another wall, with plastic bottles of water lined up in front of them.

"Does this happen often?" I asked Andrea, joining them as Abbie eased her down on the cot.

She lay back with a groan. "We get raiders every once in awhile, not often. It seems to come in spurts when it happens. But don't worry. It'll be all right. Jonah's got traps set, soldiers at strategic points all over the mountain. They'll stop them before they get too far."

"Traps?"

Andrea nodded.

I looked at Abbie. "What kind of traps?"

"Bear." She grimaced. "You may not think it, but it's lucky he found you. You might have stepped on one if he hadn't. It causes a lot of damage, can cripple someone, even kill them."

I stepped back, shocked. "All this over water?"

Andrea's eyes met mine. "It's a different world we live in now, Lizzie. It's all about the water." She hesitated, looking like she wanted to say more but didn't.

"What?" I asked.

With a shrug, she continued. "We have to protect what's ours. If we don't, they'll kill us or drive us off this mountain and take it. We'll end up homeless, wandering around, trying to survive in a world that's not survivable." She paused again, pondering something for a long moment.

I glanced at Abbie and could tell she was thinking what I was, that Andrea was keeping something from us. "You need to tell us," I said.

She finally nodded. "I guess it's only fair. Sometimes that's not the only thing they're after."

"What else?" Abbie seemed as alarmed as I was. I couldn't imagine what could be just as important to anyone as water or food.

Andrea gave us a contrite look. "Sometimes they're looking for women."

"Women?"

She nodded. "The condition of the air, the lack of food and water, millions of people have died. Some groups actively look for women for …" I watched her face redden. She grabbed my hand. "I'm so sorry, I should have insisted Jonah let y'all leave when you wanted. I didn't think this would happen. I thought you'd be long gone before we got raided again."

"They want women for what purpose?" I asked, my voice hard.

"Breeding, for one. I guess you can imagine any other reason they'd want women."

Abbie gasped. I sat down, overcome with panic, thinking, what had I done? Amanda May and Pokni had warned me, but in my selfish need to return to my life, I had only put mine and Abbie's lives in more danger.

Abbie's light kick to my shin brought me out of my self-pity. I knelt on the cot beside Andrea, watching her face contort as she bit her lip hard to keep from crying out. "Is she in labor?"

Abbie nodded. "I reckon so. Her belly's harder than a pile of rocks." My eyes locked with hers. I knew mine were filled with panic but Abbie seemed calm, in control, and didn't looked to be bothered by the fact that if these raiders came into the house and discovered us, we could be in serious trouble. When the contraction passed, she said, "How many weeks along are you, you reckon?"

Andrea panted, "I don't know exactly. I could be anywhere from 32 to 36 weeks."

Abbie looked at me. This time, I could see concern in her gaze.

"Stress can bring labor on," I said.

As if in answer to that, Andrea's eyes went wide and she looked down. "I just wet myself."

"Your water broke, most likely," Abbie said, matter-of-factly.

Tears filled Andrea's eyes and she looked on the verge of panic. "I can't have this baby, not now."

Abbie gave her a consoling pat on the arm. "I don't reckon you got any say in it, Andrea. If that baby's ready to be born, we can't stop it."

"Are you sure you've counted correctly?" I asked, wondering how in the world we could take care of a premature baby. The lungs were the last organs to fully develop, and if the baby had breathing problems, we would be helpless in treating it.

"I don't know. I was never regular before so mostly guessed." She grabbed Abbie's hand. "Is it going to hurt very much?"

"I reckon I've yet to see a birth that didn't."

I flinched when Abbie said that. What in heck had happened to the sweet, always positive young woman who had stepped into the light with me, I wondered.

When Andrea spoke, I turned back to her, noting her face was now quite pale. "Oh, God, I'll probably get us killed," she moaned.

"We'll just find you something to bite down on," Abbie said, glancing around the room. I watched her as she got up and began to search.

When Andrea groaned, I placed my hands on her abdomen, calling over my shoulder, "Look for something made out of leather."

Abbie joined me after a bit, a moldy-looking belt in her hand. "Can you wash that off?" I asked. "There's water over there."

Once the belt was clean, Abbie handed it to Andrea, who tensed when Abbie put her hands on her abdomen. "You been timing the contractions?"

I nodded. "About five minutes apart. I need to see if she's dilated."

We maneuvered Andrea into position so I could check her. "She's close. All we can do now is wait."

Abbie and I sat on each side of the cot listening for sounds on the floor above between offering consoling words to Andrea with each contraction and encouraging her to breathe while holding her hand and wiping perspiration off her face. Even though she put the leather belt in her mouth, biting down on it hard, she made enough noise I feared if anyone came into the house, they would hear and come investigate. Although I didn't know if Jonah and his soldiers were nearby, I sensed real fear from Andrea, which transmitted to me. I felt alert, on edge, every unknown sound startling, sending pricks of alarm up my spine. I glanced at Abbie from time to time, noting her composure. How did she do that? I wondered for not the first time.

I vaguely listened to Abbie asking Andrea about possible names for the baby while constantly assuring her all would be well. I wanted to scream at her, "It's not," but held my tongue. Again, I berated myself for getting us into this situation, telling myself if I ever got back to 1864, I'd be happy to remain there for life.

Feeling restless, I got up and went over to the water bottles and boxed food. The basement smelled moldy and stale, and I worried about germs. I hoped since they had stored food, there would be some sort of stove or method to heat water. Ascertaining there was nothing of the sort, I collected several large water jugs and took them over to the cot, placing them near Abbie, then went back to gather more. Once I felt I had enough to bathe the baby and to wash away blood and amniotic fluid, I began to search for rags to use, exclaiming with surprise when I found a stash of baby essentials hidden in a corner containing a pile of cloth diapers, a box of what were called disposable baby diapers, onesies, baby blankets, and a wooden crate filled with packaged baby bottles and nipples.

I took several cloth diapers and a couple of blankets over to the cot, smiling at Andrea. "Looks like you've been preparing for this."

She nodded, her eyes glassy with pain. "When Jonah goes out scavenging, he always looks for things I might need. I hope he got the right stuff. I wasn't sure myself what we'd need other than the basics. Books are pretty scarce and I couldn't find anything to tell me."

"There aren't any other mothers on the mountain who could tell you what you'd need, what to do?"

She grimaced. "Some, not many. There aren't any babies, haven't been for years. Our youngest is a teenager."

"No children? Why not?"

She looked at me, her eyes hard. "Would you want to bring a baby into this world?"

"No, but you did."

"I couldn't abort my husband's baby," she said, grunting.

"What about medical supplies? Do you have anything down here? A first aid kit maybe?"

She shook her head. "I'm not sure. Most of our supplies disappeared in the last raid. Jonah might have put some down here." She stiffened, stuffing the belt in her mouth, which barely muffled her scream.

I put my hand on her belly, feeling it tighten. Once the contraction passed, I checked her again, saying, "When you feel the urge to push, let us know." I tried smiling at her but my lips felt frozen in place. "You're fully dilated now, it won't be long."

Abbie patted her hand. "You may not feel it now, Andrea, but you're lucky. Some women go through labor for hours and hours but looks like you ain't gonna be one of those, not this time."

I touched Abbie on the arm. "We'll need something to cut the cord with. I'll see what I can find." Inside a cabinet over the worktable against the far wall, I found a pair of scissors that looked to be pretty old right next to a white plastic box with a red cross on the lid. I grabbed each and returned to Abbie and Andrea, handing the first aid kit to Abbie, who opened it up. There wasn't much inside. The wrapping on the gauze pads was yellowed and the bottle of aspirin had expired decades ago. A jar of Betadine was almost full, although it showed no expiration date. I wondered if it would still be usable. "At least we have something," I said to Abbie and Andrea. Neither looked particularly relieved.

The next hour passed in a whir of activity as the contractions came closer and we prepared to help the new babe make its way into the world. When he finally slid out of Andrea's body, into my hands, I held him close, marveling at how perfect he appeared. Since Andrea wasn't sure exactly how far along she was, I had been fearful the baby would be premature and knew Abbie shared the same concern, but this baby's coloring and loud vocalizations proclaimed good health and full-term.

When I glanced at Andrea and saw the fearful look on her face, I realized the baby was making too much noise. I quickly placed him on her chest. "Talk to him. He'll know your voice."

"It's a boy?" she said, her voice filled with joy.

"A perfect boy," Abbie told her, smiling.

As I clamped and cut the cord, Andrea gathered the baby close to her, murmuring comforting words to him. He responded to her voice at once, and I watched in amazement as he stared at her, knowing he wasn't focusing yet but still clearly he knew her as his mother. She put a finger in one tiny fist and kissed his brow. "He looks just like his daddy," she said, smiling at Abbie and me.

We froze when we heard voices above us. The baby began to fret, making mewling sounds which I knew could quickly become yowls. "Put him to your breast, see if he'll feed," I whispered.

Andrea did as I suggested and we all watched to see if the baby would latch, sighing with relief when he did.

The voices above were harsh, men shouting at one another as they moved from room to room. Andrea held the baby closer to her, placing her hand over his exposed ear as if to keep him from hearing what was going on above.

As Abbie and I began kneading Andrea's abdomen in an effort to help pass the afterbirth, we listened to loud thumps and crashes on the floor above us. I had to fight the urge to cringe with each one.

"What are they doing?" I whispered to Andrea.

Her panicked look frightened me even more. "I don't know. They must be looking for something."

"You don't think that's the guards Jonah posted outside?" I asked with hope.

"No. They wouldn't make that kind of noise. The raiders must have gotten rid of them."

"What will they do if they find us?" Abbie asked.

Andrea's face was white, her eyes huge with fear. "They'll either kill us or take us with them."

I wanted to scream. We hadn't even been in this time 24 hours yet and had been tied up and kidnapped and now faced possible death or being kidnapped again. I had to do something to stop this but had no idea what. I looked back at the stairs, noting with alarm they seemed well-lit. I leaned close to Andrea's ear. "Is there a separate light switch for the light at the top of the stairs?"

She nodded.

"Did you turn it off before you came down?"

Her eyes darted in that direction, then back to me. "I don't know," she said, with a panicked look. "I'm sure I did, I always do, but I felt that contraction and that distracted me. Oh, Lizzie, I don't know," she moaned.

"Shhh, it's all right," I whispered, afraid her voice would carry upstairs. I tapped Abbie on the arm, and when she looked at me, I pointed at me then the steps. Her nod told me she understood what I meant to do. I listened closely as I walked up the stairs, trying to locate exactly where the raiders were. At the landing at the top of the stairs, I put my ear to the door, reaching out to switch off the light, which had been left on. My mouth fell open when I realized someone was in the kitchen opening drawers, slinging cutlery and other items onto the floor. When they threw the pantry door open, I drew back with a gasp, realizing it was too late. If they saw that light, we were in trouble, but if I flipped the switch, would that draw their attention when the light went out? I didn't know what to do so simply stood there, frozen, listening to the noises on the other side.

And when the panel was flung aside, I stepped back, lost my balance and went tumbling down the stairs.

Chapter Three

August 2054

Come Go With Me

I landed hard on my left shoulder and hip. Abbie was there in an instant, kneeling beside me, asking if I'd been hurt. I sat up, dazed, feeling for a lump on my head, which had struck one of the risers. "I think I'm okay," I said, glancing up toward the top of the stairs. A man stood there, watching us, a rifle snugged into his cocked elbow.

I got to my feet with Abbie's help and backed away, noting Andrea's frightened look as she clutched her baby to her chest. Her expression told me everything I needed to know. She didn't recognize this person and that meant danger for us.

At the cot, watching the man slowly descend the stairs, I whispered to Andrea, "Do you have any weapons of any sort down here?"

Andrea shook her head, her eyes wide.

Abbie and I moved to stand in front of Andrea, shielding her from the man. He paused at the bottom of the stairway, studying us, then began to walk toward us, a smile playing about his lips. He was short and stocky with a blocky face, dark hair cut in a buzz cut and eyes pale as winter under bushy black brows. What in hell? I thought, noting the way he smirked at us.

When he reached us, he stopped, shifting the rifle so that it could easily fall into his hand. "Didn't expect to find anybody here. Hadn't been for that light ..." he gestured with the rifle toward the one at the top of the stairs "... doubt I'd even have suspected this room was down here." His gaze darted around before returning to us. "I reckon I'll score some points when I go back with you three." He peered around me toward Andrea. "Four," he amended.

"We're not going anywhere with you," I said, straightening up. I towered over him by a good three inches and knew this was not good. As a tall woman, I found short men's feelings toward me dichotomous. They either loved that about me or hated it, felt threatened by it. From the look he gave me, I could tell he fell into the latter category.

He pointed the gun at me, raising his eyebrows mockingly. "You want to say that again?"

"There's no reason for you to take us anywhere." I motioned toward Andrea. "At least not now. She just gave birth moments ago, she isn't in any kind of shape to go anywhere nor is her baby."

He shook his head, obviously irritated. "Not my problem." He waved the gun. "Get her and that baby up and let's go."

When I moved restlessly, Abbie squeezed my arm in a warning manner. "Listen, mister, I don't know who you are or where you want to take us but I'm askin you to give us a couple of hours at least to get her ready to go. She's still bleedin, she just passed the afterbirth, and if we make her get up and travel, she could hemorrhage. Then you're gonna have a death you got to explain." She tilted her heard toward the baby, adding, "He needs to nurse, we ain't got nothing else to feed him. If his mother's dead ..." She let her voice trail off.

The soldier shook his head as if Abbie were an annoying child. "Like I said, ain't my problem. She and the baby goes or she dies here and we'll take the baby." He glanced at the infant. "Or not. Better to just kill him and leave him, he'll only slow us down." He stepped around us, yanked Andrea up off the cot and shoved her into Abbie and me. "Get her ready to go."

Andrea hissed in pain, just barely managing to keep hold of her baby who let out a loud squawk as though startled out of sleep.

I clinched my fists in anger, watching Abbie steady Andrea and try to soothe the baby, whose face was red, his eyes scrunched closed. He appeared ready to let out a loud scream at any second.

A man appeared at the top of the stairs, yelling, "Come on, we got to get out of here. We don't have much time. They're on their way back."

The man in front of us poked me with the rifle, then Abbie. "Get upstairs." He turned toward the steps, yelling, "I'm sending some prisoners up."

As soon as his attention wasn't focused on us, Abbie surprised me by hitting the man with a jug of water. When had she picked that up and how had she hidden it, I wondered as I watched his head momentarily tilt sideways so severely that it lay perpendicular to his shoulder. Without hesitation, I reached out and grabbed hold of his rifle as Abbie used the jug to hit him again when he jerked his head up. This time the jug ruptured and water splashed all over the three of us. Hearing an exclamation of surprise at the top of the stairs followed by feet pounding down the steps, I jerked the rifle out of the man's hands and trained it on the soldier coming toward us, hoping my hands weren't so wet that I wouldn't be able to grip. When he cleared the stairs and began to raise his rifle, without even thinking about what I was doing, I aimed and shot him in the shin, knowing I might have possibly fractured his tibia. He shrieked, going down on one knee, the rifle he held clattering out of his hands. Andrea's baby began to scream as if in sympathy. Abbie abandoned the soldier she'd hit and went after the rifle. She grabbed it up, pointing it at one, then the other of the two men. The one who had tried to take us had fallen to his knees after Abbie hit him the second time. He slowly got up, giving Abbie a rageful look.

"Go ahead," she said, her voice ice cold. "Try it." She leaned close to him, whispering, "I want you to." I stared at her, fascinated by this new Abbie. What had happened to that sweet, gentle person who wouldn't hurt a fly, I thought, as she jabbed the man in the stomach with the rifle and told him to get over by the other soldier, writhing on the floor and screaming, then made him get on his knees.

"Lizzie, find me some rope," she said, standing over both of them, far enough away that they couldn't lunge for her, the rifle aimed at them.

I looked at Andrea first, ascertaining she and the baby were all right. She gave me a nod of assurance as she felt for the cot behind her and eased down onto it. "There's rope over by the workbench," she said before turning her attention to the squalling baby.

I hurried over to it. Finding a coil of rope on the worktable in front of the bench, I snatched it up and returned to Abbie.

"Tie em up," she said.

"You best give us back our rifles," the short one said as I yanked his hands behind his back and tied them. "We got others nearby, they'll come looking for us soon. If you want to live, you need to surrender now."

Abbie snorted with derision. "Like I believe the likes of you." Her eyes darted to his cohort. "I reckon we can handle them if they're anything like you two runts."

The short man's eyes narrowed and his face flushed an unhealthy red.

"I think you just raised his blood pressure into the danger zone," I said to Abbie.

"Hope I did." She sneered at him. "If I remember right, I asked you in a nice way to give us some time but you wouldn't even consider it. Way I see it, you're gettin what you deserve." She looked at me. "I can't for the life of me understand a man like this, can you? Thinks he's Mr. God almighty and we got to do what he says. Thinks he can decide who lives or dies." She used the butt of the rifle to hit him in the side of the head, watching blandly as he crumpled on his side. She bent down and yelled in his face, "I don't reckon so, mister." She turned to the other soldier, his screams growing louder and louder. "Shut up," she said, knocking him out with the rifle.

I felt the laughter burble up and couldn't contain it as it exploded out of me. It was part amusement but more relief at having gotten out of that dreadful situation.

Abbie stood watching as I laughed until I cried. When I finally got myself under control, she said, "You through?"

I wiped my face. "I'm sorry, Abbie, it's just, I'm so relieved. And besides, this isn't you." I gestured toward her.

She frowned at me.

"You're always so nice. You're reminding me of Sarie."

For a moment, she looked fiercely proud before the angry expression I was so familiar with settled over her features.

"I'm sorry," I said for what seemed like the thousandth time. "It's just, I'm so darn proud of you. You're like a warrior."

Ignoring me, she turned to check on Andrea and her baby. While she tended to them, I stood watch over the two men, listening for signs of life above.

After several minutes, I said, "What do we do if more come?"

Abbie turned back to me. "Go up them stairs and close the door and turn off that light. Now. I reckon if they can't see the light, they can't find us."

I went up the stairs, feeling belittled. With Abbie, I was usually the one in charge but it seemed things in that regard had changed.

I closed the door leading into the kitchen then pulled the back panel in the pantry in place. There were two light switches, side by side. I flicked the one on the left and the light above me and on the stairwell went out. Since the lights below stayed on, I figured the other one was for those, so left it on. I slowly made my way down the dark stairs, holding onto the wall. Without saying anything, I went to the baby corner, found two cloth diapers, and returned to the men, stuffing their mouths with the cotton cloths and tying ropes around them to make sure they stayed in place. The rancid smell of sweat and blood seemed to coat the air. I breathed through my mouth when I realized one of them had urinated on himself. The one with the shot leg was coming around, making high, keening noises. Imagining he must be in a lot of pain, I knelt down to check the wound. It looked like the bullet had gone through his calf without hitting bone. It wasn't bleeding enough to be concerned about, but as a doctor I had no choice but to help him.

"Shouldn't we give him something for the pain?" I asked Abbie.

She snarled. "Nope. Let him suffer."

"All right, but this wound needs to be dressed or it will get infected." I glanced at Andrea, watching us, the baby held close to her face. "Where'd we put the scissors?" I asked, finding the first aid kit and putting it aside.

"Don't know why you'd want to help the likes of him," Abbie snarled. "He ain't worth the time or effort."

"I have to Abbie. You know that."

She snorted with derision.

Ignoring her, I found the scissors we'd cut the cord with next to the cot and returned to the man. After pouring Betadine over the scissors, I cut his pants leg open above and below the wound, then poured the dark liquid over the site, trying to ignore his shrieks of pain. As I wound gauze around it, securing it with medical tape I wasn't sure would hold, I thought medicine didn't look to have advanced much from 1969 to this time. Curious, I picked up the first aid kit and studied it, finally finding an expiration date on the back. No wonder, I thought. This thing was over 60 years old.

After I finished with the bandage, I moved to the other man, who remained unconscious. I lifted each eyelid, checking to see how dilated his pupils were. "I think you gave him a concussion, Abbie."

"I don't reckon I'm too bothered by that," she answered, checking the ammunition in her rifle. "He'll live, probably. You ask me, that's too good for him."

"Yes, he'll live." I looked at the damage I'd done to the other man. "Don't know if this one will walk without limping for a time, though."

Abbie gave me a cynical look. "That ain't my problem," she said, her voice matching the short man's.

"Okay," I muttered, going up the steps to listen at the door.

"You hear anything?" Abbie asked.

"No, not a thing." I came back down the stairs. "You think they were the only two inside? It sounded like more."

Abbie walked over to the man with the injured leg, curled into a fetal position, whimpering. She yanked the rope down and pulled the gag out of his mouth. "How many were inside the cabin?" she asked, bending over him.

He ignored her, continuing to make moaning sounds.

Abbie poked the wound with her rifle. He yelped, jerking away from her.

"Answer my question," she said, her voice deadly calm, "or I'm gonna shoot you in the other leg."

He looked at her, his expression one of pain mixed with anger and fear.

"How many?" Abbie said. "I ain't gonna ask again." She raised the gun.

"Just us," he said, with a gasp. "No more, just us."

"Thought I heard that one over there say more was comin." When he didn't answer her, she reached out with the rifle.

"Wait, wait. There were two more teams. We all went in different directions. If they haven't gotten here by now, they ain't coming," he said, his voice filled with defeat.

Abbie and I exchanged looks as I walked over to join her. "Why are you here?"

He balked at that until Abbie poked him in his wound. After he quit screaming, he looked at me, sweat streaming down his face. "Please, make her stop," he said in a wheedling voice.

"She'll stop once you tell us what we want to know."

Abbie put the rifle near his leg in a menacing manner.

"Okay, okay, I'll tell you." He swallowed hard several times then used a shoulder to wipe perspiration off his face. "We were outside of Morganton, looking for clean water, and figured there'd be plenty up here."

"And?" Abbie asked.

I looked at her.

"He's holdin something back." Without warning, she jabbed the wound.

He screamed so loudly, it hurt my ears. I watched as tears ran from his eyes, wondering where in the world this hard side of Abbie was coming from.

When she made as if to poke him again, he said, "Okay, I'll tell you. Just let me get … let me sit up."

We waited as he maneuvered himself to lean against the wall behind his back. "Okay," he said, panting. He gave me a pleading look. "It wasn't me that made the decision, okay? I was just part of the group. I knew if I didn't go along, they'd kill me or leave me behind. It's too dangerous out there on your own."

"Just tell us," I said, glancing at Abbie, shifting restlessly. "We don't want to hear your rationalizations."

"We'd heard there was a community up here, figured there'd be women. We don't have any in our group. Donnel said—"

"Who's Donnel?"

"Our leader. He said we need women, you know, to help keep the men happy, maybe grow our community once we settle somewhere."

Andrea snorted with derision. "He's lying. They wanted us for rape and nothing else. If they don't have their own community by now, they won't have one ever. They're raiders and plunderers. They take what they want and leave carnage behind."

"No, no," he said, his eyes wild with panic. "That's not us. We're not like that."

"Seems to me she's right, judgin by the way you two acted when you found us down here." Abbie picked up the rifle, turned it around and hit him in the temple, butt first. "Good night," she said, walking away.

I joined Abbie, who had gone to check on Andrea and the baby. "He said there were two more teams. Want me to check to see if anyone else is up there?"

She nodded. "Be careful, though. Try to keep as quiet as you can in case they're in the house or nearby."

Without answering, I went up the stairs once more, turned on the light and slid the panel aside. I stepped into the kitchen, frowning at the mess the men had made. Why in the world did they have to do that, I wondered. What could the reason possibly have been if they were looking for people.

I stepped over the detritus littering the floor as quietly as I could, pausing every fourth or fifth step to listen for sounds of movement nearby. I made my way out of the kitchen and into the living room, which looked worse than the kitchen, with furniture overturned, the recliner Andrea had seemed to like so much upside down. I tiptoed over to the large windows overlooking the front porch and peeked out. Many of the tents around the firepit had been torn down, sleeping bags and cooking items thrown everywhere. There was no sign of anyone anywhere. Where were the guards Jonah had posted outside? Where had Jonah and his people gone? I glanced upstairs, listening for a couple of minutes, then made my way up the stairs. It was a bit of a relief to see they had not damaged anything there. I supposed they had found us before they moved to that area. Ascertaining the cabin was empty save for me, Abbie, Andrea, the baby and the two injured men, I returned to the front door and turned the dead bolt, knowing if a raider wanted inside, that wouldn't stop them, then walked back through the living room to the kitchen. Ignoring the urge to put things to right, I opened the pantry door, slid the panel back, and went downstairs after making sure to close the pantry door and panel behind me and turn off the light.

Abbie was sitting on the cot beside Andrea, still holding the rifle on the men, both of whom remained unconscious, although the man with the wounded leg was beginning to come around. She looked up when I came down, raising her eyebrows in question.

"No one's there but they sure did some damage."

Abbie frowned. "Reckon they'll just have to clean that up once the runts wake up."

I stared at her. Where had my sweet, abiding Abbie gone to, I wondered. She was beginning to scare me. I didn't think Sarie had ever been as callous as Abbie was acting.

"Are you all right?" I asked her.

She glared at me. "You push me through a light into this, this hellhole and ask me if I'm all right," she yelled.

I flinched. The baby let out a startled squawk and Andrea immediately tried to shush him.

Abbie glanced at them before turning back to me.

"Abbie, it was wrong, I know that. But please, give me a chance to make it right."

"How in the world you gonna do that, Lizzie?" She waved the rifle around recklessly. "According to Jonah, they never see the lights here. How we gonna find the one we need to get back to our time?"

"We will," I said, my voice low and determined. "We have to. I have to find Josh. I won't live the rest of my life without seeing him again."

"What happened to 1969?" she sneered. "You was all fired up to get back there, what's happened to change that?"

"He's not with me," I shouted. I glanced up the stairs, fearful someone might be up there. If so, they would have heard me. When I spoke, I lowered my voice. "Listen, I didn't mean for you to come through. I thought I was protecting you from those bushwhackers who were right at us. But I did mean for him to come. And he's not here. And I am so scared I'll never see him, Abbie. He was the love of my life. He was everything to me." Realizing I was crying, I shut up, turning away from her, wiping at my eyes.

After a few moments, I felt Abbie's hand on my shoulder. "Hush now, Lizzie, we'll find the light. We found it once, we'll find it again."

"You used to say that about my light back to 1969," I said, crestfallen. "It won't happen now just like it didn't happen then. We'll be stuck here and I am so sorry. You don't deserve this. I was so wrong, so stupid."

Abbie put her arms around me. "I reckon I'll agree with stupid, Lizzie, but it ain't gonna help crying over somethin what's already happened. We got to try, that's all we can do, and never give up."

I clutched her. "I'll get you back, Abbie. I promise on my life, I'll get you back to 1864."

"And I'll get you back to Josh," she said.

The shot man on the floor raised up, staring at us with interest. He seemed to have forgotten all about his wounded leg. "You're from the past?" he said, his voice incredulous.

"Ain't none of your business," Abbie said.

"I've heard tales," he said, grunting as he sat up, resting his back against the wall and rubbing the knot on his temple. "Always thought it was nothing but fairytales and legends, never knew it actually happened. Never even thought they existed until last night."

"Did you see the light?" I moved closer, watching his face.

"Saw something, I'll tell you that. Don't know if it was the lights you're talking about but it was different."

"Was it a light?" I insisted.

He shrugged. "Saw several, looked like. One closest to me was white with an orange glow around the edge."

Abbie and I exchanged looks. I smiled at her. "And you saw it last night?"

"I reckon I did."

A thrill shot through me. I grabbed Abbie's hand. "That might have been our light, Abbie."

She was studying the man shrewdly. "You ever seen them lights afore?"

He shook his head. "This was my first time on the mountain. Like I told you, I was part of a recon team and we were headed up the mountain when I got a glimpse of them." He shrugged. "I'm from Asheville and I reckon I've heard about em a time or two but never thought they existed." He grimaced as he tried to adjust his leg.

"Did you see us come through the light?" I asked.

"Didn't see anything. One minute the lights were there, the next, they were gone. One closest to me was so bright, you could have stepped out of it and I wouldn't have seen you. Hurt my eyes to look at it. Didn't look anymore after it vanished." He gave us a pleading look. "I'm in a lot of pain. Can you give me something to help?"

I glanced at Abbie, who shrugged. Although we had the expired aspirin which might still work, I didn't want to give it to him since it could make the bleeding worse. "I didn't see any Tylenol," I said, heading toward the first aid kit.

"What's that?" Andrea said.

"Pain reliever. Do y'all use something else?"

"Hemp oil, something called pain tabs. Don't know what's in them."

"Do you have any here?"

"If it's not in the first aid kit, we don't have it."

I couldn't find any pain relievers in the kit other than the expired aspirin. All I could offer the man was a small water bottle, which he gulped down. Watching him drink the water, I wondered if there were any herbs left on this desolate mountain. I stiffened when we heard movement above us. Abbie, Andrea, the wounded soldier and I looked toward the ceiling, listening as footsteps moved through the house and straight to the kitchen.

"Did you shut the panel?" Abbie hissed as she stuffed the gag back in the raider's mouth.

Oh, God, did I? I couldn't remember. I didn't respond as I kept my eyes on the ceiling, waiting, raising the rifle when I heard the door in the pantry open and the panel slide back. Abbie followed suit, moving closer to the bottom of the stairs with me right beside her.

We waited restlessly for whoever was coming down the steps to reveal themselves. As they got closer, I snugged the rifle in my shoulder, aiming down the barrel. We watched as first a man's combat boots were revealed, followed by camouflage pants, t-shirt, and finally the face, hearing Andrea sigh with relief when Jonah appeared. He hesitated at the bottom of the stairs, staring at Abbie and me, our rifles still trained on him. His hand rose toward the gun he wore in a shoulder holster.

"It's all right, Jonah," Andrea said behind us. He dropped his hand, his gaze moving past us to his sister. I reluctantly lowered my rifle as Jonah moved past me to Andrea, exclaiming with surprise when he saw the baby.

Abbie and I listened as Andrea told him what had happened, watching a vast range of expressions ripple across his face like wind through a wheat field. At one point, he turned and gave Abbie and me an appraising look before focusing on what his sister said.

When she finished, he kissed her on the forehead and awkwardly patted the baby's back before approaching Abbie and me, now standing side by side. "I owe you for my sister's and her baby's lives," he said, his voice filled with gratitude. "I'll make it up to you, help you get back, as soon as possible. It's the least I can do."

He walked over to where the injured soldiers were. The one with the shot leg grew rigid, watching him. Jonah knelt beside the one Abbie had hit with the water bottle, lifting each eyelid. "Looks like he took a good wallop to the head," he said casually. His attention shifted to the one with the wounded leg. "He shot?"

"I reckon so," Abbie said.

"Who shot him?" he asked, glancing at us over his shoulder.

Abbie tilted her head towards me.

"Why didn't you kill him?" Jonah said, surprising me.

"What for? All he'd done up to that point was trash your house."

"Maybe so but, like water, you're a commodity to them. They'd have killed you if you didn't do what they wanted." He glared at the soldiers. "Raped you before that, probably. Or beaten you into submission." He stood. "You should have killed him." He walked past me and up the stairs, pulling out what looked like a walkie-talkie.

"What the hell," I yelled at his back.

Although Abbie had stuffed the gag in the wounded soldier's mouth, he had managed to spit most of it out. "They're gonna kill us," he said, his voice muffled, losing his composure. "Oh, God, I didn't think it'd ever go this far."

"Kill you?" I looked at Andrea. "Is he right? Is that what y'all do, kill each other?"

"They would have killed us if we hadn't gone with them," she said, her voice hard. "It's that kind of world now, kill or be killed."

"I don't think so," I said, with determination as I walked up the steps.

I found Jonah standing in the living room, barking orders into the walkie-talkie to someone to come to the cabin. When he finished, he seemed to sense me and turned with a questioning look.

"I won't allow you to kill them," I said.

"Allow me?" He sneered at me. "You don't have any say in this."

"I do if you want me to help your sister."

Jonah's face grew hard, his lips set in a firm line. "What will it take to make you understand they would have killed you if you didn't do what they wanted you to? What do you want me to do, release them so they can return another day to finish what they started?"

"Imprison them. Trade them for something."

He shook his head, giving me an irritated look.

"Look, I'm a doctor. I can't stand by while you kill—"

"Enough," he yelled. "It's none of your business. You just got here, you don't know what it's like out there. You don't know what this world has become." He gave me a suspicious look. "If what you told me is true."

"You owe me, you said that. We kept them from taking your sister and her baby, and I expect you to at least honor my wants here."

"Your wants? Listen, if I wanted, I could keep you here forever. I'm being generous, letting you leave, not knowing who you really are or where you actually came from."

"We told you where we came from," I spat at him. "A place I thought was a hellhole until I got here."

"Well, you're right about that. This is a hellhole and welcome to it." He threw his arms up in agitation, turned on his heel and left, slamming the door behind him.

I heard movement behind me and turned to see Abbie standing in the threshold of the kitchen, watching me. "Let him do what he wants," she said in a low voice.

"Abbie ..."

"No, Lizzie, don't try to talk me into what you want. What I want is to go home, and if you mess that up for me, I'll never forgive you. Let him do what he wants so he'll honor his word and let us leave so we can go home."

We stared at one another for a long moment. "But he'll kill them."

"I reckon they knew that could happen when they come up here on this mountain to kill or take us prisoner. They made their bed, Lizzie, let em lie in it. Ain't that something you're always sayin? Let em pay for what they done."

I started walking toward the door. "I won't witness this," I said over my shoulder. "You're more than welcome to if you can bear it but I will not."

Chapter Four

August 2054

There's a Doctor

I yanked the door open and walked outside, slamming it almost as hard as Jonah had when I left. It was pandemonium in the yard, men and women trailing into the campsite, looking forlorn and bedraggled, some angrily trying to right the camp. I noted blood on several and wasn't sure if it was theirs or someone else's. I moved back toward the door, intending to fetch Abbie so we could set up some sort of triage. As I began to turn, I spied a man and woman towing an unconscious young man into the middle of the camp. I stepped off the porch, watching as they gently lowered him to the ground. When I saw he was bleeding profusely from a wound to his leg, I ran over to them.

"What happened?"

"Got knifed," the male soldier said. "I put my belt around his thigh but he's still bleeding like a pig."

The blood was flowing more than spurting, which I thought was a good sign the femoral artery hadn't been nicked. I knelt beside the injured man and tightened the tourniquet, frantically running through treatment options available to me, coming up empty with each one. I had no sutures, no way to stop the bleeding except by rudimentary methods. I looked at the young soldier. "Give me your t-shirt and go find Abbie."

"What'd you say?" he asked, leaning close.

"Give me your t-shirt and go into the cabin, find Abbie, tell her to come."

He eyed me for a moment. "Who's Abbie?"

"Never mind. Just give me your t-shirt and go," I yelled.

He hastily dropped his backpack, removed his t-shirt and handed it to me. As he turned to leave, I called after him, "And tell her to bring the Bible."

I grabbed his discarded backpack and placed it under the injured soldier's leg to elevate it, then quickly folded the t-shirt and put it over the wound, applying pressure to try to staunch the bleeding. While I waited for Abbie, cursing that it seemed to take forever for her to come, I used my other hand to apply pressure to the femoral artery, just in case it had actually been cut. I glanced around, saw Jonah heading toward us at a run, his eyes filled with shock as he stared at the young man bleeding on the ground.

"Josh … Jonah, get Abbie," I screamed at him. "She's the only one who can stop this bleeding."

He turned on his heel and hurried into the house without saying a word.

A few minutes later, Abbie flew out of the house, clutching a large white Bible in her hands. "He need a Bloodstopper?" she asked when she reached us.

I nodded. "What took so long?"

"Had to find the dang Bible," she said, thumbing through it. She glanced at the man's leg then toward the sky.

I looked up, trying to gauge the direction of the sun, which was obliterated by a mass of clouds that looked like piles of dirty cotton.

"East is that way, I think," I said, pointing into the forest.

She began to walk in that direction, reciting the biblical verse as she went.

I studied the man's face as I continued to apply pressure to the t-shirt and femoral artery. It was pale as skim milk, the veins snaking through his forehead and in his neck standing out clear as blue ice. Switching my gaze to his leg, I lifted the soaked t-shirt, watching as the blood began to slow then trickle to a stop. Is he dead or did Abbie do it, I wondered as I took my hands away and put my finger on his carotid pulse. I breathed a sigh of relief when I realized it was faint and thready but there. I glanced up, saw Jonah kneeling across from me, holding the soldier's hand, watching him. He raised his head and our eyes met.

"Did you do that?" he said in a low voice.

I shook my head. "Abbie. She's a Bloodstopper, she told you that."

He glanced at Abbie, walking back toward us. "Is that some kind of magical thing she does, from the past?"

"No, it's a gift. A gift from God. You're lucky she was here. He would have died without her."

He frowned at me. "I thought you were a doctor. Couldn't you do anything?"

"Not without the proper equipment," I snapped at him. "Just be thankful Abbie was here." I looked around, smiling when she joined us.

She handed the Bible to Jonah. "Is he alive?" she asked, staring at the young man.

"Yes, Abbie. You did it. Thank you."

Jonah reached over, squeezed her arm. "Thank you, Abbie." He caressed the young soldier's cheek in a loving manner, glanced up and caught me watching him. "This is my little brother Zachary." His gaze shifted to his brother, his expression filled with affection and concern.

"We need to get him inside," I said, rising to my feet.

Jonah called over some of the other men and they easily lifted Zachary and carried him into the house.

"Put him down on the table in the dining room," I instructed, following them in.

Once he was prostrate, after elevating the leg once more, I undid the belt above the wound, watching as blood slowly oozed. "Jostling him must have caused it to start bleeding again. We need sutures." I raised my eyes to Jonah in a questioning way.

"We don't have many medical supplies and they're old, but I'll see if there are any in there, although I've never seen any."

I put my finger in the gash in Zachary's pants and began to rip them open, away from the wound. "If not, needle and thread will do it."

He hesitated, frowning at me.

"I came from 200 years ago, what the hell do you think I used then?" I said, my voice acerbic.

Without replying, he went into the kitchen and began to search under the sink.

"I'll need scissors too," I called after him.

Andrea appeared in the pantry door, carrying her baby, looking wan and weak. Abbie immediately went to her. When Andrea noticed who we had on the table, she cried out with alarm as she rushed over to her brother.

"I think he'll be okay," I told her, "thanks to Abbie."

Andrea grabbed Zachary's hand while she held the baby with the other. Abbie reached out and took him, saying, "I'll see to him."

Tears flooded Andrea's eyes. "What happened to him?"

"They said he was stabbed. Abbie got the bleeding to stop."

"Zach?" she said, leaning close to him. "Zach?"

"He's unconscious but keep talking to him, he may hear you." I spied a laundry basket nearby filled with towels. "Are those clean?"

Andrea followed my gaze to the basket. "Yes, I was going to fold them."

"Good." I grabbed up a clean hand towel and began to apply pressure to try to stop the small amount of blood still trickling from the wound, choosing not to tell her Zachary's unconsciousness was most likely due to lack of blood. I had no idea how much he had lost before I saw him and briefly wondered if I should try to do a transfusion but dismissed that, knowing if they didn't have updated medical supplies, they would not have the equipment I needed to accomplish that task much less any method for blood typing.

Jonah returned with a sewing kit. I looked at him. "Are you kidding me? This is the 21st century, you should have more advanced treatment methods than I knew about during 1969." I glanced around, hoping no one else had heard me, but other than Jonah, Abbie, Andrea and the baby, no one else was in the room.

He shrugged. "We lost all our medical supplies in the last raid. We don't have anything left but some bandages."

I thought for a moment. I remembered reading during my time in 1969 that Vietnam war surgeons were using a cyanoacrylate glue to close wounds. "Okay. Do you have any glue around here? I need one that contains cyanoacrylate. It will close the wound and we won't have to worry about stitches. That might be better," I said, more to myself than him, "stitches can cause an infection, especially using needle and thread." I glanced at Abbie, still holding the baby, as Jonah and Andrea rushed off to try to find glue. "I doubt there are any herbs left on this mountain, Abbie. I don't know what we can do if infection sets in."

"The best we can, Lizzie, we always have." She bounced the baby a little, trying to get him to settle. All this commotion had him wailing at the top of his lungs.

I felt on edge, ready to scream at him to shut up, knowing that was illogical and would only make things worse. "When Andrea gets back, give him to her. Maybe she can feed him and that will hush him up."

Abbie nodded, her gaze shifting to the young soldier's wound. "Looks like I didn't stop the bleeding all the way," she observed.

"No, but it's not leaking much and I think it'll stop soon. He should be fine if he hasn't lost too much blood."

"I can try again. Don't know if it'll work."

"Let's wait and see. Hopefully by the time I close the wound, it'll have stopped. If not, you probably should."

Within minutes, Jonah returned with a bottle containing a clear-looking substance. "It's old but it says it contains something starting with cyano," he said, holding it out to me.

I took the bottle with one hand, continuing to apply pressure with the other, while quickly reading its contents. "Cyanoacrylate. Yes. That should do it. Abbie, I need an antiseptic. Can you fetch the Betadine from downstairs? We need to disinfect the wound first before we glue it. We'll need bandages too."

"I'll go," Jonah said, rushing off.

Andrea joined us, shaking her head. "Couldn't find any glue, Lizzie. Is there anything else?"

"Jonah found some. Listen, I need you to take the baby and nurse him or something. Try to keep him quiet, if you can."

"Of course." She took him from Abbie and put his cheek against hers, crooning to him. He immediately began to settle down. I looked at Abbie.

"I'll get her settled upstairs," she said, reading my thoughts.

I nodded with relief, turning my attention back to Zachary.

When Jonah returned, I had him apply pressure while I finished cutting the pants off Zachary, using an old pair of scissors Jonah supplied. "Okay, take off the towel and let's see if it's still bleeding," I told him. We both leaned over the leg, watching. I smiled when I realized the bleeding had stopped. "This stuff is probably a hundred years old," I mumbled to myself as I poured Betadine over my hands, wiped them on a clean towel, then washed out the wound with it, "probably expired decades ago."

"It's all we've got," Jonah said.

"You don't have alcohol?"

"What kind of alcohol?"

"Rubbing alcohol? Liquor, whiskey, anything like that? Even moonshine will do."

He shook his head. "We don't even have the basics anymore."

"Well, we'll just have to pray this works." I swabbed around the wound, trying to dry it as best I could, then pinched the skin together and applied the glue. The wound looked to be a clean cut, no jagged edges or large gashes, and it was relatively easy to hold the skin in place. I glanced at Jonah, watching me. "Without sutures, I can't stitch the skin closed but this should work. Let's hope the knife that cut him wasn't rusty or filled with bacteria, and while we're at it, that the glue won't do more harm than good."

He nodded, his mouth set in a grim line.

After several minutes, I released Zachary's skin, sighing with relief when it remained sealed shut. After bandaging the leg, I put my index and middle finger on his carotid pulse again. It seemed a bit stronger. I nodded as I stepped back. "All we can do now is wait."

"Should we move him?" Jonah said, lightly touching his brother on the cheek.

"No, let's keep him here until he's stable."

He nodded, picking up Zachary's hand and clutching it in his large ones. Hands like Josh's, I noticed as I stared at them, tears welling in my eyes. Oh, Josh, I thought, I am so sorry I left you behind. I turned away from the table and walked to the large windows overlooking the porch, trying to get myself under control.

I listened as Jonah thanked Abbie again for saving his brother, then told Andrea about the confrontation with the other raiders on the mountain. "There were at least six more, but they got away. Only ones we have are those two downstairs. We'll get as much information from them as we can." I was sure if I turned around, he would be sending a dark glare my way.

When Jonah joined me a few minutes later, it was full dark outside and I could see his reflection in the window when he stood beside me, the expression on his face wary and a bit contrite. I wiped at my eyes before I turned to him.

"I wanted to thank you for helping my brother and again for my sister." He glanced behind him. I followed his gaze, surprised to see Abbie tucking a blanket around Zachary.

"He should be all right if infection doesn't set in," I said, watching Abbie pick up Zachary's hand and hold it in hers. "He'll need a lot of rest and will be pretty weak for a while, but hopefully he'll be all right."

Jonah nodded. "I know it's asking a lot but would you at least stay until morning?" He gave me a helpless look. "Zach and Andrea, if anything should happen to them, I don't have the faintest idea how to help them and ..."

I bit my bottom lip.

"I'll go with you, I'll help you search for the light," he said quickly. "But I need to be here tonight, just to be sure they're going to be all right. It's only a few hours, Lizzie."

I glanced at Abbie again, saw she was watching us, listening. I raised my eyebrows at her. I figured she should be the one to decide. After all, she hadn't wanted to come through the light. She nodded before turning her attention back to Zachary.

"Tonight, then. That's all you get."

"Thank you." He turned to leave but hesitated. "I won't kill them," he said in a low voice, gesturing toward the basement. "I'll have to find a way to convince the others, but I won't kill them. For you and Abbie, for what you did for us." He reached out and touched my hand then walked away.

Abbie and I took turns during the night caring for Zachary. We decided to do it in two shifts, one from eight pm until two am, the other from two am until eight am. I took the first one while Abbie dozed on a large sofa that, although thrown about and upended, didn't suffer much damage. Zachary slept mostly, but the times he would come awake, I would coax him to drink small amounts of sugared water. He resisted until Jonah, dozing on and off in the canting recliner, told him he had to if he wanted to get better. I knew Zachary was more than likely feeling nauseated and too exhausted to eat or drink but only in doing so would he begin to feel better and gain his strength back.

At two am, I woke Abbie and took her place on the couch, turning my back on the room and pulling the blanket over my head. At some point during the night, I came awake to hear Abbie laughing softly. Laughing? I thought to myself. Surely not. I slowly slid the blanket off my face as I turned over, listening to a low conversation going on over at the table. Was that Jonah, I wondered? I turned my head and saw Abbie and Zachary, their heads close to one another, talking while holding hands. What the ... I thought, my gaze switching to Jonah, in the recliner, his eyes hooded but watching them, just like I was. As if sensing my gaze, he looked at me. When our eyes met, he raised his eyebrows in a sardonic gesture. What the heck does that mean? I thought, frowning at him. I turned my head away, listening to the murmuring voices, occasionally pierced by laughter, before falling back asleep.

Chapter Five

August 2054

Take Me Back to the Sweet Sunny South

A crying baby woke me the next morning. I opened my eyes, momentarily forgetting where and when I was, doing what I did each morning, making a mental tally in my mind of what all Abbie and I needed to do that day on Brown Mountain. Another loud squawk had me trying to remember where the baby came from. Had Abbie delivered one during the night and I hadn't heard? I froze when I realized this was not 1864 but almost 200 years in the future in a time of greater turmoil than the one we had left.

I pushed the blanket off as I sat up, using my fingers to comb my hair off my face and neck. I glanced toward the table where Abbie sat, feeding what looked to be pudding to Zachary, who was smiling at her. I heard Jonah in the kitchen, talking to whom I assumed to be Andrea, since that's where the baby's wails were coming from. Tears flooded my eyes and my throat burned as I tried to stifle my feelings and come to grips with what had happened. It'll be all right, I told myself. We'll find the light, go back, and it will be like this never happened. When thoughts of what that could possibly do to Jonah, Zachary, and Andrea and her baby began to creep into my mind, I got to my feet quickly, telling myself to Stop!

Abbie turned and smiled at me. I stared at her in surprise, noting the anger and hostility that had stayed with her the day before seemed to have disappeared. "Mornin, Lizzie."

I forced my lips to turn upwards. "Morning." I walked over to join them at the table, placing the back of my hand against Zachary's forehead. "How's our patient?"

Zachary gave me a weak smile. "I woke up during the night and thought I'd gone to Heaven and been greeted by an angel." His eyes darted to Abbie.

Oh, God, I thought, how corny.

Abbie smiled with pleasure as she squeezed Zachary's hand. "I been feedin him the most amazing food, Lizzie. It's called chocolate pudding and it tastes wonderful."

I kissed her cheek. "It does," I agreed. Straightening, I glanced toward the kitchen, where Jonah stood, watching me. I focused back on Abbie. "Do you need anything? I can watch him if you want to eat or go shower or …"

"I'm fine, you go on and eat breakfast. I done ate." She turned back to Zachary, giving him a look I'd never seen on Abbie before, one of intrigue and wonder. In all the years I'd known her, she had never shown any particular interest in men and I always assumed that was due to the harsh treatment she had received at her father's hands. Or listening for years to Sarie's rather opinionated views on the vileness of men. She likes him, I thought, with panic, as I watched her. That can't happen, not here, not now.

Jonah appeared by my side, startling me. "You hungry? We have some eggs and toast."

I nodded as I followed him into the kitchen, noting how tidy and organized it was. "Who straightened up in here?"

Jonah shrugged. "Me. Couldn't sleep very well last night so figured I might as well be of good use somewhere." He gestured at a small banquette set in a nook in the kitchen beneath a window overlooking the straggly forest. "Sit. I'll get your food for you."

I glanced out the window, checking the weather. Noting a soft golden glow to the trees, I figured the sun must be shining somewhere. When the baby made another squawk, I glanced around at Andrea, standing in the middle of the room, swaying from side to side.

Noticing my attention, she gave me a wan smile. "He's cranky, Lizzie. I can't figure out what's wrong with him."

I got to my feet, reaching out for the baby. When she handed him to me, I placed him on the table and began to unswaddle him. "Nice job," I told her.

She shrugged. "Jonah did it."

I glanced at Jonah, thinking, well, I sure didn't know you had that in you. As if sensing my thoughts, he shrugged, giving me a crooked smile. Just like Josh. My breath caught and I forced myself to look away from him. Turning my attention to the baby, I began to move his arms and legs in a circle. Realizing I hadn't done an Apgar after his birth, I quickly did this, checking his heart rate, respiration, skin color, muscle tone and response to stimulation. Afterward, I said to Andrea, "He's as normal as can be." I undid the diaper in order to check the stump of the umbilical cord which was hidden beneath. I noted it seemed red, irritated. "We need to keep the stump as dry as possible," I told her, picking up a napkin and blotting around it. "Keep the diaper folded underneath so it doesn't cover it up and irritate it. It should fall off in a few days.""

"Oh, I didn't know that."

"Not many new mothers do." I smiled at her. "He's fine, Andrea. Just some irritation but that will clear up soon. Has he nursed this morning?"

She nodded, watching me re-swaddle him. When she took him from me, she reached out and clasped my hand. "Thank God for you and Abbie. You saved Zachary's life and I don't think I would have survived having this baby on my own."

I squeezed her hand. "You'd be surprised what you can do on your own, Andrea. Don't underestimate yourself."

Jonah put a plate on the table along with a cup of coffee. I sat down and dug into the eggs, realizing I hadn't eaten the night before and was famished. "These taste fresh. Do y'all have chickens?"

Andrea settled in the seat across from me. "Yes, along with several cows and goats for milk and cheese, and greenhouses not too far from here for produce. We protect those above all else except the water."

"And women," Jonah added.

She ignored him. "As for things like coffee, tea, flour, sugar, all that, Jonah and his troops go scavenging, raid abandoned food warehouses and stores, or trade with other communities. A lot of the stuff has expired but it seems pretty good. At least no one's died from eating it."

"Yet," Jonah said, grinning at her.

She shook her head with irritation.

As I ate, I listened to their banter, seeing Jonah in a different light, noting when he was with family, he was more relaxed, not as harsh and commanding as when he was with his troops or strangers like me and Abbie. Well, he loves them, I told myself. That counts for something, I guess.

After breakfast, I went upstairs to shower and brush my teeth. The day before, Andrea had allowed us to take long, hot showers but Jonah made it a point to tell Abbie and me they tried to conserve water in every way possible, so showers were limited to five minutes. I was shocked I actually washed my hair and body within that time fame. After brushing my teeth and dressing in fresh clothes which Andrea provided from the basement, I repaired downstairs where I found Abbie sitting by Zachary, listening as Jonah told him about the outcome of the prior day's raid. Andrea sat in the recliner, which someone had apparently fixed, as it wasn't canting to one side any longer, the baby nursing under a blanket she had placed over one shoulder.

I touched his pink fist, clutching a tendril of her hair. "He doing all right?"

She smiled at me. "Not as fussy now. It must have been the irritated cord."

I shrugged. "Or just baby. They tend to fuss a lot, as you'll find out soon enough."

She gave the baby an indulgent smile.

"Can I get you anything?"

She shook her head.

I knelt beside her. "You need to remember to take care of yourself as well or you won't be of much use to him. Be sure to stay hydrated and eat regularly. Get as much rest as you can, which won't feel like enough in the coming days since you're nursing him, but when he sleeps, try to sleep then too."

"Yes, doctor," she said in a teasing voice.

I glanced up, caught Jonah watching me. I raised my eyebrows at him. His mouth set in a hard line but he nodded his agreement. "Since I made the promise, I reckon it's time we let Abbie and Lizzie find that light they keep talking about."

Abbie looked up startled. She turned her gaze on me.

"You ready?" I asked.

She glanced at Zachary. "I don't reckon now's a good time to leave, Lizzie. He's feeling a mite feverish. I reckon we ought to stay one more day, just to make sure Andrea and Zach are set." She gestured toward Zachary. "He ain't out of the woods yet."

I frowned at her, feeling my blood pressure rise. "But I thought you wanted to go back as soon as we could. Sarie and Amanda May are alone back there, with bushwhackers on the mountain. They might need our help."

She shrugged. "I reckon what's happened has already happened and we can't stop it. Besides, Josh is there. He'll help em, you know that."

I gave her a disbelieving look. "But you were so anxious to get back yesterday, Abbie. I don't—"

Her eyes darted toward Andrea. "I reckon Sarie made it through whatever happened, Lizzie." She glanced at Jonah and back to me. "And Josh."

I stared at the floor, the need to leave, to get back to Josh so strong I could literally feel it pulling me toward the door.

Jonah stepped toward me. "I need to do a perimeter check. Why don't you come with me? If you see the light, I'll leave it up to you as to whether you want to wait on Abbie or go ahead and go."

I nodded, not looking at Abbie, who I felt had betrayed me in some way. "All right. Let's go." As I walked toward the door, I said to Abbie over my shoulder, "Take care of them until I get back … if I get back." I slammed the door behind me and stalked into the yard.

Jonah came out moments later and quickly caught up with me at the edge of the clearing. He touched my elbow. "We need to go this way."

Without replying, I turned and followed him. We walked in silence for some time before he turned his gaze on me. "You really love this Josh, huh?"

I nodded, tears flooding my eyes. I swiped at them, blinking hard to clear my vision. I did not want to cry in front of this man. "We were planning to be married. He's my life, he means everything to me. He was supposed to come with us but the bushwhackers must have caught him."

He raised his eyebrows, looking interested. "Bushwhackers? What happened?"

As we walked along, I told him about how the outliers had found us, how Josh held them off while Abbie and I went through the light, how my fingers had grazed Josh's as he reached for me right before the light took me.

"And Sarie? Abbie's sister? Were they after her?"

"We heard a shot from her cabin. We were afraid they were there." I shook my head. "Sarie's tough, absolutely the strongest woman I know. I pray she was able to protect Amanda May and herself."

Jonah made a sound in his throat. "Who's Amanda May? Is she Abbie and Sarie's sister?"

"No, that would be Maggie. She's married and doesn't live with Sarie. Amanda May was bonded over to Sarie to learn healing from her."

"Bonded?"

"Given to Sarie so she could learn about herbal healing in exchange for room and board."

He nodded. "If Sarie's as tough as you and Abbie, I have no doubt she was able to take care of matters."

I stared at him, unsure if he was teasing or actually meant it.

He gave me back a serious look. "The way you handled those men yesterday," he said in a low voice. "That took guts."

"They were trying to take Andrea and her baby. We couldn't let that happen. She'd just given birth, she wasn't in any shape to travel."

"You didn't owe it to her to protect her. I hadn't been very charitable to you and I wouldn't have blamed you if you'd just left."

"We couldn't do that to her. She was alone, had no one to help her. Neither one of us is that callous." I gave him a look, meaning not like you. He had the grace to look contrite.

"I did what I did for my family," he said, glancing away.

"What happened to the guards you posted outside the door?" I asked.

"They left to help Zach's group, who were pursuing the raiders." His expression darkened. "They'll pay for that, believe me. If they'd been there, they could have taken care of those two who got inside."

I decided to ask him something I'd been wondering about. "I'm curious why you left us alone in the house with Andrea yesterday. Obviously, you didn't believe our story and for all you knew we could have been with the raiders."

He darted a glance at me. "I was short on manpower or I would have also posted a couple of guards in the house, but Andrea said she trusted you and Abbie. She ... I've learned to trust her instincts. She has this way of knowing things about people."

I nodded. "Abbie's like that. Must be a Collins thing."

We each were silent for awhile, thinking our own thoughts. I finally turned to him. "Do you believe us about the light now?"

He shrugged. "Personally, I don't know what to think. It sounds a bit too paranormal for me. I guess I'll just hold judgment until I actually see one."

"And still remain suspicious of us until you do."

"No. You proved yourselves yesterday. You may not be spies and I still have no idea who you are, if you're who you claim to be, but my sister and brother trust you so I will too." He gave me a speculative look. "For the time being."

I noticed we were heading to the top of the mountain. "Where are we going?"

He glanced at me. "We have greenhouses up there. I want to check to make sure the raiders didn't find them and do any damage."

I stared at the dirty sky, the sun barely visible through the haze. "Are you able to grow anything?"

He nodded. "Takes a lot of work but we've figured things out. We're pretty self-sustainable. Don't eat meat, of course, because most of the animals are gone and the ones we have we use for other purposes." He shrugged. "But we produce enough food to keep us alive, at least."

"Aren't there any grocery stores, places you can buy food?"

"In the cities, sure, and there's a black market but not here. Doesn't matter anyway. No one has money nowadays, at least not away from the cities."

"So that's why you raid?"

He frowned at me. "Scavenge."

"What about Morganton, is it thriving?"

"It's a ghost town. Hardly anyone lives there now. Most people headed toward the larger cities when things started going bad. Not many survived."

I considered this for a moment. "How many are left, do you know?"

He shook his head. "I have no idea."

"What about the government? Isn't one in place?"

"If you can call it that, but they're more concerned with the areas with the most population, I guess."

"I'm surprised they haven't claimed the mountains for the water."

He shook his head. "Before the asteroid strike, the government built large desalination plants along the coastlines, turning seawater into fresh water to address ongoing water shortages within the larger cities. I imagine those that are still thriving are continuing to be supplied with that. The smaller towns and communities were left to deal with the water issue on their own, and that hasn't changed that I know of. We're pretty isolated here, which is a bonus, but what we have is what others want so we're forced to deal with the raiders."

I contemplated this as we walked along, thinking I couldn't have picked a worse era to come through the lights. Well, no, that wasn't quite true if what Amanda May's grandmother had told her. Darker days loomed ahead, days when America itself would be threatened by another country.

My gloomy thoughts were interrupted when Jonah called a halt for rest beside a meandering creek filled with rocks and boulders. The day had turned hot and the creek looked so inviting, I took off my socks and boots and stepped into the water, sighing as silky wetness rushed over my feet, cooling me instantly. I knelt down, cupping water in my hands, splashing my face and the back of my neck, slick with perspiration, while Jonah walked a few yards upstream to refill our canteens. When he came back, he handed me one then sat down on the bank beside the stream. Spying a flat rock at the water's edge nearby, I made my way to it, then sat down. I eyed the canteen. "Is it safe to drink?"

He gave me a curious look.

"The water, it's not contaminated?"

"Hasn't affected us so far." As if to prove his point, he took a long swallow. "The water comes from an underground spring and the rocks are a natural filter."

After I took a drink, I lay back on the rock, gazing up at the sky. I could just make out the sun through the haze and cloud mass. "Is it like this all the time?"

Jonah gave me a questioning look.

"This hazy, this polluted looking."

He shrugged. "In the past year, it's gotten better than it was. Some days we can even see the sun clearly." He poured water from the canteen over his head, swiping at his face with his hand. "We're actually pretty lucky here. The air cover isn't as bad as it is west of us. There's hardly anything left there, the fallout is so thick."

"How far does it extend? I mean, does it affect only America or other countries as well?"

"From what I've heard, it only affected America. With satellite interference and no internet reception, I have no idea how bad it actually is."

"How have people survived this?" I said, with despair.

"I'm not sure. I reckon millions have died."

"From starvation?"

"That along with diseases, suicides, other causes."

The way he said that got my attention. I looked at him. "Such as?"

When his eyes met mine, I could see pain reflected in the depths. "Like I told you, it's almost a war-like state. I'd say most of the people who've died have been at the hands of others."

I sat up.

He nodded. "It's man against man. Don't know how we've managed to survive all this as long as we have but I intend to keep this mountain and its water safe as long as I'm alive."

I eyed the gun tucked into a holster he wore around his shoulder. "I'd think you'd have more modern weaponry than that. That looks like a gun from my time, back in the 1960s."

"A little bit more modern than that, but not by much." He took out the gun, ejected the magazine, checked it, then reloaded it. "Back about 30 years ago, guns were banned in America. The government confiscated a lot but there were many more that people hid away they didn't get to."

I nodded.

"Weaponry of any kind's in short supply. We're always looking for more, for protection."

"Andrea said there's around a hundred people here."

"Give or take. We're scattered all over the mountain. You'll meet some today."

I watched him for a moment, mentally comparing him to Josh. When he glanced at me, I asked something that had been on my mind but I'd been afraid to know the answer to. "What about those two men yesterday? What happened to them?"

He shook his head, grimacing. "I kept my word, don't worry. Not too popular now because of it, but it is what it is."

"Where are they?"

"I had a couple of men escort them down to Morganton this morning."

"Do you think they'll come back?"

He looked at me then, his gaze hard and cold. "Yes. They didn't get what they came for. You can bet they'll be back, with more men, probably."

"I hope not. I hope the fact that you showed mercy will count for something."

He didn't answer and we sat in silence for awhile. I pulled the band holding my ponytail out, smoothed my hair back, then rebound it, more than aware that he watched me. When I looked at him, he said, "What did Abbie mean when she looked at Andrea and said she figured Sarie was all right? Is it the same with her as me? She looks like someone y'all knew?"

I hesitated, unsure what to say.

"Does Andrea look like Sarie?" he asked, his voice pressured.

"Yes, a little. I didn't actually see it until she smiled but she has her smile." I shrugged, unwilling to meet his gaze. "Sarie has blue eyes and Andrea has brown, and there are differences, unlike you and Josh. You could be his twin." I stopped.

He nodded. "Andrea likes genealogy, talks about it a lot. I remember she dug back through our family line, saying something about a Hampton marrying a Collins centuries ago." He stared at me. "That's his last name, isn't it, Hampton, like mine?"

I nodded. "The plantation's still there?"

He reached down, splashed water over his lower arms. "Hasn't been lived in in years but it's there."

"It's not your family home?"

He shook his head, grimacing. "We lost it well over a hundred years ago, I guess. Had a relative who liked to gamble. Word is he lost it in a poker game." He lifted the canteen to his mouth and drank. Putting it beside him, he wiped his mouth with the back of his hand and when he spoke his voice was low and hard. "So if you make it back and stop the marriage between Sarie and your Josh, that wipes out my entire family from that point on." He looked at me. "Right?"

I shook my head, glancing away from him. "Probably. I don't know. Maybe you'd be one of my descendants, mine and Josh's."

He uttered a huffing noise. "You know that's probably not true. You said it yourself yesterday, when you threatened me with not existing anymore after you went back."

"Josh had two brothers, maybe one of them will marry ... married Sarie," I said, knowing that was highly unlikely. Josh's brothers had favored their mother, who was dark-headed and had brown eyes and olive skin. Both were also under the age of ten, a good deal younger than Sarie.

A bird flew overhead, making a loud, squawking noise. I jumped, startled. Glancing up, I spied a black crow circling above us. "Birds made it, looks like."

When he didn't answer, I looked at him. "Look, it bothers me, too. I've met you and Zach and Andrea, and helped deliver her baby. I wouldn't want that to happen to you all, not at all. But I love Josh, I don't want to lose him. Am I to just remain here in this horrible time and place and let him marry her and live the rest of his life with her, if that's what actually happened ... or will happen? Is that what you want me to do?"

He stood, an angry look on his face. "I reckon it's up to you. If you want to leave, I won't break my promise to you. I won't stop you." He hooked his canteen to his belt. "Looks like our lives depend on you, Lizzie." He turned and walked away, leaving me to hurriedly put on my socks and shoes and follow him.

At the top of the mountain, we emerged into a large clearing housing three roomy rectangular greenhouses, all with some sort of reflective material on their domed tops. I stopped, my gaze drawn to wind turbines sprinkled around the meadow, their blades slowly turning in the breeze. Jonah unclipped what looked to be a walkie-talkie from his belt and clicked in three times, followed by twice more after a slight pause.

"Walkie-talkies made it through, I guess."

He grimaced. "Only way we can communicate nowadays. Wi-fi doesn't work. At least, not here."

I frowned at him. "Wi-fi? What's that?"

He gave me a disbelieving look. "You must be from the past if you don't know about wi-fi."

"I'm from 1969 then 1859."

He nodded, a smile playing around his lips. "Wi-fi is a way to connect to the internet. You know, for PCs—"

"You've lost me. I have no idea what an internet is, much less a PC."

"I can understand you not knowing about the internet if you're actually from 1969, but they didn't have PCs back then?"

"What's a PC?"

"Personal computer."

I felt my eyes widen. "People had personal computers?"

He smiled fully this time. "Sure did. Laptop computers, computers on their cell phones and watches, even small writing pens."

"Cell phones?"

"Small phones you carried around with you everywhere, about the size of a pack of playing cards. They were like minicomputers. You could use them to turn lights or any appliance on and off, unlock and lock doors, have face time with a friend or relative."

"Face time?"

"You could see who you were actually talking to."

"No way."

He smiled. "You could research anything you wanted on the internet, send text messages ..."

"Text messages? Internet?" I shook my head. "Dang. I really missed a lot."

He started to reply but something caught his attention and he turned from me, waiting. In moments, several people seemed to melt out of the wooded area around us, all armed with weapons, walking toward us. "We're good," he said. "Let's go."

We stepped into the meadow and began to make our way to the greenhouses, joined by what I assumed were members of his army. Jonah greeted them as they approached, asking for status updates. Each cast a suspicious glance at me but didn't inquire as to my presence, ignoring me while they talked to Jonah. "Where's Lem?" Jonah asked at one point, glancing around.

A young woman wearing a tank top and camouflage pants tucked into Army boots shrugged. "He was here just a minute ago. Must be taking a bathroom break."

Jonah nodded. Turning to me, he said, "I was hoping you could take a look at his leg. He limps pretty badly from an injury he sustained several years ago."

I nodded. "I'll be happy to, although to be honest, I doubt I could do anything for that. I'm not skilled in orthopedics."

"Just a thought," he said, leading the way to the greenhouses.

I scanned the meadow as we walked along, surmising Jonah had guards posted all around this area, and when I stepped into the first greenhouse knew why. The fecund odors of rich topsoil and growing vegetation surrounded me as I walked down row after row of vegetables, noting the bright red of tomatoes, sweet peppers of orange and yellow and red, the deep green of cucumbers, peppers, zucchini and green beans, large stalks with yellow and white corn barely showing through the husks, pale-yellow squash along with rows of leafy lettuce and cabbage, others bearing signs of carrots and potatoes and onions, eggplant, okra, beans, peas, and strawberries, their blooms dainty and white. It went on and on. I turned to Jonah, following me. "Are all three greenhouses like this?"

He nodded.

I turned around in a full circle, admiring the neat rows, breathing in the heady air. "Where are the bees?"

Jonah, whose gaze was focused outside, turned back to me. "Pardon?"

"The bees? Some of these are self-pollinators but I think most have to be cross-pollinated. Please tell me you have bees. Honey is a great antibiotic."

He shook his head. "Very few. We lost most of the bees back in the 2020s, so we self-pollinate."

"How in the world do you do that?"

He smiled at me. "It's relatively easy. We use small artist brushes to transfer the pollen from the male flower to the female, or wind's a pretty effective measure. We can pollinate ourselves as easily as brushing against the plants as we walk by or turning on fans." He gestured at the ceiling, from which hung several large industrial fans as well as a plethora of artificial growing lights. He turned back toward the entrance. "You said honey can be used as an antibiotic. We have herbs in the smallest greenhouse. Maybe we'll—"

"Herbs?" I asked, delighted, hurrying to catch up with him.

"Yes."

"Well, that's even better. We can make medicine." I suddenly felt a sense of purpose.

He smiled. "Really? You can do that?"

I nodded. "Sarie, Maggie and Abbie taught me. Abbie knows a lot about herbal medicines."

"That would be great. We haven't had any herbalists on the mountain in years."

"It'll give me something to do until I leave." I floundered on this last word and when I glanced at him saw the hard look back on his face. I turned away, my cheeks reddening, wondering if I was cruel enough to end three, no four, lives by going back. Was my love for Josh worth that? Suddenly the humidity and smell got to me and I turned and ran out of the building. I went around the side, away from everyone, and bent over, my hands on my knees, breathing deeply. When I heard movement nearby, I looked up. Jonah. "I'm sorry. I shouldn't have said that. It makes me sick, thinking of it."

He nodded, his mouth set in a grim line. "Come on, let's go to the herb greenhouse. Like I said, it's the smallest but only because we didn't know what to grow, so we just got seeds and started planting them, mostly to flavor food, but hoping one day we'd know if they could be used for anything else."

I caught up with him, my interest in the herbs overriding my concern for Jonah's and his family's fate. "There are books, you know. You could have researched."

"Good luck with that."

I stopped. "What's that mean?"

He paused, turning back to me. "We don't have wi-fi anymore. At least not here. No one can access the internet to download the ebooks we would need."

I frowned at him. "What's an ebook?"

"An electronic book you can read on a phone, computer, or ebook reader, even a watch."

"What about paper books? Don't they exist anymore?"

"They were around, but everything was pretty much electronic. Not many people actually read, much less bought, dead-tree books."

"Why not?"

"Convenience at first. Easy to carry a small reader around with you with thousands of books stored on it than a heavy book. Then when pollution got so bad, there was a massive effort to save trees so very few dead-tree books were printed." He ran his fingers through his hair. "And now, well, look around you. There aren't many healthy trees."

"Wouldn't there be some dead-tree books around? Like, say, at a library?"

"Maybe. Probably not."

"Why?"

"Afterward, after the asteroid strike, it was utter chaos. People looted buildings, trashed them, burned them. If you stay long enough, I'll take you into Morganton so you can see for yourself what they did. It's like they went crazy. Grocery stores were ransacked, warehouses broken into and torn apart. Even the museum in Morganton was trashed, the library burned to the ground." He shook his head. "It was madness." He scratched at his jaw. "And still is." He stopped in front of the building, gesturing me inside.

Like the first greenhouse, it was laid out neatly, row after row filled with plants. I walked along, reading the signs, recognizing many, noting there were dozens of herbs in the greenhouse but not nearly what we would need to treat different infirmities. I was glad there was an abundance of garlic, which was a good natural antibiotic, antiviral and antibacterial. Near the back of the building, I asked, "Where'd you get the seeds or bulbs?"

"We found a co-op a few miles away. They had some stored in a shed in the back that had been overlooked."

"Were there any more than this?"

He shrugged. "I can't remember, to tell the truth. Like I said, we mostly got these for flavoring food."

"I can tell that." I opened the door and stepped outside, studying the spindly forest surrounding us. "Maybe there are some still left," I said more to myself than him. "Joe Pye weed, ginseng, yarrow." I glanced at the sky, gauging the position of the sun, glowing like a scuffed white ball behind trailing clouds that looked like dirty linen. Well into the west by now, it wouldn't be long before dark. I felt movement behind me and knew Jonah was there. I said over my shoulder as I walked away, "Can you take me farther into the woods as we go back? I'd like to gather if I can find any herbs."

He glanced at the sky. "We don't have much time but we can do that," he replied, his voice friendlier than it had been.

The outskirts of the forest were bare, the trees offering little shelter from what sun managed to filter through the clouds overhead. The air, which was humid and stale, seeming trapped by the clouds above, instantly cooled when we entered the forest. As we walked deeper into the woods, the canopy overhead multiplied and I noticed many of the trees here looked healthier, their leaves green and abundant. I glanced around, wondering what was different about the inner forest. Stopping to rest beneath a large poplar, I couldn't keep myself from putting my arms around it and hugging it while resting my forehead against it. Jonah stood by, watching me with curiosity. I glanced up, caught this. My face reddening, I said, "I'm a tree lover," as I peered closely at the ground, searching for herbs.

"This planet would die without them, I reckon."

"It's good to know they're surviving. At least here." I looked at him. "Why is that, I wonder."

He glanced up at the towering trees. "Due to the Wood Wide Web, I imagine."

I looked at him. "The what?"

"Trees communicate with each other through an underground network of fungus roots. It's called the Wood

Wide Web. Adult trees can share food with younger trees and sick trees can send their remaining nutrients to the healthy ones." He gestured around us. "I'd say that's happening here, they're closing in, helping the ones that might stand a better chance of surviving."

I smiled at this. "Makes sense to me. How do you know so much about trees?"

He shrugged. "I love em too."

I began to walk along, resting my hand on trees we passed as I searched for herbs, and finally stopped, spying a cluster of ginseng nearby.

Jonah joined me when I knelt down beside them, reaching out to touch a red berry. "What's that?"

"Ginseng. It's a good anti-inflammatory and detoxifier." I studied the plants, recalling Sarie's instructions as to the mature ginseng. "It has to be 12 to 24 inches," I told him, "with four or more leaves and these." I touched one of the crimson-colored berries. "Pokni taught me the way of the Catawba, which is to take one out of every three."

"Pokni?"

"She's a Catawba woman I knew back … when I went back to the 1800s. She taught me a lot about healing." I shrugged. "Well, a lot about life." My voice cracked and tears sprang to my eyes as I remembered the little old woman whom I had loved like a grandmother. I blinked hard to clear them. "One out of three won't deplete them, so they can continue to multiply. We'll also need to replant the seeds."

"Okay. What can we dig them up with?"

I glanced around the forest floor, searching for something.

"Will my knife do?" Jonah asked, removing it from the sheath on his belt.

I nodded as I prodded the ground, hard as a rock. "For now, let's just take a couple of plants. We'll mark this spot. That is, if you can remember it?"

Jonah stood, looking around. He finally withdrew what looked to be a large compass from the pack strapped to his back and took bearings, committing them to memory. Afterward, he removed a red rag from his backpack and tied it to a limb low to the ground. "We should be able to find it," he said, bending down to help me with the plants.

After we harvested the ginseng roots and replanted their berries, watering them from our canteens, we resumed our trip. Jonah handed the plants to me which I stuffed into my backpack.

"We need to hurry," he said. "It's getting dark."

I glanced up, noting the forest seemed starker now, the tree boles and leaves a dark gray, their color leached from lack of sunlight.

Using his compass, Jonah guided us to a path he recognized and we began the trek home, barely speaking to one another. My thoughts had returned to Pokni. As I walked along, I said a silent prayer to God, thanking Him for her presence in my life, then reached out with my mind, as I so often did, searching for her. Are you there, Pokni? I asked, remembering her words to me that she would look in on me from time to time as she continued her life's journey.

Although I had hated the 1800s, with its primitive living and brutality, the way women were looked at as chattel instead of actual persons, I realized with a start that my time there had actually been one of the best of my life. I had grown as a person, learned the art of healing from my best friend and surrogate grandmother and sisters, and grown to love those around me, feeling as if they were part of my family. I fell in love with a wonderful man and had begun to plan a future with him. Why in the world were you so anxious to leave, I asked myself. If I hadn't been, I would be back there with Josh, planning our wedding, our life together. A loud cracking sound brought my attention back to the real world. I started, looking up, noting Jonah had probably stepped on a limb or twig. And what about him if you go back? my mind whispered as I watched the way he moved, so like Joshua yet so Jonah as well. Will you kill him and his family with your selfish desire to be with Josh? Shut up, I mentally shouted, making a frustrated noise in my throat.

Jonah glanced back. "You all right, Lizzie?"

I tried to smile but my lips wouldn't move. "I'm fine," I finally managed to croak.

As we broke through the trees into an area I was familiar with, I debated not returning to the house with Jonah but instead continuing on and searching for the lights. Thoughts of leaving Abbie behind, along with concern for Zachary's wound and Andrea's postnatal condition, quickly led me to decide I should stay, at least for the night. Close to the house, I stopped, listening. It's so silent here, I thought. No dogs barking, no birds calling, no cicadas chirping or whatever the heck they did, which used to drive me nuts, they were so loud.

"What about dogs?" I said, catching up with Jonah.

He raised his eyebrows.

"Did they survive? Cats? Horses?" I asked with a pang, remembering my beloved Beauty, sending a silent prayer to Sarie back 190 years ago to please take care of my sweet stallion.

He nodded. "Some. Not many. We have several dogs on the mountain. There are a few domesticated cats and I've seen feral cats roaming around but they never come close. Horses." He smiled at me, and I couldn't help but smile back. "We have horses."

My pulse quickened and I felt my smile broaden. "Oh, lovely. I had the sweetest horse back ..." I gestured with my arm. "Tall, I bet he was 16 or 17 hands, black as midnight, with the sweetest temperament. Although he was a male, I called him Beauty. No other name fit."

Jonah grinned at me. "It's apparent he meant a lot to you."

"I loved him." I blinked away tears. "I miss him."

"You'll see him one day," Jonah said, his smile faltering.

I shrugged. "Maybe."

The encampment came into view and I pointed, glad for the distraction. "Looks like we're here."

He nodded before turning away to greet the sentry coming forward to meet us.

Chapter Six

August 2054

That's How I Eat

I paused when I stepped inside the cabin, sniffing the delightful odor of some sort of bread baking as I took off my backpack and placed it on the table by the door. I noticed Abbie and Andrea had managed to move Zachary to the couch. I walked over to him and placed the back of my hand against his cheek, which felt very warm. "How are you feeling?"

He squinted at me. "Weak, a little tired, but I'm okay."

Abbie joined me, saying, "I think he's feverish, Lizzie."

I nodded, glancing toward Andrea who was approaching sans baby. "Have you got a thermometer?"

She nodded. "An old digital one. Will that do?"

"Digital?"

She smiled. "Oh, that's probably after your time. I'll go get it."

I squeezed Abbie's hand. "Jonah took me to the greenhouses. They've got one just for herbs, Abbie. Not many I could see we can use but on the way back we found some ginseng."

Abbie nodded, her eyes on Zachary. "You reckon he's getting an infection?"

I knelt beside him, saying, "Let me look at the wound," as I peeled back the light blanket covering his leg and removed the bandage. I studied the gash, the skin around it swollen and bright red. I didn't like the looks of it. "If it's not, it's going to be." I thought a moment. "There's garlic in the herb greenhouse, maybe they'll have some here."

Abbie nodded. "A garlic poultice would work."

"They have medicine for fever, the aspirin we found yesterday. Have you given him any today?"

Abbie shook her head. "Andrea and I didn't know how much to give him. We figured we'd wait till you got back."

"Okay, we'll …" I reached out to take the thermometer from Andrea, staring at the cylindrical white instrument, wondering how in the world it worked.

"Here, I'll do it," Andrea said, pushing a button as she moved the wand across her brother's forehead. When it beeped, she studied the readout, then held it out to me.

Red numbers across the back showed 101. "He's definitely feverish. Abbie, can you go get the medical kit we used yesterday? We can give him aspirin. Although it's expired, it may still be potent." I glanced at the wound again. "Bleeding's stopped, I think it's safe enough." As she hurried off, I handed the thermometer back to Andrea, who was watching her brother with a worried look. "Wish we had some willow bark. It contains salicylic acid, the same ingredient as aspirin. The aspirin we have is expired. I'm not sure if it will work."

"Is he going to be okay?" she whispered to me.

"Yes. We just need to treat the fever and infection. Have you got any garlic here?"

"You mean garlic salt or powder?"

"No, the actual vegetable."

She thought a moment. "We might have raw garlic in the pantry. I'll go look."

I followed her, noticing she was moving much better. "How's the baby? How are you?"

She smiled at me over her shoulder. "He's great. I put him down for a nap half an hour ago. I'm feeling fine. I managed to nap this morning when he did."

We found some wilted garlic on a shelf in the pantry. I held it up, studying it. "This might help. We can at least try it."

Andrea followed me into the kitchen. "What are you going to do with it?"

"Make a poultice."

She stood beside me as I took a broad knife and crushed three cloves of garlic. I rummaged through a drawer holding dishtowels, saying over my shoulder, "Do you have a cheesecloth?"

Andrea shrugged. "Not sure what that is."

I found a loosely woven dishcloth. "This will do." I wrapped the crushed cloves in the cloth, then placed it in a bowl of warm water for several minutes. After wringing it out, I returned to the living room, knelt beside Zachary, and put the poultice on his wound. Andrea watched all this with interest while Abbie busied herself trying to make Zachary more comfortable. I noticed she seemed awfully solicitous of someone she didn't know very well.

She eyed my poultice, saying, "I seen Sarie put garlic right on the wound a time or two. Seemed to work well enough."

"We may have to do that but for now let's use the cloth. As you know, garlic can irritate the skin."

"It's a bit harsh but Sarie used it when nothing else would work."

I nodded, remembering how she had treated a young conscript suffering a pustulant bayonet wound with a garlic poultice after placing fly larvae on the wound to ingest the dead tissue. Abbie lightly touched Zachary's shoulder before turning her attention back to me. "You was telling me about the ginseng you found?"

"Yes, in the woods. Most of the herbs in the herb greenhouse are for food flavoring but hopefully we can find some seeds and bulbs at the co-op where Jonah found the herb seedlings. Deeper in the forest, the trees look better and there's ground covering. I figure if we go gathering, we might be able to find some things."

Abbie gave me a curious look.

"What?"

"Seems to me you're planning on staying awhile, Lizzie."

I froze at this observation. Was I? I turned away from her. "Until I find the light." I could feel her staring at me and glanced over my shoulder. I grew uncomfortable at the look she was giving me so smiled at Andrea, saying, "Let's go see the baby, I need to check the umbilical cord," doing my best to ignore the accusation in Abbie's eyes.

When Jonah came inside shortly afterward, Andrea asked him to help move Zachary to his bedroom upstairs, where she felt he'd be more comfortable. I couldn't help but admire Jonah's strength as I watched him pick up his brother as if he were a child and carry him up the stairs, not seeming to strain under the weight. After we got Zachary settled, I returned downstairs to help Andrea with dinner, ignoring Jonah when he told Andrea he would be gone until later.

After he left, I glanced at Andrea, staring at the door, a peculiar expression on her face. "He got a date or something?" I said, in a teasing way.

"Date?" She shook her head. "If you can call it that. He's gone to see Clancy, probably. They're not exactly boyfriend and girlfriend but as close as you can get to it, I guess, without actually being it."

I nodded, not sure what she meant. When Jonah hadn't returned by dinner, I suspected Andrea wasn't expecting him until much later as she didn't put out a plate for him.

When we sat down to eat, I closed my eyes and breathed deeply, sniffing in all the delightful aromas. My mouth watering, I picked up a piece of oven-warm bread and lathered butter on it, then bit into it, moaning with delight. Abbie sat watching me, as if waiting for something. I gave her a questioning look but she simply stared. I looked down at my plate and then up at her. "It's easy to eat, Abbie. Just take your fork and twirl the linguini around it, like this." I coiled the pasta coated with tomato sauce spiced with oregano, garlic, onions and green peppers around my fork then popped it in my mouth. "Oh, it's good," I said, "try it."

Without commenting, she imitated what I had done and put it in her mouth, slowly chewing. I watched as her lips turned upward. "It's right good, I reckon."

I turned to Andrea. "We didn't have linguini back in the 1800s." I shrugged. "Well, not that I know of. Didn't make it, anyway."

"You could have," Andrea said, using her fork to pierce salad greens. "You had flour back then, didn't you?"

Abbie nodded, busy twirling more linguini around her fork. "If we was lucky enough to be able to afford it from the grist mill. A-course, Josh kept us pretty much supplied with things like flour and sugar ..." Her voice trailed off as she darted a glance at me.

I put my fork down on my plate, my appetite dissipating. I had forgotten about Josh and that bothered me more than anything else.

"I'm sorry, Lizzie, I didn't mean to talk about him."

"No, it's all right." I wiped my mouth with my napkin, trying to smile at her and Andrea. "I'm going to go check on Zach. I'll be down in a minute."

Zachary seemed a bit cooler and was resting more comfortably. I had him drink sugared water after checking his wound and ascertaining it wasn't worse looking than earlier, which I took to be a good sign. When I returned downstairs, I found Andrea in the recliner nursing her baby and Abbie filling the kitchen sink with water preparatory to washing the dishes. "Here, let me help," I said, nudging her aside and picking up the dishcloth. I eyed the dishwasher, which looked much more complicated than those from my time, wondering if I would have been able to figure it out if they actually used it instead of saving water by doing dishes by hand.

Abbie stepped back, watching me as she picked up a dishtowel. "Life would've been a lot easier if we had running water back then. I can't get used to bein able to have hot water in an instant, Lizzie. Don't know if I'll ever get used to it."

I smiled at her over my shoulder. "You will, Abbie. Before long, it will seem normal to you."

She nodded. "I reckon it ain't so hard understandin why you wanted to go back so bad."

"Well, this is one of many reasons." I sighed. "But I'd give all these luxuries up in an instant if I could find my way back to Josh."

"I know." She touched my shoulder. "I'm so sorry I was so mad at you, Lizzie. I know you thought you was protectin me and did what you thought was best."

"I'll make it up to you, Abbie. I'll get us back, I swear it."

She didn't answer, which puzzled me. I looked at her, wondering if she was beginning to like this time and place enough to want to stay. She seemed to have lost her enthusiasm for finding the light and wasn't as anxious to leave as she had been the day before. What had changed? When I saw her eyes shift upward, the thought occurred to me she may have formed some sort of connection to Zach. She seemed more concerned about him than I'd ever seen her act with a patient before.

Her face reddened when she caught me staring at her. As if to explain, she said, "I moved our things into a bedroom upstairs. It's the last one on the left."

"Oh, that's great, Abbie. We can sleep in an actual bed."

She grinned. "There's two of em up there, Lizzie. We each get our own. I lay down on mine and I never felt anything so soft and comfortable. I reckon we'll sleep well tonight."

I smiled back. "I reckon we will, Abbie."

After we finished the dishes, Abbie took a light supper upstairs to Zachary while I returned to the living room, where I joined Andrea in admiring the baby. When the door opened, Andrea and I both looked up. Jonah stepped through, followed by a young, exotically beautiful woman with black, silky hair hanging low down her back. I vaguely thought everything about her was black and white, from her dark eyebrows and eyes to the white shirt and black jeans she wore. Jonah touched her elbow as he introduced her to me. "Lizzie, this is Clancy. Clancy, Lizzie."

I smiled at her, thinking what a contrast she was to Jonah. "Nice to meet you."

Her eyes traveled over me in an appraising way. Apparently not liking what she saw, she gave me a brusque nod before turning her attention to Andrea and the baby. As I watched the way they interacted, I surmised at once that Andrea did not like this woman. I glanced at Jonah, his eyes on me. He quickly looked away.

After a few moments, Clancy walked toward the door, ignoring me as she passed by. "It was nice meeting you," I called after her but she acted as if she didn't hear me.

Jonah smiled at Andrea before following Clancy out.

"That was weird," I observed.

Andrea shook her head. "Don't let her get to you. She isn't the friendliest person in the world, especially if you're a woman and anywhere near Jonah."

"Jealous, is she?"

"Overly so." Andrea rolled her eyes. The baby made a squawking sound and she turned her attention to him, rocking him slightly as she sang softly to him. I sat on the sofa watching her, wondering why some women were so much more maternal than others. I had met several on the mountain who had children but who seemed to resent that fact and took their feelings out on them in harsh ways, or simply ignored them as much as they could, leaving them to their own devices in regards to eating and having basic needs met. But there were so many others who, from the moment the baby was born, even conceived, fell in love with their child and relished their role as mother, as nurturer.

Andrea glanced up, caught me watching her. "I think I'll name him Joseph, after his father." Tears shone in her eyes and she quickly looked down at the baby. "He looks like him."

"It's a beautiful name for a beautiful child."

"Yes," she whispered, "it is. And he was." She stroked the baby's fine hair. "I understand why you want so desperately to return to your Josh. My separation from Joseph was not of my choosing, as yours wasn't, and I know how hellish it is wanting to be with your love once more and not being able to." She glanced at the door. "Jonah's never loved anyone like that. It's hard for him to understand. But he made you a promise, and if I know one thing about my brother, he'll keep it come hell or high water."

"I hope so," I said, rising to my feet. I touched her on the shoulder. "I'm tired, I think I'll go upstairs and go to bed. Call me if you need me."

She placed her cheek against the back of my hand for a moment. "I will, Lizzie. Sleep well."

I looked in on Zachary, being watched over by Abbie. She smiled when she saw me. "I think his fever's gone."

"Good. I'm going to bed. You staying up for awhile?"

"I think I'll sit with Zach a bit longer, then Andrea promised to show me one of them movies you kept talking about back …" She grimaced. "Sorry, Lizzie."

I smiled. "You'll love it, Abbie. Have fun. If they have any popcorn, have her make you some, with butter."

Chapter Seven

August 2054

I'm a Stranger Here

Feeling more rested when I woke early the next morning, I rolled over and checked the bed against the opposite wall. Abbie was there, on her side facing the wall, breathing evenly. Moving as quietly as I could, I got out of bed and walked over to the window to peek out at the day. The grayish tinge to the sky told me it must be just past dawn. I opened the door, wincing when it squeaked, squeezed through and walked across the hall to check on Zach. Realizing he still slept, I stood over him, staring at his face for a long moment. Unlike Jonah, who resembled Josh so much, and Andrea, who favored Sarie in facial expressions and mannerisms, Zach looked nothing like either the Collins or Hamptons. His hair was a deep chestnut color and his eyes so brown they appeared black at times, which made me wonder if there wasn't Cherokee or Catawba in his bloodline. He wasn't as tall as his brother and had a stockier build, the muscles in his arm bulging as if he worked out with weights. When he opened his eyes suddenly, startling me, I blinked then placed the back of my hand on his forehead.

"How are you feeling?" I whispered.

"Better," he whispered back.

I lifted the blanket and removed the garlic poultice. Although the skin around the wound remained red, it didn't look as bright and the swelling had gone down. I smiled at him. "It's looking better."

"Feels better." His gaze shifted toward the door. "Is Abbie awake yet?"

I smiled to myself, thinking he must like her about as much as she seemed to like him. "She's still sleeping." I didn't miss the disappointment on his face at this news. "I'm sure she'll check on you when she wakes up. Can I get you anything?"

"I'm fine. I'll wait for Abbie." He closed his eyes, dismissing me.

I patted his arm. "Okay." I returned to our room, crossed over to the dresser, on which Abbie and Andrea had placed fresh clothes, picked up a tank top and jeans and went down the hall to the bathroom. Emerging ten minutes later, refreshed and clean, I luxuriated in this feeling. Back in the 1800s, freshening up in the morning usually consisted of simply splashing water on my face, and I could not deny how wonderful it was to step under a hot shower, sluice away dirt and grime and perspiration, and emerge feeling ready to face any challenge put before me.

I returned to our bedroom, collected all our dirty clothes, then tiptoed downstairs in search of the laundry room, figuring I would wash our clothes while the others slept. Jonah was sitting at the table, drinking from a steaming mug. I jerked when I saw him, startled at the sight of anyone other than me awake this early.

He held up his cup. "You want some coffee? It's fresh."

I raised the clothes in my hands. "After I find the washing machine. Andrea said you had one. Is it down here?"

He nodded. "It's behind those louvered doors next to the pantry."

I found the machine, placed my load inside, then spent a few minutes trying to figure out how to work the darn thing. There were no knobs to turn but plenty of options to push. After punching different ones then changing my mind and punching others, I finally settled on what I thought would work, added some kind of weird-looking gel tablet that was in a box labeled laundry detergent, and pushed start. When I heard water gushing into the machine, I figured I'd apparently got it right.

By the time I returned to the kitchen, Jonah had poured a cup of coffee and set it on the table. I reached for it, took a sip and sighed with pleasure. "So good," I murmured, sliding the chair out across from him and sitting down.

"Better than coffee in your time?"

"In the 1800s, if we didn't have any real coffee, which was a lot, we'd make it out of acorns or chicory." I made a face. "Not the best taste in the world. Not even real coffee back then tasted this good because of all the grounds floating around. But this, this is bliss." I inhaled deeply from the cup, savoring the smell as I eyed the coffee machine on the counter which looked about as complicated as the washing machine.

He smiled at me. "You figure out the washer?"

"Took awhile but, yeah, I think I got it right. In my time, the 20th century, washers had knobs you turned, not all these different buttons."

"Is that right?"

"And the detergent was in powder form, not those multi-colored tablets y'all have."

His mouth twitched. "Wow, must have been harsh back then."

I looked at him, saw the grin playing around his lips.

Smiling back, I said, "Not as hard as the 1800s. Try scrubbing clothes against rocks in streams to get them clean or boiling them in a big pot over a fire. Not to mention, having to use lye soap." I shuddered, looking at my hands, which always appeared red even though I used a special lotion Pokni had taught me to make. "It was horrible, grueling work. I always dreaded it."

"How'd you dry them?"

"Abbie and her sisters were draping them over bushes when I first arrived but I showed them how to make clotheslines using rope. Big difference."

He grinned at this. "I could imagine."

I noticed he seemed more at ease today. Clancy must have been of some benefit to him, I thought.

We sipped in companionable silence for a bit, staring out the window at the struggling forest, beginning to take shape as light found the trees. After awhile, Jonah put down his mug and turned his attention on me. "I have a favor to ask."

"If I can do it, sure."

"We have some people on the mountain who aren't doing so well. I was wondering if you'd take a look at them, see if you can help them."

"Just to set things straight, I'm not really a doctor, you know."

His eyebrows shot up at that. "I thought that's what Abbie said."

"During her time, you could say I qualified as a doctor, certainly more than some of the quacks I met. But during my time, in the 20th century, I was only a medical student. I hadn't graduated med school and gotten my medical degree."

"Maybe so, but I'd say if experience counts for anything, calling you a doctor isn't far off the mark."

I was unexpectedly pleased at the compliment. "We can look for the light as we go along. And if you don't mind, I want to go to my cabin, see if it's still standing. I really loved that place."

"No problem. We'll start out after breakfast. Speaking of which …" He rose to his feet. "I better get started."

I put down my mug and stood. "I'll help."

After breakfast, as I was packing the first aid kit into the backpack Andrea had given me, I asked Abbie if she wanted to go along. "Jonah wants me to take a look at some people who aren't feeling well and I thought I'd go check on our cabin."

Her eyes lit at that. "Oh, Lizzie, I hope it's still there." She glanced upstairs. "I reckon I ought to stay one more day and see to Zach. Just to make sure."

I wanted to argue with her, tell her he was out of danger, but didn't have the heart for it. It was obvious to me by now that she had developed some sort of feelings for the young man. I stared at the contents of my backpack. "Andrea, do y'all have any latex gloves I can use?"

"I think there's a box in the pantry. I'll go look." When Andrea pushed the baby into Jonah's arms, he looked down at his nephew as if he had no idea what to do with him. His expression was so comical, I had to turn my head so he wouldn't see my amusement.

"What's latex gloves?" Abbie said.

On the mountain, of course, we never had that luxury and it was one I had certainly missed, always fearful of contamination to the patient or me. "Thin rubber gloves you wear when you examine patients. It's safer for everyone."

Andrea returned with a box of rubber gloves, explaining they were supposed to be used for painting or home projects. I pulled one out and examined it, deciding it looked thin enough to do the job while protecting me. "Thanks. This will work." I stuffed several in the backpack then picked it up and put it on. "I'll let you know what I find," I told Abbie as I hugged her, then followed Jonah out of the cabin.

He turned toward me, saying, "First, I want to show you something."

I followed him around the house into the tree line which was just that, a row of trees hiding a meadow, in the middle of which sat a roomy barn with a fenced-in corral to one side and a large pasture on the other boxed in by barbwire tacked to posts made out of what looked to be the stout limbs of trees.

Following my gaze, Jonah said, "That's been there since before my time, probably over a hundred years from the looks of it. Don't know who put it up but they did a good job. It's never broken down."

Nearby, a chicken coop sat inside a small area fenced with chicken wire, at least a dozen chickens clucking away and pecking at the ground while a rooster strutted around as if king of the castle. In the meadow grazed several goats, cows and two horses, one that looked to be a quarter horse, chestnut in color with a black mane, the other a dapple grey that might have been Arabian. When the horses spied Jonah, they ambled toward the fence. I couldn't help but smile at him as I hurried toward them. I threw my arms around the chestnut as he leaned his head over the top rail, burying my face in the side of his neck, breathing in deeply. "Nothing smells better than a horse."

Jonah laughed. "For the most part."

"Are they yours?" I asked, thinking he had a nice laugh.

He nodded, feeding each a carrot. "Mine and Zachary's. Andrea had one too but she died a year ago. Been looking for another one for her ever since."

"Do you ride them much?"

"Occasionally if we're traveling over the whole mountain. We won't be needing them today."

My smile faltered.

He caught that. "Disappointed?"

"A bit."

"We'll ride soon, I promise."

I rubbed my hand beneath the mane of each horse, wondering if I'd get the chance before I left. "Let's go."

Jonah led me down the mountain, on a narrow path I didn't recognize. I looked around at the scenery as we passed by. "Nothing looks the same. I can't even find the trails we used to travel when we made our rounds on the mountain."

He stopped to remove a limb that had fallen across the way. "What about when you were here back in 1969?"

"We were camping then. The mechanic working on our van gave us a ride from Morganton up to the overlook on Brown Mountain and we walked in from there. It was almost dark by the time we got here. I didn't see very much, to tell you the truth."

"Well, over the years, roads have been paved on the mountain along with some driveways, although a lot of people elected for gravel instead. I'm sure as time went on, the eco system has changed somewhat."

I stared at the spindly trees. "You can say that again. It never looked this sparse."

"Hopefully that will change once the air clears." We both looked at the sky, a sullen beige color.

When he stopped and turned to me, I gave him a questioning look. "What are we going to tell people?"

"I don't understand."

"About you and Abbie. We can't tell them you came from the lights. People don't believe in those things, at least not anymore."

"Well, what'd you tell Clancy and the others?"

"Simply that you showed up here looking for your family's old homeplace, and when we found out you were a doctor and Abbie a midwife, we asked you to stay to help with Andrea."

I shrugged. "Sounds good enough. We'll stick with that." I gave him a look. "For now. You can figure out what to tell them after we've gone."

He didn't reply to that, simply turned and began walking again, pausing every now and again to hold back a limb from smacking me in the face. Finally, he pointed to a spacious looking house ahead. "That's our first stop." Other than the white paint peeling off its planks, the house looked sturdy and in good condition, standing tall and stately among the trees. I figured it must have been built after the 1800s since it didn't look familiar at all.

I followed Jonah up a gravel drive to the wraparound porch and stood behind him as he banged on the wooden door. Muffled footsteps told me someone was home. The door was opened by a woman who looked to be in her 80s with a severe dowager's hump that I assumed must be from osteoporosis.

She grinned widely when she saw Jonah. "Well, hell's bells, if it ain't our esteemed leader Jonah Hampton. What brings you to my door this fine day?"

"Helen," Jonah said with a smile, acknowledging her ironic referral to him. "You have any problem during the raid?"

She shook her head. "Bishop alerted me in time to hide. Don't think they even come this far over, to tell the truth. Never heard anybody."

"That's good. This here is Lizzie." He took my elbow and drew me to stand beside him. "She's a doctor. I thought I'd bring her by, see if she can help you with your rheumatism."

Helen peered up at me from beneath wiry white eyebrows. "See you got you another tall un." She glared at Jonah. "You sayin she's a doctor?"

"Yes. Why don't you let us in? Maybe she can help you."

Helen studied me a moment longer, then shrugged, causing her head to almost disappear between her shoulders. "Come on in then."

We stepped into a wide foyer with a wooden staircase on the far side. The plank floors glowed with polish, the side table near the door gleaming in the weak light pouring in through the doorway. "You have a beautiful home," I said to Helen as she walked ahead of us into a spacious living room filled with a comfortable-looking sofa and chairs.

"Thank you," she said rather primly. "My Horace built this house 60 years back. Built it well, too. Ain't had to replace much as the years have gone by, just a few boards on the porch and a-course the roof when it started leaking."

"He did a beautiful job," I said watching her gait as she walked, which was stiff and awkward, her upper back so rounded, she seemed to be staring down at the floor. I thought it must be frustrating looking down all day.

Helen poked a large mound dozing on the sofa, saying, "Get up, old man, we've got company." With black hair and huge paws, I crazily thought at first it might be a bear. When it jerked to attention, standing on all four paws, looking ready to attack, I backed away then realized it was only a dog. When the mongrel saw Jonah, he panted, wagging his tail, then turned his gaze on me. I held out my fist for him to sniff, figuring if he was dangerous, I would have been warned by Jonah and Helen. Apparently passing muster, he licked the back of my hand then got off the couch and went to Jonah, who scratched his ears, the dog groaning in bliss.

Helen sat in a chair across from the couch and gestured for us to sit. After we were all settled, including the dog, who sat between Jonah and me, leaning heavily against Jonah, I said, "Why don't you tell me about your rheumatism?"

She shrugged. "Ain't much to tell. Hurts like the dickens most days."

I reached out with my hands. "Do you mind if I look at your hands, Helen?"

She glanced at Jonah before putting her arms out. I took her hands in mine, studying the red, swollen knuckles, her fingers so twisted her hands were almost claw-like. "Do you take anything for this?"

"Nope. Don't have anything to take. I put heat on it from time to time. Don't seem to help much, tell the truth."

I dug in the backpack. "All I've got is some expired aspirin but it will help with the pain. Would you like some?"

She waved it away. "You keep that, use it on somebody else. I've dealt with this pain for so long, it's part of me now. I reckon I can bide for now."

I turned to Jonah. "Isn't there medication for this?"

He nodded. "When I go scavenging, I always check pharmacies, but medicine is in high demand, there's never anything on hand to help her."

"I doubt you'd have anything in your herb greenhouse. Black cohosh is good for this. So is juniper or willow. Surely there are junipers and willows in the forest?"

"Should be plenty of those."

"If you have sweet basil, also called St. John's wort, in your greenhouse, that could help with the pain."

"I'll check." He got up, pulling the walkie-talkie off his belt, and walked outside.

Helen watched him go, a smile on her face. She looked back to me. "You his girlfriend?"

I shook my head. "No, I've only just come here. I think he already has one."

She pursed her lips. "Clancy," she said, with a sneer. "I wouldn't call her that."

I didn't know what to say to that so busied myself pulling out a pad and pen and writing notes about Helen's predicament. "I'll go gathering for herbs as soon as I can. I should have something for you very soon, Helen, which I think will help a bit."

"I do thank you," she said, rising to her feet.

I followed suit, looking toward the door when Jonah returned. "We don't have it," he said, glancing at Helen.

"There are probably herbs in the forest that will work. I'll look for them."

"You ready to go?"

"Yes." I turned to Helen. "It was nice meeting you. I'll see you soon."

Helen nodded as Jonah held the door for me, waiting for me to precede him outdoors. I bent down to pet the dog before leaving, smiling when he licked my face. As I went outside, I heard Helen say to Jonah, "Don't know where this un come from, but she's a whole site better than that Clancy hanging on your arm."

Jonah murmured something I didn't catch. As we walked away, I wondered what the deal was with Clancy. When my mind turned to Helen, I said, "What's his name?"

Jonah gave me a curious look.

"The dog."

"Oh. Nobody knows. He showed up here one day a few years back, half-starved, so afraid of people he wouldn't let anyone get near him. Helen put food out for him every day but didn't think he'd hang around, so never gave him a name, just called him Old Man. Even though he eventually started trusting her and never left, she still calls him that." He shrugged. "Don't guess the dog objects too much, that's what he answers to."

"Do you have a veterinarian on the mountain?"

He shook his head. "Wish we'd had one last year when Andrea's horse went down. Lord, how she grieved that horse."

"What happened?"

"We don't know. I think she got into something, a plant or some such that must have been poisonous. It wasn't pleasant."

"Well, if you need a vet, Abbie's as good as any I've ever known. She has a way with animals."

He darted a smile my way. "That's good. We can use her." His smile dropped. "Well, as long as y'all are here."

Jonah led me to a small cabin farther down the mountain, where he introduced me to a young black woman named Evelyn, who was five months pregnant and terrified. After she assured Jonah she hadn't had any problems with the raiders, he told her I was a doctor and could help her.

She grabbed my hands when Jonah introduced me. "Oh, I've prayed for someone who would know what to do," she said, tears in her eyes.

"You'll be in good hands," Jonah said. "Lizzie and her friend Abbie helped Andrea when she gave birth yesterday."

Evelyn squealed with delight. "Is she all right? Is the baby? What'd she have, a boy or girl? I bet it was a boy."

"You're right and they're both fine, thanks to Lizzie and Abbie," Jonah said.

I squeezed her hands. "You don't have anything to worry about, Evelyn. I'm here and so is Abbie. She's the best midwife I've ever known." Well, other than Maggie, I added mentally. I looked around at the cabin. "I recognize this place," I said to Jonah. It had belonged to the Gruber family back when I was here with Abbie and her sisters. They had lost their infant son to influenza during one particularly harsh winter.

"You've been on the mountain before?" Evelyn said, Interrupting my thoughts.

Oh, shoot, I thought, avoiding Jonah's eyes. "A long time ago. My family used to live here, way back when. Jonah is going to take me to our cabin today. I'm anxious to see it, actually." Realizing I would begin to ramble if I didn't stop, I gestured at the small interior, consisting of one main room, a small galley kitchen tucked into a corner, with a tiny bedroom and bathroom off to one side. "Why don't we go into the bedroom where I can check you, make sure everything's all right?

Jonah's face reddened. "Uh, I think I'll step outside for this part," he said, backing away.

I had to hold my laughter. He looked so uncomfortable, and an embarrassed Jonah was a new one to me. "That's a good idea," I said, with a smile.

I had Evelyn lie down on the bed, admiring the colorful quilt covering it. "It was my granny's," she said with a proud look. "Only thing I ever asked of her before she died was to give it to me."

"It's beautiful." I traced the stitchery, remembering quilting bees back before. I had never been a skilled seamstress but had eventually become good enough to sit in on one or two. "Jonah says you're about five months along." I put my hand on the slight abdominal bulge, wishing I had a tape measure to measure the fundal height. "Have you had any problems?"

She shook her head. "I've been trying to eat healthy."

"Any alcohol?"

"No."

"Good. Don't. What about smoking?"

"You mean like vaping?"

"Cigarettes?"

"Hardly anyone smokes those things anymore. Doubt they could get them if they wanted. They're illegal, you know."

"Right. What about drugs?"

"You mean like medicine?"

"That, and illegal drugs, like marijuana and cocaine and such."

"No." She gave me a look before saying, "Marijuana's not illegal, you should know that."

"Right, but it's better if you don't smoke it."

"What about cannabis pills or oils?"

"I wouldn't risk it."

She smiled. "Don't take it anyway."

"Any bleeding, pain?"

"No, none."

"How old are you, Evelyn?"

"19. Why? Is that too young?"

She seemed so anxious, I worried it would affect her pregnancy. "No, actually, it's a very good age for having a baby."

I did a quick pelvic exam to check for effacement or dilation as well as the position of the cervix. Everything seemed normal. "You're good," I told her, peeling off the gloves and placing them in a trash can in the bathroom. Returning to the bedroom, I said, "Do you have any questions?"

She gave me a beaming smile. "No, I'm just glad you're here. I can't tell you how relieved I am knowing you'll be here when I have my baby."

I didn't know what to say to that since my one hope was that I would not be there in four months' time but would instead be back where I belonged. And where is that, my inner voice sneered. Back with Josh, where you eliminate a whole family, or maybe back where you really belong, with your father? I forced those thoughts out of my head as I smiled back at Evelyn, trying to offer her some reassurance while not committing to staying.

When I left, I told Evelyn she wouldn't need to be seen for a month unless she developed problems along the way.

"Are you sure?" she said, glancing anxiously at Jonah. "Don't you need to see a pregnant woman every week or so?"

"No, that only happens at the last month. Up until then, the norm is monthly unless you're having any problems. You should do well. You're young, healthy, doing all the right things." I reached out and touched her arm. "But if you get scared or have any questions, get word to me and I'll come see you. How's that?"

She pulled me into a tight hug. "Thank you, Lizzie."

When we left, I led the way, saying over my shoulder. "I know where we are. I can find our cabin from here."

Jonah gestured with his hand. "Lead on."

We walked single file until the trail widened, then he stepped up beside me.

I asked something that had been troubling me. "Where's the father? It looked to me like Evelyn's living alone."

His mouth tightened for a moment. "Gone. When he found out she was pregnant, he took off." He shrugged. "Didn't want the responsibility, I guess."

I shook my head with disdain as I veered off the path. "How'd she take it?"

"Badly. She wanted to abort the baby but no one wanted to help her."

"I gather there aren't many abortionists around." There hadn't been back in 1969, either, since it was illegal. Most women had to resort to back-alley doctors if theirs weren't amenable to it. And when they were, the reason had to be hidden behind a medical issue.

"Nowadays, there are pills you can take in the early days. She asked me to find a pharmacy that had them. I lied and told her I checked at several but there were none to be found."

"You lied?"

The bushes rustled nearby and Jonah and I stopped, looking that way. I prayed it wasn't a snake intent on sinking its fangs in my ankle. When the noise ended, we resumed our journey, returning our eyes to the path ahead as Jonah continued. "Andrea thought Evelyn wasn't putting things in the right perspective at that exact moment. She felt if we gave her a chance to get used to the idea, let her know we would be there to help her, she'd warm up to it and change her mind."

I smiled. "Must have worked. She seems relatively happy and looks to be doing the right things to make sure her baby is born healthy."

He nodded but didn't say anything.

"Does she have anyone, any close friends, relatives, who look in on her?"

He nodded. "Her brother's married, lives close by. He checks in with her daily. So do others on the mountain." He glanced back at me. "We all look out for one another."

I decided to ask him a question I'd already asked Andrea, just to get his perspective. "Andrea said that other than her baby, there aren't infants or toddlers on the mountain. Why is that?"

He shrugged, saying, "Would you want a child at a time like this?"

"But Andrea had her baby, you wanted Evelyn to keep her child. Why now?"

He glanced at the sky. "It's getting better, the sky is clearing. Plus we're more able to take care of ourselves now and can offer them a more normal life, not one where they might starve to death or die from unnatural causes."

"Meaning raiders?"

"That, and hopefully with a doctor and healer on the mountain, they'll stand a better chance of surviving."

Until I leave, I thought but didn't voice.

His raised eyebrows told me he knew what I was thinking.

I looked ahead, quickening my pace, knowing we were close to where my cabin was. I was nearly running by the time I stepped into the clearing where it had been. I stopped suddenly, staring. Jonah caught up with me but remained silent as I looked around.

The fence Abbie and I had put up around the small corral was gone as was the barn we had put so much time and effort into, aided by Joshua. My cabin was still there, looking desolate and abandoned. I heaved a sigh of relief when I realized no one appeared to be living in it. I slowly walked toward it, studying the outside. The logs were more weathered but looked to have held up well. Our small front porch, where we had placed two rocking chairs side by side, where Abbie and I used to sit of a night and talk about this or that, or she would listen while I told her about my world or the movies I had seen or books I had read, was entirely gone. The front door tilted downward but opened easily enough when I tugged on it.

I stepped inside, smiling with delight when I saw that Luther's woodwork on the mantle over the fireplace remained. As I looked around, I noted several of the wooden floor planks had rotted and a thick layer of dirt and dust lay over everything. At some point, the cabin had been updated somewhat. The kitchen area now contained a black double sink along with a refrigerator and stove and oven combination, surrounded by a modern-looking black and white countertop with sleek white cabinets overhead. An extension had been built onto the back, with a spacious bedroom and master bath with toilet, vanity and shower. I was disappointed to see that the headboard Luther had carved so beautifully was gone.

"Is it changed much?" Jonah said behind me.

I glanced at him, tears in my eyes. "Yes and no." I walked over to the mantle, traced the lovely carving so intricately set into the wood. "The cabin originally belonged to a man named Luther who came to North Carolina to mine gold but all he got for it was lung cancer. He built this mantle and a headboard with carvings to match. When he died, he gave the cabin to me, along with his mule Jonah." I wiped at the tears falling down my face. "Oh, how Abbie and I loved that mule and this place. We worked on it a lot, even built a bigger barn and fenced in a corral. With Josh's help." I turned my back on him, wiping my eyes.

"I'm sorry," he said in a low voice.

I turned back to him. "What for?"

"That this happened to you, that you ended up here." He gestured toward the outside of the cabin. "That you lost your home and your horse and mule and Josh."

"That's all my fault. I shouldn't have pushed Abbie into the light, knowing it was the wrong one."

"Sounds to me like you were only trying to get to safety."

I shook my head, walking away from him, out the door. When he left the cabin, he shut the door behind him softly then rejoined me at the edge of the small clearing. I pointed to the right, near where the corral had been. "Abbie and I had our garden there. Oh how I hated weeding that blasted thing but loved what we grew. Our days were so busy here, I barely had time to think, and when I did, all I could think about was getting back to 1969, to my time, where things were so much better. Electricity, hot and cold running water, indoor toilets."

"I imagine it must have been a huge culture shock going back to that time," he mused, kneeling down to move dead leaves away from a small blue flower trying to poke its way through.

I couldn't help but laugh. "It was horrible. But looking back now, I realize it was probably the best time of my life. I learned herbal healing from Pokni, Sarie, Abbie and Maggie. I helped people, had a lot of experiences, good and bad. I participated in a bit of history by helping Josh help slaves escape through the Underground Railroad," I said with a bit of pride, adding, "Even went to the Battle of Gettysburg."

He leaned his head back and looked at me then, his expression one of astonishment. "How'd you end up in Gettysburg?"

"Josh was spying for the North, and when he was asked by a friend to join the Confederacy as a courier for his regiment just before the Battle of Gettysburg, he agreed, hoping to gather information that could be of use. Abbie and I went along as field nurses."

"What happened?"

"A lot at the time, but that was the extent of our involvement in the Civil War. Josh got injured and was sent home, so we went back with him."

Jonah stood up, squinting his eyes at me. "I'd love to hear what all happened sometime."

I frowned at him, not sure what the look he was giving me meant. "Sure. It'll take awhile. Later?"

He gave me Josh's crooked grin. "What else interesting happened to you then?"

"I fell in love, real love."

He cocked an eyebrow at that.

"I had a boyfriend back in 1969, who I thought I was in love with but that wasn't like what I felt for Josh. Anyway, that's the reason I was in Morganton when our van broke down. We were headed to Woodstock."

He smiled widely at that.

"You've heard of it?"

"Only the best rock concert ever."

I gave him a questioning look.

"My granddad's dad was there. He purchased a video of the entire concert which my dad transferred to a flash drive. Andrea, Zach and I watch it all the time."

I vaguely wondered what a flash drive was but didn't pursue it, more interested in the goings-on at Woodstock. "Would you mind if I watch sometime? See what I missed?"

"No problem."

I found myself smiling widely at him, thinking how awfully handsome he was when he lost the stern look on his face. Realizing what I was doing, I stopped smiling and looked away from him.

"We'd best be on our way," he said, in a low voice. "There's someone else I'd like you to see."

"Oh, sure. Let's go." I looked at the cabin one last time then turned my back on it and walked into the forest.

After a bit, he said, "Did you find the light near here?"

I shook my head. "It was closer to Sarie's cabin." I glanced at him. "I can't understand why you've lived here all your life and never seen them."

"It may have something to do with the sky. Up until a few years back, it was like twilight most days. Like I told you before, it's getting better."

As we walked farther down the mountain, I kept looking around me, hoping I'd recognize familiar points. Occasionally I'd see a cabin but rarely saw anyone. When we did, they'd hail Jonah while giving me questioning looks but never engaged in conversation with either one of us.

"You said you have sentries all over the mountain. I haven't seen any."

His lips twitched. "They're there, but you won't notice them. They're well-hidden but see everything. I guarantee our progress down the mountain is being relayed as we pass each sentry point."

After he said that, I kept feeling eyes on the back of my neck, as if the sentries were staring hard at me. I knew it was just paranoia but couldn't shake the feeling.

"What happens when raiders are on the mountain?" I asked. "How do you let everyone know they're here and what happens after that?"

He glanced at me. "Everyone carries walkie-talkies. If a sentry or anyone spots a raider or stranger, they key in a code which goes out to everyone. We all have hidey-holes we can go to, places they hopefully won't find us."

"You mean like your basement?"

He nodded. "First time they've found it. I guess we'll have to come up with something better."

Near the bottom of the mountain, Jonah turned into a paved driveway leading up to a small clapboard cottage. The wooden door was open but a screen door barred our entrance into the cottage. Jonah knocked a couple of times before opening the door with a loud screech. A middle-aged woman stepped out of what I assumed to be the kitchen, a drying towel in her hands. She smiled widely when she saw Jonah, but when he stepped aside to reveal me, her expression changed to one filled with suspicion.

"You have any problems during the raid?" Jonah asked, drawing her attention back to him.

She shook her head. "Got the alert but I didn't see or hear anything." She stared at me with an insolent expression.

"Angie, this is Lizzie," Jonah said quickly, catching her look. "She's a doctor. I brought her to see Avery."

Angie studied me for a long moment. "Where'd she come from, Jonah?"

"Her family used to live here, years ago. She asked me to show her the cabin they owned and I said I would. When I found out she knows about healing with herbs and such, I thought I'd have her take a look at those on the mountain who are ailing."

Angie nodded but thought about it for a long moment. She finally sighed. "Well, if you vouch for her, I guess she's all right. He's in his bedroom. I'll take you there."

She walked down a short hallway to a doorway on the right and opened the door without knocking, saying, "Avery, Jonah's here."

Jonah stepped into the room, speaking to Avery in a friendly tone. His shoulders were so broad, he filled the doorway and I had to stand patiently outside in the hallway until Jonah explained who I was and what I was there for. He finally moved aside, motioning me into the room. I stepped through the door, smiling at the young teenager sitting in bed, a book on his lap. Although his black hair was tousled and unkempt, he had on a clean t-shirt and jeans. He removed his glasses, revealing dark-blue eyes framed with thick black lashes. I smiled at him as I approached, my gaze scanning his body, which appeared emaciated and undernourished.

I pulled over a chair at a small desk beneath the window and placed it beside the bed. Sitting down, I said, "Why don't you tell me what's going on?"

Avery glanced at his mother, who I assumed nodded her approval, before answering. "I don't know, honestly. I'm thirsty all the time, can't get enough water. Even though I eat, I'm losing weight."

"And he sleeps a lot," his mother put in.

I picked up his hand, put my fingers on his inner wrist, checking his pulse, then placed my hand on his chest, watching him breathe. I checked the carotid pulse, felt for swollen glands beneath his jaw. "Do you ever run a fever?"

He shook his head.

I wished I had a stethoscope so I could listen to his heart then inwardly sighed when I realized I was right back to 1864, without any sort of medical instrumentation to help me make diagnoses. Leaning close to his face, so I could smell his breath as he talked, I said, "Tell me your age, what you like to do."

"I'm 16 and my favorite thing to do is read, I guess, although there aren't many books around. Used to like to play sports but I don't feel up to it anymore."

"Do you have to pee a lot?" I asked.

He nodded.

"How about your vision? Any problems there?"

"Well, I have to wear reading glasses to read." He held up the glasses, which looked ancient and I assumed must have belonged to an ancestor.

"Tingling or numbness in your hands and feet?"

"Sometimes."

"What about when you get a sore, does it take long to heal, or do you get infections a lot?"

"He gets colds all the time," his mom said. "A lot more than he used to."

"And sores?"

Avery rolled up his sleeve and pointed to an open sore on his arm. "Got that from a mosquito bite. It's taking a long time to scab over."

I leaned back, patting his hand. "Okay, thanks, Avery. Let me talk to your mom, all right?"

His forehead furrowed. "You can tell me what you think's wrong with me. I'm old enough to hear it."

I glanced at Angie, whose eyes darted to her son then back to me. She seemed to deflate as she nodded.

"Okay, that's fine." I addressed Avery as I spoke. "From your symptoms and the fact that your breath smells very sweet, I think you have diabetes. Of course, I can't confirm that without medical tests but I doubt that can be done here. In any event, I'm fairly certain it's diabetes. I'm sorry, but I don't know of an herb that can help with that." I turned to Jonah. "Can you get insulin?"

He scowled. "What's that?"

"It's a medicine to replace the insulin your body produces."

"For what?" Avery said.

"Insulin is a hormone produced by your pancreas that allows your body to use glucose, or sugar, from the carbohydrates in the foods you eat for energy. It keeps your blood sugar from getting too high or too low and helps glucose get into the cells of your body. Diabetes is when your body doesn't properly process the food you eat for energy. With diabetes, your body either doesn't make enough insulin or can't use its own as well as it should. This causes sugar to build up in your blood. I think you have type 1 diabetes, or insulin-dependent diabetes mellitus, more commonly called juvenile-onset diabetes."

"I've heard of diabetes before but not insulin," Jonah said.

"How did you all treat it?"

"They would just replace the pancreas with an artificial one," Jonah said.

Angie stiffened. "Wait a minute. If she knows about healing, she should know that."

Well, shoot, I thought.

Jonah glanced at me, giving me a warning look. "Lizzie was living off the grid, using herbal medicines in the community where she lived. They didn't have facilities for any modern medicine."

Angie stared at me, the suspicious look back in her eyes.

I stood. "I would suggest you limit Avery's carbohydrates, that should help some."

"What foods are those?"

"Breads, fruits, mostly. And nothing sweet, like cookies or cake. I know you don't have meat but most vegetables are low in carbs as well as eggs and nuts."

"So anything that can help him gain weight, he can't eat," Angie said in a tart tone.

"I'm afraid so. If we can get his blood sugar regulated, he should at least feel better." I turned back to Avery. "I'm sorry, Avery. I wish I could do more for you."

He gave me a wan smile. "It's okay. At least I know what's wrong."

I glanced at his mother, who was giving me a skeptical look. "I'll ask Abbie, see if she knows what to do."

Her expression darkened. "Who's Abbie?"

"My friend. We're both here."

She glared at Jonah.

"They're fine, Angie. Abbie and Lizzie delivered Andrea's baby and helped save Zach's life. They know what they're doing."

She looked off as if unwilling to accept this but finally nodded. When she spoke, her tone was harsh. "I'll take your word for it, Jonah. But you know what's happened in the past."

He held up his hand. "This is different. I promise."

"All right then. Now, if y'all don't mind, I reckon Avery needs to rest a bit. He looks a bit tuckered."

Although Avery protested this, he did look tired and weak, so I left him after promising to check in on him weekly.

Angie escorted us to the door, and once we were on the porch, said, "You don't need to come back, I'll tend to my son." She closed the screen door, then the wooden one, cutting off any response we might have made.

As we walked away, I said, "What's up with her?"

Jonah shook his head. "Her husband found a man on the mountain, a stranger. He believed his story about having family on the mountain, so he brought him home, fed him, and he repaid him by killing him while they were eating dinner. Angie picked up a knife and stabbed him in the throat or he would have killed her and Avery." He grimaced. "It was too late for her husband. We couldn't save him. Anyway, since then, she doesn't trust anyone. So don't take it personally."

"Well, I hope she'll let me check on Avery at least," I said, turning onto the path. When I realized Jonah wasn't behind me, I looked at him over my shoulder. "What?"

"You're talking like you're intending on staying."

"Well, no, I meant just for now, while I'm here."

He nodded. "It's getting late, I guess we better head back."

Walking along, I said, "That guy we shot told me he was part of a recon mission."

"That's what he told us."

"What did he mean by that?"

"I imagine they were looking for our vulnerable spots, trying to figure out where we place our sentries, where we keep our water."

"But they came inside the house."

"Those two were looking for plunder, I guess." He gave me a sidelong glance. "Or women."

"When one of your sentries caught sight of the others, that's why you left?"

He nodded.

"And you didn't catch them?"

He shook his head. "All got away except the two you all caught."

"I heard you tell Andrea there were six more."

"I did."

"And you think they'll be back."

He glanced away from me. "I'm sure they will," he said in a curt tone.

Goosebumps broke out on my arms. "Shoot," I said softly.

"Exactly."

Chapter Eight

August 2054

Commotion

That evening after supper, I went outside to sit on the porch. I wanted to be alone for a bit to think about the day and this place and the dilemma in which I had placed Abbie and myself. I settled in a corner of the porch, leaning my back against the house, looking at the night sky, pondering the differences in time. In 1864, the sky had been littered with so many stars, they seemed endless. In 1969, pollution and city emissions concealed so many of them, at times there seemed to be none at all. And here, in this time, the mass of ash and pollution hovering over this part of the world made the atmosphere above look more like the dirty ceiling of a room, no stars or moon visible to the naked eye most nights.

I inhaled, vaguely wondering what damage was being done to our lungs as we breathed in this poisoned air. This turned my thoughts to cigarettes and I found myself lustily wishing for one, one of those Virginia Slims I smoked back in the 20th century or even one of Pokni's homemade rolled cigarettes during my time in the 1800s, which were so strong they stung my eyes but sweetly flavored with a hint of the honey she used to seal the husk she wrapped the tobacco in. I almost got up and went inside to ask Andrea if she knew where I could get a cigarette or one of those vapes Evelyn told me about but quickly changed my mind. It was peaceful out here, whereas inside, there were baby noises and the babble of voices to contend with.

I glanced at the screen door when it creaked. Abbie stepped out onto the porch, looking around. I ducked my head, remaining quiet, hoping she wouldn't see me and would go away. I was feeling guilty enough without Abbie adding to that burden.

It didn't take long for her to spy me. She made her way toward me, not saying anything until she reached me. "I was lookin for you," she said as she sat down beside me.

"I just wanted to be alone for awhile."

Ignoring my subtle hint, she leaned her shoulder against mine. "I'll say one thing, it sure is different here at night than it was back ... then."

I gave her a questioning look.

"Can't hear all the insects and birds, much less a hoot owl. Remember how loud them cicadas could get? And the bull frogs at night? Law, sometimes I thought it'd drive me crazy, they were so loud."

I smiled at this. "I miss it, Abbie. I didn't know it, but that had become my time. I wish I'd realized that before I put us in that light. I can't tell you how sor—"

She elbowed me lightly in the side. "You hush. You've said I'm sorry so many times, I'm sick of hearin it. Besides, if we hadn't gone through, I wouldn't have ever known about all them things you told me about, the electricity and hot showers and television and such. It's a pure miracle, you ask me. Why, today, Andrea showed me how to wash clothes in that washin machine they got inside then dry em in that dryer. Lord mercy, I sure didn't know what I was missing." She laughed softly.

I turned and stared at her. "If I didn't know better, I'd think you were beginning to like it here, Abby."

She shrugged but didn't say anything.

"When we came through this time, we were close to where you found me the first time, right?"

"We were right close, Lizzie."

"I think that's where we should keep looking, in that area. We can go in that direction and search for it. I know how to get there from here."

"Tonight?"

"Why not? Maybe we'll get lucky."

It was too dark to see her expression, but I sensed she wasn't happy with this. "What is it, Abbie? What's wrong?"

She remained quiet for so long, I didn't think she was going to answer. Finally, she said, "It's just, Lizzie, if you go back and stop what's going to happen, what will that mean for Andrea, Jonah and Zach?"

She didn't say it but I knew there was a reason she listed Zach last. Oh, God, I thought to myself, could I really do that? "I don't know," I mumbled.

"You'll kill em," she said, her voice low, almost a whisper. "You said it yourself. You'll put an end to them if you keep Josh from marrying Sarie."

"Abbie, we don't know for sure they're descended from a marriage between Josh and Sarie. How can we? I mean, she could have married one of his brothers."

"I do."

I turned to her. "How?"

That Bible I used to stop Zach from bleeding? It's their family Bible and it's recorded right there, Joshua Lee Hampton marrying Sara Elaine Collins, back in November, 1864."

"1864?"

She nodded, placing her hand over mine. "I'm sorry, Lizzie. A-course, we don't know why they married but they did. Maybe they was both so grief-stricken over losing us, they turned to one another for comfort. Maybe—"

"I don't want to hear it, Abbie. Josh loves me, he wouldn't just marry her without trying to find me. He wouldn't."

"There's a reason he didn't, Lizzie, one we don't know. But if you go back there and put a stop to it, you're killin four innocent people and you know it."

I moved away from her. "What do you want me to do? Stay here, in this ungodly place and time? It's worse here than it was in 1864."

She sighed.

"What?"

"Back then all you could talk about was gettin back to 1969, now it's gettin back to 1864. Lizzie, if you want to go back, go back to 1969, to your Ben and your pa. Let Josh and Sarie get married, have their children, live their lives. He didn't come after you but there's a reason for that, so you just got to accept it's a just reason and move on."

I stood. "No, I won't. I can't. I love him, I can't lose him."

When she spoke, her voice was filled with such sadness, it brought tears to my eyes. "Oh, Lizzie, you done lost him, don't you know that? You lost him when you went through the light."

I strode past her.

"Where are you goin?"

"To find the light." I spoke harsher than I meant. I paused on the top step when I realized she wasn't following me. "You coming with me?"

Abbie stood and her tone told me she was frowning. "No. I won't do what you're plannin on doing."

"So you want to stay here?"

"For now."

"Why, Abbie?" I walked back to stand in front of her, glancing at the window she stood next to, checking to see if anyone inside was listening. "Why are you so het up on staying here all of a sudden when just two days ago you couldn't stand being here and wanted to leave right away?"

From the light leaking through the window, I saw her eyes dart toward the inside of the house. I nodded. "Oh, it's Zach, isn't it? You're falling in love with Zach."

She glared at me.

"Don't deny it. I see how chummy you two are, how much time you spend with him."

"I ain't in love with him," she said, harshly. "But I like him well enough and I feel connected to him in some way. Maybe it's because he's related to Sarie, I don't know."

"If he's related to Sarie, he's your I don't know how many times great-nephew, Abbie."

She ignored this. "Like I told you before, whatever happened back there the night we came through is over with and Sarie and Josh both survived it. Way I see it, she don't need me anymore. Neither does Maggie, she's got Randall, and Amanda May's got Tommy. Here, I can help people, Lizzie, do something important maybe, be part of something, even if there is a war comin like you said."

I shook my head. "Tell yourself that all you want, but Zach's the reason you're staying, the reason you won't go." I turned on my heel and walked down the steps.

"Think about what you're gonna do," she called after me, her voice strident. "Think about who'll you'll hurt by what you do, Lizzie."

I ignored her as I stalked away into the forest, too irritated to really pay attention to where I was going. Before long, I realized I had walked off the path and was lost. Trees began to close in and it grew so dark, I couldn't see my hand in front of my face. I had never liked the darkness of the forest at night and fought a sense of panic as I groped for the flashlight I carried in my backpack. Clicking it on, I cursed myself for not carrying a flashlight with a stronger beam. I looked up at the sky, hoping to find the Northern Star so I could get my bearings, but there was no moonlight tonight, no visible sign of any sort of light up there. I turned around, shining my flashlight on the ground, searching for signs of recent passage, but could see no trampled leaves, no broken limbs, not even a pathway used by animals. I finally gave up and started walking again, hoping to eventually come out of the forest or run across a trail. I slowly began to realize with a tingling sense of horror that there were no sounds at all inside the trees. Before, I should have been able to detect the rustling of bushes as small, nocturnal animals rooted for food or the hoot of an owl in the trees, waiting for prey to reveal themselves. I remembered the bobcat that lived near Abbie and me and the way it had scared us at times, sounding like a woman screaming or a baby crying. But here, it felt as if the world had died around me and I was the only living soul on it.

I stopped to rest, leaning against a tree, perking up when I heard low voices nearby. It sounded like two men talking to each other, their footsteps making shuffling noises in the dead leaves covering the ground. I was on the verge of stepping out and calling to them when something made me hesitate. As they made their way toward me, I clicked off the flashlight and moved behind the tree in order to hide, figuring if they were people I recognized, I'd reveal myself. If not, I'd simply follow them to wherever they were going, in hopes of finding Jonah or someone who knew me. Aware by now that more than a few people on the mountain viewed me with suspicion, I wasn't sure what sort of greeting I'd receive from them so deemed it in my best interests to wait.

The two men walked past me, one limping badly, putting most of his weight on his uninjured leg. Startled, I realized these were the two raiders Jonah had promised not to kill. What are they doing back on the mountain, I wondered, as I moved away from the tree and began to follow them. And where were the two men Jonah had sent with them as escorts? Deciding they were up to no good, I tried to get as close to them as I could without revealing myself, hoping to hear what they were saying. Whatever they were up to, it couldn't be good.

I trailed them down the mountain, noting the two men remained just inside the tree line, never stepping outside the forest, never following a trail. They were speaking to one another in low voices and at first I feared they'd hear me as I crept behind, but when I stepped on a twig, my foot causing it to snap in two with a loud crack, they didn't falter or even look back. Deciding they weren't paying attention, I picked up my pace, drawing closer.

When they stepped out of the forest, I recognized the road they were on. This was the one that led to Josh's father's plantation, one I had ridden on and walked numerous times. I remembered Jonah had told me the plantation was now vacant, hadn't been occupied in years. Could this be their destiny, and why? Near the entrance to the plantation, they stopped in the roadway, looking around, waiting. I crouched down in the shadow of a tree, hoping they wouldn't look back and see me. A few minutes later, two other men appeared out of the darkness and they all met in the roadway. After conferring in low voices for a few minutes, they proceeded on toward the plantation. When they turned down the drive, I knew that had to be where they were going. Without hesitating, I wheeled around and flew back up the mountain, hoping to attract the attention of a sentry.

I hadn't gone very far up the trail when a shadow stepped out of the forest and into my path, barring my way, startling me enough to elicit a stifled squeal as I dropped my flashlight. I felt something hard poke me in the chest. Without thinking, I put my hand on it, trying to push it away. The feel of a long rod of smooth, cold metal told me this was most probably a rifle.

"What are you doing?" a male voice asked as the brilliant beam of a flashlight pierced my vision, blinding me as to the identity of its bearer.

I put my hand in front of my face, squinting my eyes, trying to get a glimpse of whoever stood in front of me, wondering if he was one of Jonah's people. "Who are you?" I said in a breathless voice, my heart beating furiously in my chest.

"Where are you going, Lizzie?" a man answered, his tone low.

His question told me he knew who I was but I had to be sure. "Do you know me?"

"You were with Jonah, he said you were okay."

"You're one of the sentries?"

He didn't respond.

I debated for a minute. Could I trust this man? "Listen," I finally said, "I need to know who you are, what you're doing here."

"That's what I need to know from you."

I kept my eyes down, away from the bright beam of the flashlight. It cast enough light around us that I could see the walkie-talkie on his belt. Without thinking, I reached out and snatched it away from him.

"Hey," he said, bringing the rifle up to aim it at my face.

Praying he was one of the good guys and wouldn't shoot me, I clicked the signal Jonah had used when we went to the greenhouses. Someone clicked back immediately. The man with the rifle reached out to snatch the walkie-talkie back but I backed away from him as a man said, "What's going on?"

"I need Jonah," I said into the walkie-talkie.

The man with the rifle hesitated when he heard that.

The walkie-talkie buzzed with static then the man said, "Who is this?"

"This is Lizzie Baker, the healer who was with Jonah. I need to speak to Jonah."

"Let me talk to whoever's walkie-talkie this is."

I held the walkie-talkie out to the sentry. He snatched it out of my hands with a baleful look. "Bishop here. I caught her coming up the mountain." He glared at me. "She got her hands on my walkie-talkie but I've got my rifle on her."

"Oh, for Pete's sake," I hissed. "Tell him those two men y'all took to Morganton are back on the mountain and I followed them down to the Hampton plantation."

"The what?"

"The large farm near the bottom of the mountain. It was called the Hampton plantation when I was here. Jonah knows where it is."

I waited impatiently while he relayed this.

"Hold on," the man on the other end of the walkie-talkie said. He was back within seconds. "Bishop."

Bishop put the walkie-talkie to his mouth, never taking his eyes off me. "Yeah?"

"You at your station?"

"Yeah."

"Jonah's on his way down. Keep her there."

"No problem." He keyed off, gesturing with the rifle for me to precede him back into the trees, where he turned off his flashlight. As we waited in the dark for Jonah, he whispered, "Are you talking about the two men who broke into Jonah's house?"

"Yes, the ones who tried to take Andrea, Abbie and me."

"They're here, on the mountain?"

"I saw them in the woods. I couldn't figure out what they were doing here so followed them down to the road that goes to the plantation. When they turned in the drive, I came back to find someone."

He cursed under his breath. "I knew it was a mistake to let them go free." I surmised Jonah hadn't told them I was the reason behind the men's freedom when he spoke with no hint of malice in his voice. "I'm Mike Bishop, by the way. Nice to meet you." He gave me a curt nod.

Feeling ludicrous at playing niceties during this time of danger, I nodded. "Same here."

"I'm sorry if I got rough with you back there," he continued, his voice low. "Couldn't figure out what you were doing down here."

"I was trying to find you."

"Find me?"

"Well, a sentry who could help me get in touch with Jonah."

"Oh, right. He should be here shortly."

After that, we waited in silence. When Bishop perked up, turning to look behind him, I wondered what got his attention. I hadn't heard a thing.

"Lizzie," Jonah said, touching me lightly on the elbow, startling me.

"Hey," I said, clicking on and shining my flashlight upwards so I could see him, feeling safer than I had since I got lost in the forest.

"Tell me what happened."

So I told him about spying the two men on the mountain and following them down.

"What were you doing out here?"

"I was going to try to find the …" I trailed off, remembering Jonah's warning about mentioning the light. "To find my cabin," I finished lamely.

Jonah's mouth tightened but he didn't say anything to that. After a few seconds, he said, "What were they doing up on the mountain, do you know?"

I shook my head. "I tried to listen to what they were saying as we came down but I couldn't get close enough."

Jonah looked at Bishop. "I thought we had someone trailing them."

Bishop shrugged. "That's what I thought. They must have lost them."

"Why wasn't I told?" Jonah said, his voice harsh.

Bishop shook his head. "I don't reckon anyone knew, boss. They're still not back."

Jonah glanced toward the road, pondering. He turned to me, taking my flashlight out of my hand and turning it off. "Can you find your way back?"

"Probably."

"Go on back, we'll take care of this."

I shifted away from him. "No."

"Lizzie, there's no deal to be made here, not this time. Go on back."

"Listen, I saw where they went. Have you ever been inside? Do you know the layout?"

"No."

"Well, I do. I know that place like the back of my hand. I can help y'all."

I could feel Jonah staring at me as he hefted his rifle off his shoulder and into his hands. "This is dangerous. They're here for a reason and it's not a good one. You need to go back. I don't have time to argue with you."

"Yeah? Well, way I see it, there's just you and me and Bishop here."

"Others are coming."

"Maybe, but they're not here now. I know how to use a gun. Besides, I'm a healer. If anyone gets hurt, I can help them."

"Not those two, I won't let you this time."

I thought about it. "Okay, I'll do what you say. I just want to make sure they don't get their grimy hands on Abbie and Andrea."

Without responding, Jonah drew a gun from his shoulder holster and handed it over to me along with my flashlight. "Be careful. Do what I say."

After securing the flashlight in my backpack, I made sure the safety on the gun was engaged then tucked it into the back of my pants. "I will."

He gestured with his rifle. "Let's go."

I turned on my heel and stepped into the roadway. We made our way slowly down the road, keeping to its outer boundary. I paused at the head of the driveway when Jonah put his hand on my arm.

He leaned close to whisper in my ear. "We'll go ahead of you. Stay behind and try to be as quiet as you can. If anyone starts firing, hit the ground. When it stops, run back up the mountain, alert everyone you see as you go."

I nodded, thinking, no way. Jonah and Bishop picked up their pace, jogging up the driveway, staying close to the rail fence that ran its length. I followed, determined to see this through, spurred by my guilt over having talked Jonah into letting those two go. If they hurt anyone, it would be my fault.

Jonah called a halt when the house came into view. The gibbous moon overhead cast enough light to reveal the mansion had suffered some great damage at one point. I could see leaning chimneys and large, dark gaps in the roof that looked like huge holes. What had once been a magnificent plantation manse now looked like a rambling, broken-down hovel.

"What happened here?" I whispered.

"Most of it burned down some time ago," Jonah said.

"Was it still in your family?"

He shook his head, his attention returning to the plantation home. "Like I told you, we lost it way back in the early 1900s."

I looked back, noting very few lights shone through the windows, all on the first floor.

Jonah pulled me closer to him. "Tell me the layout of the house," he whispered.

"First floor, when I knew it, had a large entryway with a grand stairway in the center leading to the upper floors, and a large parlor, drawing room, living room, whatever you want to call it, to the left at the front of the house with a study and library behind. The kitchen is at the back of the house on the right, with a huge dining room in front of it and a butler's pantry behind it. All of the bedrooms are on the second and third floors." I wanted to qualify my answer by telling him it was almost 200 years since I had seen the house but Bishop was with us and he didn't know my truth.

Jonah nodded at the house. "Where are the lights coming from?"

"The entryway and parlor."

He stared at the mansion for a long moment. "All right. I see windows low enough we should be able to try to get a look inside. Follow me but move quietly. I don't see any but they probably have sentries posted."

Without waiting for our response, he moved away, melting into the darkness. I followed by listening to Jonah's and Bishop's muted footsteps. When we reached the house, we went around to the side and gathered beneath a large window, shielded by a row of prickly bushes. Luck was with us as the window had no pane and we could easily hear voices from the interior of the house. We each tried to peek inside but the window was covered by a heavy cotton curtain. I reached out to pull it back an inch or two in order to see indoors but Jonah covered my hand with his, stopping me. He made a hand gesture to Bishop, who nodded then melted into the darkness. I wondered where he was going but didn't say anything in case our voices carried and someone could hear us.

Jonah and I leaned against the house, our shoulders touching, listening to the conversation going on in the parlor. I caught only bits and pieces but it was enough to put together what they were planning. Apparently the two Abbie and I had injured had been on the mountain trying to find the encampment again but hadn't had much luck. Voices raised in argument as the men inside debated on how best to proceed. Jonah stiffened when we heard one man, who sounded alarmingly like the one Abbie and I had encountered, the one she had knocked out with the water jug, demand to be the one to take Abbie and me into custody. "I got plans for those two," he said, his voice a low growl. When the other men laughed, I clenched my fists.

"Over my dead body," I said sotto voce.

Jonah must have heard, because he reached out and squeezed my arm.

We listened to voices berate the man for letting us get away from him, while others teased him about his plans and whether he would be able to follow through. My face felt hot and my body tensed as they discussed Abbie and me like we were objects to be used and discarded, not living, breathing bodies.

Finally, Jonah pulled me away from the window and around the back corner of the house. He crouched down, hauling me down beside him. "Don't worry about what they're saying, it won't happen," he said, his voice pitched low.

I breathed in and out slowly, trying to calm down. "I can't believe I talked you into letting them go, Jonah. It was so stupid of me."

"It's not your fault. You don't know what it's like now. But concentrate for me. We've got to put an end to this before it gets started. How many do you think are in there?"

I thought about it for a long moment. "We know at least the four I saw, but I heard several others laugh at what that idiot said. I don't know, I'd say maybe six or more."

"That's what I figured." He glanced around us. "The others should be here soon. But if these people leave, we're going to have to move and move fast. You understand?"

I nodded then realized he probably couldn't see me. "Yes."

"We have to stop them, Lizzie. That means shooting them, and I don't mean to injure. They're here to kill us at worst, harm us at best. We can't allow that to happen."

"Where'd Bishop go?" I asked, suddenly afraid I'd have to pull the trigger on another human being, someone I didn't even know.

"He's at the gate waiting for the others so he can bring them to us."

We heard a shot nearby and both abruptly stood, looking around.

"Did that come from inside?" I asked.

"No." Jonah hefted his rifle into his hands. "Their guards might have found Bishop. Let's go." He grabbed my hand and broke into a run, pulling me along behind him. We circled back toward the front of the house just in time to see several men shoving through the front door and onto the porch, flashlight beams sweeping the grounds. We both drew up but not before the men saw us and stopped. A couple ducked back inside but the others pulled guns and aimed them at us.

Jonah immediately raised his hands after pushing me behind him. "We're not here for trouble," he began but then a shot rang out and I watched as the lead man, who was coming down the steps, his gun pointed at Jonah, jerked back and fell. Jonah grabbed my hand and pulled me toward the back of the house, both of us ducking our heads as shots rang out all around us.

We ended up in the same bushes from whence we started, both breathing heavily, listening to gunplay at the front of the house.

"You think that was Bishop?" I whispered.

"I'm sure it was. We need to do something. He won't know about the two that went back inside."

I stood on tiptoe, reaching for the windowsill. Jonah pulled me back. "What are you doing?"

"Hoist me up, I can climb through the window."

"No."

"We need to get in there, stop them before they shoot our people, Jonah." Our people, my inner voice whispered. When did they become *our* people?

"I'll go," Jonah said, interrupting my thoughts. Before I could say anything, he had grabbed hold of the sill and pulled himself up and through the window.

"Help me through," I said in a loud whisper.

He pushed the curtain aside, leaned his head out, said, "Stay there," and was gone.

I waited, feeling energized, agitated, wanting to do something, needing to do something, wondering if this was what it felt like during a battle. The gunshots at the front of the house soon stopped and I couldn't hear a thing going on inside. I put my hands on the sill with the intent of going through the window, then made myself stop, thinking Jonah might mistake me for one of the raiders and shoot me.

After what seemed like an eternity, a shadowy figure came around the side of the house. I crouched down in the bushes, hoping it wasn't one of the raiders. They stopped in front of me and when Jonah said, "It's okay, Lizzie, it's over," I raised up, breathing a sigh of relief.

"Did you find the two inside?"

"They won't be a problem anymore."

"Where are the others?"

"They're all in the front. Come on." He took my elbow and guided me around the side of the house. Although it was shadowy and too murky in places to see anything, I noted dark bulks littering the ground in front of the mansion, figures mulling about among them. "Is that ...?"

"Don't look," he said, steering me around the front lawn and onto the drive. When we were near the road, he stopped and waited.

"Look, if anyone's injured back there, I need to see to them," I said.

"No one's injured." His voice was harsh and curt, and I was glad I couldn't see his expression.

"What are we waiting for?"

"Clancy's on her way down. She'll take you back up the mountain."

"No. I'll wait."

"You'll go, Lizzie. We need to ..." he glanced back behind him. "We need to take care of that back there. You don't need to be a part of it."

"What about your people, Jonah? Was anyone injured? Can I help anyone?"

"We're good. A couple of flesh wounds, nothing more."

I didn't want to leave but, even more, didn't want to be escorted back by Clancy. Although I had had few dealings with her, it was obvious by now she bore ill feelings toward me and, to be honest, I didn't really like her, for a reason I could not have named other than her blatant hatred for me.

"If you insist, I'll leave, but I can get back on my own. I know this mountain, I know the way back."

We both turned at the sound of footsteps, watching a slim figure walk toward us carrying a flashlight. When she drew near, I could see this was Clancy.

She stopped in front of us, staring at Jonah.

"I need you to take Lizzie back up the mountain," he said, without any preamble.

She stared at him for a long moment. I knew she didn't want to do this as much as I didn't want her to.

"Now," he said, in a voice that brooked no argument.

Taking time enough to send a glare his way before turning on her heel and saying, "Come on," in a voice cold and harsh, she walked away without waiting to see if I followed.

"I'll go get my medical supplies together for the injured. Be sure to bring them to me when you're finished here."

He nodded, his eyes darting toward Clancy's departing back.

"I'll see you later," I said as I fell into step behind her, wishing he had called anyone but Clancy.

We walked in silence for a long time. When we were about halfway up the mountain, she said, over her shoulder, "What were you doing there?"

I had been replaying that horrid scene on the front lawn in my mind and not paying attention to what she said. "What?"

"What were you doing there?" she said in a loud voice. "With Jonah?"

"I saw the two men from the raid going down the mountain so followed them. When I saw them go to the Hampton Plantation, I found a sentry and had him notify Jonah."

"So you get to play heroine again," she said, her voice bitter.

I gave a harsh laugh. "I doubt that."

She stopped suddenly and turned to me. "Just what are you doing here, Lizzie? That's your name, right, Lizzie?"

That got my dander up, the way she said my name, like it offended her. "If by here, you mean on the mountain, talk to Jonah if you have a problem with that, Clancy," putting as much derision in my voice at her name as she had mine.

"Oh, I've asked him already, you can believe that. But I don't buy what he tells me." She stepped closer to me. "You might have him fooled, along with that silly sister of his and his naïve little brother, but I don't buy it for a minute. There's a reason you and that redneck hillbilly are here, one we haven't found out yet, but I will, and you better hope you're both gone before I do."

I laughed simply to keep from doing what I wanted to, slapping the fire out of her. How dare she denigrate my best friend. "Redneck hillbilly? Is that how you see Abbie?" I shook my head. "She has more class in her little finger than you'll ever have. I don't see you helping people on the mountain, treating the injured and sick, making their lives better."

She stepped back from me and I could see the anger in her stance.

"What is this, anyway? Are we a threat to you? Or more specifically, am I a threat to you in some way, Clancy? If so, I'd sure like to know how because your attitude is unwarranted. So, why don't you do both of us a favor? You stay on your side of the mountain and I'll stay on mine, and we'll get along fine. If it's Jonah you're worried about, he's yours, I have no interest in him, so stop acting like we're all in high school and I'm trying to steal your boyfriend. Because believe me, if I wanted to, I could." I leaned close to her. "In a heartbeat." I shoved past her and walked away.

"Leave him alone," she shouted after me. "He's mine."

I stopped walking and turned around. "What is this? Has the world devolved to this point? When … where I come from, women are independent, they don't need a man to fulfill them or make their life more meaningful. So what happened to you, Clancy, that you have to threaten someone to leave your man alone?"

I half-expected her to come after me, ready to grab my hair and rake my eyes. But she didn't, which was a great relief. I had never been in a fight with a woman in my life and didn't intend to unless it was a matter of self-defense. And to tussle over a man. For Pete's sake, I told myself, who would do such a thing?

Instead she said, "If you know what's good for you, you'll leave this mountain. You don't belong here."

"I don't need you to tell me that," I sneered at her. I stalked away, wondering if women of the 21st century had regressed back to the 19th century.

I was in a state by the time I reached Jonah's house. Abbie and Andrea were up, waiting anxiously in the living room. When they saw me, both ran to greet me, asking questions over one another.

"Let me get a drink of water then I'll tell you what happened," I said, going into the kitchen.

"I'll fix us some tea," Abbie said, snatching the kettle up and pouring water in it. "You sit down. You look right agitated."

"I am right agitated, Abbie," I said, although it wasn't for the reason she thought.

So as the kettle boiled, I filled them in on what had happened. I didn't mention Clancy and my conversation with her.

"Did they get all the raiders?" Abbie asked.

I nodded. "I suppose. Jonah didn't say otherwise." I glanced away. "I'm glad it wasn't daylight. I'm glad I didn't see those bodies in the daylight."

Andrea put her hand on my arm. "Lizzie, you don't understand. If it wasn't them, it would be us. You saved our lives tonight. I hope you can see that."

"It's the least I could do after I talked Jonah into letting those two go. I feel bad about that."

"I was concerned something like that would happen," Andrea said. "Jonah sent scouts after them to trail them to see where they went, but we haven't heard anything."

"They haven't come back?"

She shook her head. "We've been worried about them but no one's heard anything that I know of."

I suspected she wasn't telling me something. "What were they going to do once they got to where they were going?"

Andrea's gaze darted to Abbie then back to me. "What do you think, Lizzie?"

"Kill them?" I looked at Abbie, could see she was aware of this.

"Did you think they'd just go away?" Abbie said. "That they wouldn't try to come back? We have what they want."

"Surely you can't be that naïve, Lizzie," Andrea said. "They made their intent known." She leaned toward me. "They threatened to kill my baby."

I sat back in my chair. "We've gone from one brutal world to another," I said to Abbie. "From one set of raiders to another set, same objective, different centuries. This is surreal." I rose to my feet, feeling agitated, restless, and began to pace to ease my frustration. An overwhelming sadness came over me. "My God, it never stops. We're always going to be prey, a commodity, whether we're there or here. Probably anywhere."

Abbie glanced at the door. "Lizzie, this ain't the time to bemoan the fate of them two men. We need to think about our people." She leaned toward me. "Was anybody injured, any of ours?"

"Jonah said only flesh wounds. I guess when they get back, we'll be pretty busy." I stood. "I'll go get supplies together."

It was almost dawn before Jonah and the others came back. Abbie, Lizzie and I had piled medical supplies on the table and were just putting on coffee when we noticed Zachary, who had come downstairs without us noticing, looking pale and weak as he limped toward the door. "They're coming," he said.

Abbie made a small sound in her throat as she went to him and took his arm. He turned to her and I watched them hug one another, feeling utter defeat, knowing she'd never go back with me now. Although she said she felt connected to Zachary, this looked to be more than that. Their feelings for one another seemed to vibrate, like an electric current shimmering through the air. How did that happen so fast? I wondered as I watched them.

The door opened and Jonah's face appeared behind his brother. He gave a weary smile as he gently pushed them aside, patting his brother on the shoulder. I watched him walk toward us with that panther grace of his, admiring the way he moved. When he gave me a look as if he knew what I was thinking, I glanced away from him, down to the medical supplies, waiting until after he hugged Andrea hello and assured her he was fine.

"Are the injured coming?" I asked.

"They're on their way. Should be here any minute."

I nodded, refolding a gauze bandage I'd folded dozens of times now. He put his hand on mine. It was warm, solid, comforting. I didn't like that. "Thank you," was all he said before he moved away and into the kitchen.

I raised my eyes to watch him and caught Andrea studying me. She tilted her head, smiling at me. I frowned at her then went toward the door, where people were beginning to mill.

Chapter Nine

Fall 2054

Motherless Child

My life settled into a routine as the days passed and summer gave way to fall. With Andrea's encouragement, I opened a medical clinic in the basement where those who were suffering from minor illnesses or injuries could be treated. Afternoons were spent on the mountain checking in on patients too ill to come to the clinic or helping Andrea can produce for the upcoming winter. Freed from that, I would go into the forest to gather herbs. Although I never saw them, I sensed Jonah had people following me at all times when I was by myself on the mountain. Even though I wondered about that, I didn't say anything. After our confrontation with the raiders, I felt safer knowing someone had me in sight.

Abbie spent most mornings with me and afternoons I didn't need her help gathering herbs or checking on patients would often go off with Zachary after lunch, working beside him as a sentry or patrolling the perimeter or running errands for Jonah, who doled out daily duties to his troops. Late afternoons, she would train with the others and quickly stood out for her ability to handle and shoot guns as well as her expertise with a bow and arrow. When she began to dress in camouflage gear and wear a gun on her hip, I teased her about looking soldierly but she only seemed proud of that fact. She rarely accompanied me at night when I went in search of the lights, which confirmed to me that she had no interest in returning to her time. Occasionally Jonah would join me for an hour or so. This bothered me. I didn't know if he was doing that so he could stop me from going through if I found the light or if he truly wanted to help. But how could he, I would ask myself, if it might mean his nonexistence? I tried to act aloof with him, not to like him, but at times would find myself laughing at something he said or simply smiling when I saw him. Less and less, he reminded me of Joshua and more and more I began to see him as the man he was, and I didn't know if that was good or bad. I didn't want to feel friendly toward him at all, I didn't want to look upon him as a friend. But he seemed to always be around me, sitting across from me at breakfast in the morning, checking in at the clinic to see if we needed anything, and at dinner, teasing his sister and brother and playing with his nephew, who was a happy baby and evidently a great joy to his family, even dour Jonah.

At least once a week, Jonah rode his horse over the mountain visiting families, checking to make sure all was well and they had everything they needed. He began to invite me to accompany him on these treks, offering Zachary's horse for me to ride, which was the beautiful chestnut I admired. I couldn't help but marvel at the scenery as we rode. Although most of the trees on the mountain were not as bountiful and massive as they had been back in the 1800s, their dying leaves painted the mountain in shades of orange and red and brown and amber, and I imagined it looked as beautiful as a handmade patchwork quilt from above. I found myself looking forward to these outings with Jonah and at times would surprise myself by feeling happy and contented, exuberant and free, laughing with delight as we galloped along the flat roads near the bottom of the mountain. Afterward, I would be overcome with guilt, telling myself this was not where I wanted to be, this was not where Josh was, ignoring my inner voice whispering what it would mean if I went back.

As the days shortened and warm weather fled, I began to become vested in the people on the mountain. I looked forward to my visits with Helen, who would regale me with tales of her life with her husband, who traveled the world before the asteroid hit and everything changed. I worried over Evelyn, whose pregnancy was progressing nicely but who remained fearful no one would be there for her when she went into labor, and Avery, whose diabetes was life-threatening. Several had lung problems which I presumed were from the dirty air and there were a couple I suspected might even have lung cancer, but I couldn't do anything for them other than try to make them more comfortable.

I began to focus on finding more medicine. Although my supply of medicinal herbs was steadily growing, I knew they were not adequate for the number of people on the mountain. Jonah had returned to the nursery where he found the seedlings for the herb greenhouse but found it empty, which was a huge disappointment. So, I constantly pestered him about taking me scavenging with him to try to find drugs for the mountaineers. He kept telling me he'd checked everywhere and there was nothing to be found, but I persisted, suggesting we might meet with some success if we went inside abandoned homes.

One morning in late fall, while haranguing him at breakfast, he put his head in his hands. "Are you ever gonna stop asking me?" he moaned.

Abbie laughed. "You don't know Lizzie. Once she gets an idea in her head, she won't let it go until she's got what she wants. Best to just give in and let her have her way."

Jonah rubbed a hand over his face, giving me a wary look.

Zachary grinned at his brother. "We are getting close to winter, which means we'll get a respite from raiders—"

"What do you mean, a respite?" Abbie asked.

"Winter's a good time for us. On the mountain, it can be 60 one day and one heck of a snowstorm the next. No one wants to get caught outside on this mountain in a snowstorm, not even those who live here, due to the danger of getting stranded. So far, we've yet to be raided during the winter. Right, brother?"

Jonah glared at Zachary but didn't respond.

I smiled at Jonah. "There've been no sign of raiders lately, right? Everything seems pretty stable on the mountain. What do you say?"

"Okay, I'll take you into Morganton just to get you to stop haranguing me about it."

"Today?"

He nodded. "After breakfast." He looked at Zachary. "You and Abbie can go with us if Andrea doesn't need your help."

"Y'all go on ahead, I'll be fine," Andrea said. "I was planning to take Joseph to visit Helen today."

Jonah pushed back from the table. "Okay, we'll leave after breakfast. Be sure to bring food and water in your backpacks." He touched Andrea on the shoulder. "We'll have the walkie-talkies. Contact us if you need us or anything happens."

"Will do, brother," she said with affection.

After we secured a rusty old pickup truck from the meager motor pool, we set out, Jonah and me in the front, Abbie and Zachary sharing the back seat, sitting so close together they were almost on top of one another. As we rode down the bumpy mountain road, our bodies jerking and shifting with the motion of the truck, Jonah and I sat in silence while Abbie and Zachary spoke to one another in low tones. I stole a glance at Jonah, wondering what he thought of the budding relationship between his brother and Abbie, whether he approved or disapproved. Most of the time, he treated Abbie the same way he treated most, with an aloofness that sometimes bordered on cold disregard, until she was with Zachary, then he would relax and speak to her in a friendlier tone.

Jonah glanced at me, caught me watching him. He smiled, his lips barely moving.

"Listen, I know you don't think this is a good idea," I said, "but we might get lucky. You never know."

"I doubt it, but it's worth a try, I guess."

"Have you tried doctors' offices?"

He nodded.

"Medical clinics, hospitals?"

"We've gone everywhere. Of course, we were looking for medications we knew. There might be some left that you'd recognize."

"I hope so, although I'm only familiar with medication from the 1960s. Maybe we'll find a PDR, that should help."

"What's that?"

"'Physicians' Desk Reference'. A medication guide that contains information on all the drugs licensed by the FDA."

"Good luck with that. Like I told you, there aren't many dead-tree books around anymore."

"One can only hope," I said with a sigh.

Once we reached the foot of the mountain, it didn't take long to get to downtown Morganton. Jonah stopped beside a brick building that had apparently been vandalized. All the windows were broken out, decaying trash scattered about the parking lot which was beginning to buckle in places.

After I got out of the truck, I glanced at the sky, more blue today than beige. Winter is definitely coming, I thought, as I buttoned up my jacket against the chilly wind blowing my hair about my face.

"What building was this?" I asked Jonah.

"The Chamber of Commerce. A good place for tourists to visit if they wanted to find out more about Morganton and Brown Mountain."

"I remember this place. We stopped in here when our van broke down. This is where I learned about the Brown Mountain lights."

He raised an eyebrow at that. "I don't recall them having any information on that, but then, I only came here as a child."

I turned around. "If I remember right, the library was over that way," I said, pointing.

Jonah nodded. "I'll drive you over, although there's nothing left."

"And wasn't the museum near it?"

"Sure was. Within walking distance. It's been vandalized too."

As we drew nearer, I began to remember that library, how beautiful and stately it was, with a large front porch for sitting and conversing or reading. Now there was nothing but charred remains, tumbled down brick, and more detritus littering the ground. I stared at it, wondering what would beset anyone to burn down such an elegant edifice containing so much valuable information.

"Pretty sad, huh?" Jonah said in a low voice.

"Pretty sickening. Have you sifted through the debris to see if there are any books left?"

He nodded. "Several times. There's nothing." He pointed to his right. "The museum's right over there."

I walked toward it with a sense of dread, knowing before we reached it that there was nothing to be found there.

When Jonah joined me, I said, "Let's move on, this is just heartbreaking."

He pointed to a row of houses nearby. "As you can see, there are houses all around us. We can each take one." He turned to Zachary and Abbie. "Check cabinets in the bathrooms, kitchen, anywhere you think they might have stored medications. Don't worry about going through any you find, just put them in your backpacks. We'll sort through them later."

"And while you're at it, search for a book called the PDR, 'Physicians' Desk Reference'," I said.

Abbie kissed Zachary on the cheek then turned and walked to a house at the far corner of the street. I followed, going into the house beside the one she entered, Jonah and Zachary entering the two on the other side of me. The inside of the small cottage looked like it had been torn apart. Blinds had been ripped from windows, furniture overturned, large holes punched in walls, dishes and cutlery tossed about. As I stepped over and around the mess littering the carpet, so soiled I couldn't tell its original color, I couldn't wrap my mind around why someone felt the need to destroy something in such a violent way. I found the one bathroom, which was tiny and cramped, containing a small one-sink vanity, broken toilet and grimy shower stall. There was no medicine cabinet and the vanity had been emptied. In the galley kitchen, I searched through all the cabinets, most of which contained nothing but mouse droppings and dust, smiling when I found a Lazy Susan containing several bottles of medication. Without reading the labels, I dropped each into my backpack, hurried outside, and went down four more houses.

We had completed several blocks by the time Jonah called a halt for lunch. While we sat on the lawn in front of the library munching on sandwiches and drinking water, we made comparisons about our hauls. Zachary had found the largest stash so far but said he didn't recognize any of the names on the medication bottles. We agreed to just take everything back with us, hoping I'd be able to identify what some of the medicines were for.

"Be sure to look for a PDR," I reminded them when we split apart for another search.

By late afternoon, we had covered at least a dozen blocks and had more medicine than we could haul in our backpacks. "Most of this has probably expired," I said as we tossed the bottles into a large trash bag Jonah had found in one of the houses, "but they still may have some potency." I looked at the others. "No one found a PDR?"

They shook their heads.

"Do you think we could stop at a doctor's office or medical clinic on the way out?" I asked Jonah. "I could look for a PDR there."

He nodded. "There's a clinic not far from here. Like everything else, it's been vandalized but maybe they left that."

The clinic was housed in a small building that had obviously once been someone's home. The front door had been yanked off its hinges and discarded in the tiny yard. Inside the small waiting area, chairs had been ripped open, stuffing pulled out and thrown about. The door into the inner sanctum was missing as were most of the doors leading into exam rooms. I easily located the doctor's office, where the desk had been overturned, paperwork strewn all over the floor. I exclaimed with delight when I spied bookcases lining two walls but quickly lost my enthusiasm when I saw that most of the books had been ripped apart. "Who would do such a thing?" I said to no one in particular.

"It should be a sin to do that to a book," Abbie said with derision.

I knelt down to study the books on the floor in front of the bookcase, lifting up broken bindings with the papers inside ripped away, shaking my head with disdain. I glanced back at the others, watching me. "Look for anything that has information about medicine," I said, gesturing at all the loose papers. "We can take those and I'll go through them and see if I can match anything up with the medicines we found."

Abbie joined me on the floor while Zachary and Jonah began to search the upper shelves on the adjoining wall. By the time we had gone through all those books and loose papers, it was growing dark outside. Although we didn't have much, we did find a PDR several decades old with a lot of pages missing.

"We need to leave," Jonah said. "We don't know if anyone's still here in Morganton but I doubt they'll be welcoming after dark."

I nodded. "Do you think we can come back again, go through other doctors' offices?"

He reached out a hand to help me to my feet. "Sure. Maybe not right away, but soon."

I smiled at him. "Thank you, Jonah." Lifting the book in my hand, I said, "This may not be much but it's a start."

It was almost full dark by the time we left the building. Jonah had parked the truck right outside the door, and when we exited, we all stumbled into one another, staring at a group of people gathered around the truck, all bearing weapons.

Jonah cursed under his breath as he stepped in front of us, resting his hand on the grip of his pistol. "What's this?"

A middle-aged woman moved away from the truck, her gun aimed at us. She had a stocky build, heavy through the breasts and thighs, and a voice that bespoke years of smoking. "I might ask you the same," she said in a belligerent tone.

"We're here for medicine," Jonah said, his voice low and hard.

She motioned to another woman—it was then that I noticed with something of a shock that they were all women—who stepped forward holding up the bag.

"You mean *our* medicine," the leader said.

"Didn't see you there to claim it when we found it," he said.

"Didn't need to be. This is my town and you're trespassing."

"Didn't see your name on the town marker," Jonah said, his voice now pressured, his stance rigid.

"Doesn't need to be."

Without any sort of signal I could detect, the other women straightened, aiming their guns at us. Jonah, Zachary and Abbie all drew their guns.

Fearful this was going to get out of control, I stepped around Jonah, holding up my hands. "Listen, we didn't know this was your town or that you had claim to the medicine we found, but we need this desperately. We have some sick people on the mountain I need to treat and no medication."

The attitude of the group of women changed as they all looked at one another then their leader. She studied me for a long time before saying, "You're a doctor?"

"Yes."

She glanced at the woman next to her then back at me. "Take her." Five of the women stepped out of line and began to advance toward us.

"She stays with us," Jonah said, his gun aimed at the leader.

The women stopped in unison, waiting for instructions from their leader.

"You're outnumbered, cowboy," she said, "there's no way you're gonna shoot all of us."

"But we can make a dent, at least. And you'll be first."

I looked at him, awed at how determined he was. "It's all right, Jonah. I'll go with them." I moved toward them but he put his hand on my arm and held me firm.

"No."

"I can't let you all be killed simply because she wants me to go with them," I said, my voice low.

"You ain't goin," Abbie said, glancing from the women to me. "No tellin what they got planned for you."

"Why do you want me to go with you?" I said, ignoring Abbie and Jonah. "If someone is ill or hurt, I'm more than happy to help. It's my duty. You don't need to take me by force."

She took her time answering. Finally, she nodded to the other women, all watching her, and they put down their guns. An immense sense of relief washed over me. "If you'll go willingly, we won't force you," she said, "but we need you and I can't let you leave without helping us."

I turned to Jonah, placing my hand over the one holding me back. "I'll be fine, Jonah. I need to go."

He gave me a look as if he thought I had betrayed him before focusing his attention back on the leader. "Wherever she goes, I go."

"Us too," Abbie said.

Zachary made a noise of affirmation.

The leader didn't look too happy about this but finally nodded her assent.

"And we keep the medicine," Jonah said.

"It's ours, we'll keep it."

Feeling tensions rise once more, I said, "Why don't we go with them, I'll help treat their sick or wounded, and then we can all look at the medication we found and decide who needs it most?"

Jonah and the leader locked gazes for a time before she finally said, "I think we can do that." She turned on her heel. "Follow us."

As we fell into step behind the group, it wasn't lost on me that several of the women detached themselves and moved around so they were to the rear, as if herding us. The leader led us to a two-story house on the outskirts of town. The downstairs was roomy and comfortable looking, and I wondered if this was where the women lived, although quickly determined not all, since there were several more inside, milling about the kitchen and dining room areas. They watched us with curiosity as we came through the door before all eyes turned to their leader, who ignored them as she led us up a narrow stairway to the second floor. I could hear a baby crying behind a closed door, and this is where she headed. Inside the tiny bedroom, a woman sat in a rocking chair holding the baby, wrapped in a blanket, trying to soothe it. The leader went to her and took the baby from her then turned to me.

"Is the baby ill?" I asked, my eyes scanning the tiny thing, noting the pallor of its skin, the sunken eyes. I undid the blanket, placing my hand over its chest, timing the rise and fall, feeling the tiny heartbeat.

"Starving," she answered curtly.

I looked at her.

"Her mother died during childbirth," she said, and I could see pain flicker in her eyes.

"How long ago?"

"Yesterday."

"Do you have a cow, goats?" I asked her.

She shook her head.

"No nursing mothers?"

She shook her head.

"I take it you have water here?"

She nodded. "We have several wells."

"Have you tried sugared water or honeyed water?"

"We did but she doesn't seem to know how to suck." She shrugged. "Doesn't matter anyway. She can't live on water."

"For now, we need to get her hydrated. If you press the nipple against the roof of the mouth, the liquid will spurt out and she'll swallow it."

At a signal from her leader, the woman who had been holding the baby hurried out of the room.

I turned to Abbie, wondering if she was thinking the same thing I was. She nodded in confirmation. I raised my eyebrows at her. She shrugged. "It's either that or let her die," she said.

I looked back at the leader. "Can I talk with the others in private, please?"

She gave me a curious look.

"I think I might have an idea. I just need to confirm it with them."

She walked out without responding.

After she left with the baby, I turned to Jonah. "Andrea's nursing her baby, she can help with this."

"No," he said.

Zachary nodded in agreement.

"If she doesn't, the baby won't live, Jonah."

"It's not our problem, Lizzie."

"Listen, if we help them, they'll be more prone to help us. Abbie and Zachary can take the baby to Andrea and hopefully she'll have enough milk for the two babies."

"And what if she doesn't? What if the baby dies?" Jonah raised his eyebrows. "What if that happens? They'll blame us, you know that, and probably try to kill us for it."

"We have goats, we have cows if Andrea can't nurse her," I insisted. "There's little time left and we have to try, Jonah. They'll know we tried to help if we do it. They can't fault us for that."

Abbie put her hand on Zachary's arm. "She's right, Zach. We have to try."

The brothers looked at one another. "What do you think?" Jonah asked Zachary, surprising me.

"We need to do it. If it will buy goodwill and save the baby, it's worth it." He glanced at the door. "Besides, we might need their help one day. They've got people, weapons. We don't need more enemies right now, Jonah."

Jonah sighed. "All right. You and Abbie take the baby back, see if Andrea can do it." He hesitated. "If she wants to."

Zachary nodded. "I don't like leaving you all here. We'll get back as quick as we can."

I opened the door and stepped into the hall. The leader was there, the baby in her arms, holding a baby bottle filled with water in its mouth. "Is it working?"

She smiled at me, obviously relieved. "So far."

"I'm Lizzie, by the way."

She nodded. "Meredith."

"And the baby's name?"

"We call her Pearl," Meredith said, looking lovingly at the infant.

"We have a young woman who's nursing her baby back at our camp. If she has enough milk, she can also nurse Pearl. I can't guarantee she'll be able to, though, you have to understand that, but I think it's worth a try."

Her stance relaxed a little as she moved toward me. "Okay."

"Abbie and Zachary will take the baby back. Jonah will stay to help me. Is that all right with you?"

She nodded as she turned and gave the baby to Abbie who was standing beside me.

Abbie settled Pearl in her arms, holding the bottle up. I was relieved to see Pearl seemed to be taking the water well enough. "We'll take real good care of her, I promise," Abbie said.

"I'll send one of my soldiers with you," Meredith said.

Jonah stepped up beside me. "No."

She frowned at him.

"There's no need to. They'll come right back and let us know whether or not it's working. If not, they'll bring the baby back."

I looked at him, wondering why he didn't mention the cows or goats. Knowing he didn't want this group to learn of our place on the mountain, I decided he also didn't want them to know about our livestock. I was prepared to step in to intercede if they got into an argument about one of Meredith's soldiers going with Abbie and Zach, but she simply nodded as she said, "Don't see as I have any other choice." She moved back, watching as Zachary and Abbie hurried away with the baby.

After they left, Meredith said, "We have others who need your attention. It's this way."

I glanced at Jonah, frowning at me, then followed after her.

They had apparently turned the house into some sort of infirmary, as each of the bedrooms upstairs had at least one patient. The next person I saw was a woman I placed in her early 50s, who complained of shortness of breath and fatigue. She coughed often and wheezed when she breathed, and it was obvious she was in much distress. When she confirmed her nails and lips would turn blue with any activity, I suspected she had emphysema, probably caused by the dirty air we all breathed. "Did you see a bronchodilator in those medicines we found?" I asked Jonah.

"What's that?"

"An inhaler."

"I don't recall." He looked at Meredith. "Where's the medicine?"

"I'll get it." She left, returning shortly with the bag.

"Empty it on the table over there," I said.

After she had, we sorted through the prescription bottles but I couldn't find any inhaler of any sort. "Do you have coffee?" I asked her, as I picked up the PDR.

"We do."

"Make some, strong. It will help with her breathing."

"Coffee?" Jonah asked with disbelief after Meredith left.

"It's in the same chemical class as theophylline, which is a long-acting bronchodilator. It will help her some. Back ..." I glanced at the ailing woman ... "we used hyssop or jimsonweed for asthma which should help but I haven't found any yet." While we waited, I had Jonah read off the names on the prescription bottles which I then looked up in the PDR but found nothing for breathing problems. Once Meredith returned, I had the woman, who told me her name was Sofie, drink the coffee. It seemed to help her breathing some but I knew it was only a matter of time before her symptoms grew worse, resulting in death if we could not find a way to stop the progression of the disease.

After assuring Sofie I would research other ways to help her, Meredith led me to the next patient, a young man named Eddie suffering shingles on his upper torso. He was in immense pain and couldn't stand clothing of any sort to touch the area. "Aren't there medications for this?" I whispered to Jonah when Meredith's attention was turned to another matter.

"Shingles was cured years ago," he whispered back. "Before the asteroid strike, there was a vaccine for it. He's too young to have had it."

"A salve made out of hyssop might possibly help but, like I said, I haven't found any on the mountain yet. Let's see if we can find some old medication."

Jonah, Meredith and I poured through the medication bottles, matching them with information we found in the PDR. I finally found an old bottle of pills prescribed decades ago to treat shingles. I explained to Eddie that the pills had long expired and might do more harm than good, but he was in so much pain, he insisted on taking them. Saying a silent prayer the pills would help and not hurt him, I handed them over, telling him if he tolerated the first dose, to take one a day until the shingles cleared or he ran out, whichever occurred first. He thanked me profusely for helping him which only made me feel worse because I felt so inept in this time and place.

I saw several children, male and female, all together in the same room, apparently suffering from respiratory infections with deep, rumbling coughs.

"It's been going around," Meredith told me.

"Didn't we find some pediatric antibiotics?" I asked Jonah.

He nodded. "They're outdated though."

"We can try that as a last resort." I glanced at the light overhead, burning brightly. "I see y'all have electricity. Do you have hot water?"

Meredith nodded.

"Turn on the hot water faucet in the tub or shower with the bathroom door closed and get it as steamy as you can. Let the ones who are coughing sit in the steam for ten minutes or so. It might offer them some relief." Meredith nodded at a young woman, who hurried out of the room. "Do you have any herbs?"

"Herbs? No, I don't think so."

"Garlic? Honey?"

"Both but the honey's old."

"Honey could probably last for centuries. Both are good for coughs and as an antibiotic."

Meredith nodded. "I'll go get them."

I was wary of using medications that had expired but knew no other recourse if the honey and garlic didn't help. Abbie and I hadn't had time to build up our stock of herbal medicines to the point where we had an overabundance of any one herb, and I suspected Jonah wouldn't want me to use what little we had on this group of people, who were not his own. I had by this time learned how much he cared for the people on the mountain and how responsible he felt for their safety.

By the time Abbie and Zachary returned with the good news that the baby was nursing and Andrea was happy to accommodate her, I was on my last patient, an elderly woman in great pain whom I suspected was very close to dying of cancer. I was relieved when Jonah found pain tabs among the medication bottles we had taken from the houses. After dosing her, I held her hand until they took effect, trying to distract her by asking her about her life and family, and was thankful when she at last slipped into a deep sleep. "It won't be long now," I told Meredith as I released the woman's hand and rose, giving her the bottle of pain tabs. By this time, I could tell by Jonah's actions that he was anxious to get back to the mountain. I was more than aware that he was never comfortable being away, fearful that raiders would attack or he would be needed for something, and we had been gone almost 24 hours.

Before leaving, I checked in on the sick children, some of whom appeared a bit better, others with no obvious change. I told Meredith she might want to try the antibiotics if any got worse. She merely shook her head as she held out her hand, saying, "Thank you for your help and for saving my niece."

"Oh, I didn't know. I'm so sorry for the death of your sister," I replied.

She shrugged. "Sister-in-law but she was family."

"You're welcome to come visit your niece anytime," Jonah said. "Just head up the mountain. One of the sentries will spot you and bring you to her."

"Thank you." She turned to me. "I trust you'll see that Pearl's well taken care of."

"Of course."

"And when she's weaned or we have another way to feed her, we get her back."

"I wouldn't have it any other way."

She eyed Jonah with suspicion for a moment then with a sigh handed over the bag filled with medicines. "I reckon this is yours."

"Don't you want to split them?" I asked.

"There are other houses we can look through. We probably wouldn't know what to do with them anyway. If it's all right, when we need a doctor, we'd like to come find you."

"I'd like that. Just do what Jonah said, find a sentry and they'll bring you to me or me to you. If any of the children get worse, send for me right away."

"I'll do that."

I looked around. "I've been wondering, where are all the men? The only males I've seen have been adolescents and younger."

"Most got killed by others, some ran off." She shrugged. "We decided to keep it mostly women. We don't need men and can fight our own battles well enough without em." She gave Jonah a defiant look.

He surprised me by laughing. "I reckon you can, Meredith."

After we said our goodbyes, we piled into the truck for our return to the mountain. On the way back, I sifted through the bottles of medicine, wondering about their uses, frustrated that the truck's inner light didn't work so I couldn't read what illnesses they treated.

Once we arrived at the house, just before we walked inside, Jonah pulled me aside. "Thanks for handling that so well back there."

I smiled at him. "No problem. I'm just glad there wasn't any violence and we parted on good terms."

His lips tightened. "Yeah, well, that may be, but next time, do what I say. Don't contradict me." He glared at me for a moment before turning on his heel and entering the house.

I watched him go, fighting the urge to kick his backside. Instead, I followed him inside, moving around to stand in front of him, stopping his progress.

"Don't contradict you? Do what you say?" I yelled at him, vaguely aware of Abbie, Zachary and Andrea all turning to us with surprised looks on their faces. "You can forget that! I'm not going to stand by meek and taciturn when you make bad decisions. If I'd done that, we'd all be dead on the front porch of that doctor's office."

He glared at me as he folded his arms, stepping back. "Dead? That's what you think?"

"Yes. You'd have had us in a gunfight if you kept on like you were, acting all macho and tough and unwilling to compromise, which I offered, by the way, and which was accepted, and which was the best decision to be made at that point."

He pointed his finger at me as he leaned toward me. "Which could have gone wrong at any point in time. We didn't know who they were, what they really wanted. They could have used you, then killed you, killed all of us right there in the midst of that whole group. So no, that wasn't necessarily the right one. I'm the leader here, I make the decisions and don't need you contradicting them."

"Not if they're bad ones."

"Who's to say that was a bad one?" he shouted. "It hadn't played out when you stepped in and offered to go with them."

His nostrils were flared, his eyes narrowed, his fists clenched but that didn't stop me. "Still a bad decision, like the one you made when those raiders came on the mountain and you left your sister, pregnant by the way and close to labor, while you went chasing after them. You left her, Jonah, with two complete strangers, two prisoners," putting emphasis on this word, "not knowing what we'd do in that situation. But Abbie and I made the right decision. We controlled that situation, without anyone dying, no thanks to you."

"And because I listened to your next decision, which was to let those two idiots live, they were back on the mountain with their team the next night, ready to attack."

"Which I stopped by the way, so you're welcome."

"Only because you were in the woods searching for your damn light," he yelled. I inwardly flinched. "Which would have led to your next bad decision, to go through that light, find your boyfriend and stop his marriage to Sarie, ending a whole line of descendants, including my brother and sister and baby nephew."

I stepped back from him. "But I wouldn't have done that," I said, my voice low. "I couldn't. Not now, not knowing you all, caring about you all."

He straightened up at that.

Shoot, I thought. "So don't assume that the decisions I make will be the wrong ones, Jonah. Just know that for me, they're the right ones, a lot righter than the ones you choose to make. And as for following your orders, I'm not one of your soldiers, I'm a visitor at best for now, and I will only do that if I think they're the right ones. If not, then I'll make my own, and there's nothing you can do to stop me."

He watched me for a moment.

"What?"

"Are you finished?" His voice was low, hard, curt.

"Yes."

"Good. I've heard all I want to." He turned on his heel and left, slamming the door behind him.

I closed my eyes, feeling so tired, irritated I'd let myself get angry with him. When I opened them, I noticed Abbie, Andrea and Zachary exchanging amused glances.

"What?" I said, my face growing red.

"Nothing," they each said, looking away.

"Oh, for Pete's sake." I picked up the bag of medicine and the PDR and stalked upstairs to my bedroom.

Chapter Ten

Late Fall – Winter 2054

The Letter

There were no more arguments between Jonah and me after that, but the tension between us was almost tangible. I tried to stay away from him as much as I could, although there were occasions, of course, when we were in the same room and had to interact. I would catch myself watching him and at times find his eyes on me, his expression unreadable. I vacillated between wanting to apologize and wanting to hit him and could never decide which one so spent most of my time frustrated with myself. Abbie, Zachary and Andrea found all this highly amusing, which irritated me to no end. Abbie told me we were like two wild animals prowling around one another, seeing who was going to make the first move, while Zachary and Andrea kept silent on the matter but the looks they gave me spoke volumes.

I was thrilled that Abbie got to experience a modern-day Thanksgiving, which Andrea told us was one of the most important holidays the mountain people celebrated. I immersed myself in helping Andrea decorate the house and prepare foods for Thanksgiving dinner, grateful for the distraction from thinking of Joshua and past Thanksgivings I had shared with him. Jonah invited people on the mountain who had no family to share it with, and I was glad to see Helen and Evelyn arrive together but surprised to see Avery and his mother Angie, who actually smiled at me. I noticed Mike Bishop, the sentry who had stopped me when the raiders were back on the mountain, paying solicitous attention to Andrea and her baby and found myself hoping things might work out for them.

During the day, people came and went, bringing food or partaking, and the atmosphere was relaxed and cordial. For once, I felt accepted on the mountain and was startled at how much that had come to mean to me. The harmonious mood changed when Clancy showed up. Sensing tension in the air the minute she stepped through the door, I wondered about that, but my curiosity quickly changed to unease when I noticed the glares she sent my way and overheard the snide comments she made about strangers who didn't belong, knowing she was talking about Abbie and me. Most everyone ignored her, and when she eventually took her leave after what looked to be a heated argument between her and Jonah outside, I breathed a sigh of relief. Although it was apparent to everyone by now that Clancy didn't like Abbie and me, even more so that she didn't trust us, I hadn't realized how much so. I didn't know how in the world I could change that and, to be honest, didn't find her an important enough person to try, so quickly forgot about her.

The mountain scenery changed as fall gave way to winter, the spindly deciduous trees stretching their skeletal limbs toward the sky, dry pine needles littering the ground, the grass in the meadows now brown and stiff. The air had a constant bite to it, chafing cheeks and lips as the wind seemed to constantly blow. Between working in my clinic, treating patients on the mountain, and compounding medicines from the herbs Abbie and I had gathered, I stayed quite busy. At night, I continued to search for the lights when the weather permitted, but this decreased considerably as the temperature plummeted and we seemed to be constantly bombarded by either rain or snow showers.

By this time, Evelyn had become more agitated with her pregnancy, terrified she would go into labor and have her baby without anyone there to help. In early December, I talked her into moving into Jonah's house, where we set up a private area for her in the basement, away from the medical clinic. That way, I assured her, Abbie and/or I would be available at a moment's notice if she went into labor. As it turned out, this was the right decision. On a freezing, snowy Christmas day, as we ate Christmas brunch around a live fir Jonah and Zachary had brought into the house and Abbie, Andrea and I had decorated, we were all startled when Evelyn let out a screech, her hands cradling her abdomen. Abbie and I exchanged glances as we simultaneously rose and went to her. With Jonah's and Zachary's help, we got Evelyn to the basement, where several hours later we welcomed a baby girl into the world.

When Jonah and Zachary came downstairs to see the baby, I was holding her in my arms, running my finger over her smooth-as-silk cheek, admiring her perfectness. Glancing up to see Jonah watching me with a look I had never seen on his face before, I raised my eyebrows at him.

His expression changed as he smiled at me, something he rarely did. "Life," he said.

I smiled at him. "Yes, life."

I insisted Evelyn stay with us until she felt comfortable enough with motherhood to return to her cabin. I worried about her taking care of an infant alone, knowing how stressful and overwhelming that could be, but after a month, she insisted on leaving. "My brother and his wife want me to come live with them," she said, smiling widely. "They don't have any kids and love Chloe so." She squeezed my hand. "I'll … we'll be fine, Lizzie."

"I'll check in with you weekly," I said, giving her a hug, my eyes tearing, already knowing how much I'd miss them.

One afternoon near the end of winter, I decided to visit my cabin, thinking I could live there temporarily until I decided what to do. Abbie found me standing in the yard, staring at it, remembering how it had looked when we lived there.

"You thinkin about movin in?" she said when she joined me.

I smiled at her. "Not really. Well, maybe. But just now, I was thinking of all we had done to it, how pretty it looked back then."

She took my hand and led me toward the cabin where we settled just inside the doorway, away from the wind, looking out over the land. Although the days were usually cold and at times bitter, this was one of those winter days that teasingly let you know spring was coming but not for awhile yet. The sun shone brightly in the sky, something we all were grateful for, and the temperature was warm, although the wind had a bite to it that brought tears to your eyes.

"I miss Beauty and Jonah so much," I said, my voice low.

Abbie sighed. "Oh, Lizzie, I grieve for Billy and Bob, all our fine animals. And friends and family too. I reckon I always will."

"I just wish I knew what happened."

She darted a glance at me. "I reckon you're still thinkin about goin back."

I shook my head. "I vacillate. Sometimes I think maybe I could be his mistress, you know, but Josh would never agree to that and I wouldn't want it, to be honest. Plus it wouldn't be fair to Sarie." I didn't tell her that at times I thought if I had some way of knowing if Sarie died before Josh, then I could go back afterward and he'd be mine. But that was so macabre, I was ashamed of thinking it. I looked at Abbie. "I know how Jonah feels about me going back but Zach and Andrea never say anything. Doesn't it bother them, the chance that I might?"

She shook her head, giving me a solemn look. "They trust you, Lizzie. They know you'll do the right thing."

"Whatever I do, I won't interfere with the marriage between Sarie and Josh, Abbie. I promise you that."

We were silent for a time, then she gave me a mischievous look. "Have you checked your tree?"

I frowned at her. "My tree?"

She grinned. "You and Josh thought you had the whole mountain fooled, leaving them love notes for one another in that big old oak, but most of us knew about it."

At my shocked look, she hurried on. "A-course, none of us read your letters." She shook her head. "'Twouldn't be right to do that."

I sat back, wondering how in the world I had forgotten about that tree. It was conveniently placed, the midway point between my cabin and Josh's plantation and close to the church we both attended. We frequently left messages for one another there, promising to meet at a specified time and place or just expressing our love. I closed my eyes, thinking of the countless rendezvous we had there, thinking it our secret place, our special tree, but apparently not as private as we thought. I looked at Abbie. "Do you think?"

She shrugged. "Why not? Could be he'd want you to know why he didn't follow you through the light, why he decided to stay behind." She glanced away. "And marry Sarie."

I jumped to my feet.

"Where you goin?" She squinted up at me.

"To the tree."

"But I thought we were going gatherin with Zach."

"I'll catch up." I dashed off into the forest, hearing her calling after me, "Good luck, Lizzie. I hope you find your answers."

Once inside the tree line, I was forced to a fast walk. As I hurried along, toward the site where the church used to be, I prayed Josh would have thought to leave me something, some explanation as to what had happened. As I drew closer to the site, I began to hope maybe he hadn't. Maybe I wouldn't like the reason he didn't try to find me, maybe I wouldn't want to know what had happened between him and Sarie.

I stepped into the clearing, glancing toward where the church had stood. All that remained now was a towering stone chimney leaning alarmingly to one side, looking as if a puff of air would send it toppling to the ground. I looked beyond it, searching for the charming little house occupied by Preacher Hennesy and his wife Freda, but there was no indication it had ever existed. I turned to my west, to the trees at the edge of the forest, now nothing more than a scraggly thicket, wondering as I walked toward them if that large, elegant, beautiful oak still stood. Inside the forest, everything had changed so much, I found myself wandering back and forth, searching for the tree, growing more and more desperate. I finally stopped, telling myself the oak couldn't possibly still be alive, it had lived many years before Josh and I chose it as our tree. It's probably dead and rotted away, I thought with despondency, walking back toward the clearing. As if by magic, I heard a bird calling and looked toward the sound. And there, towering above all the other trees was the massive oak, looking as elegant and stately as ever.

I ran to it, threw my arms around it, and kissed the bark, saying, "Oh, I've missed you, old friend." Realizing how ridiculous I must look, I glanced around, embarrassed, hoping no one had seen or heard me. Jonah's sentries were well-hidden and I had no idea if one lurked nearby. It was bad enough most of his troops didn't trust me, but to think me loony on top of that was almost too much to bear. Stepping back, I stared at the hollow in the trunk of the tree, one that looked shallow but was actually several inches deep, deep enough to hide a secret missive. Taking a breath, I put my hand inside the hole and felt around. When my fingers touched something smooth, I jerked my hand out, making a squeaking sound. You idiot, I told myself, as I forced my hand back into the hollow, grasped the smooth object and hauled it out. When I recognized Josh's plantation's stamp on the piece of leather that had been wrapped around a thick packet, I dropped it as if it were on fire.

I stared at the package for a long time, eventually lowering myself to the ground and sitting beside it, terrified to open it. The leather had aged over the years to a deep, crackled brown. The string around it had rotted through in several places, and when I reached out a finger and barely touched it, it fell apart as if it had only been waiting for that gentle touch. Steeling myself, I removed the twine and unwrapped the packet to find a thick piece of canvas tied around something shaped like a letter. Expecting only one, I was surprised to find several inside the canvas wrapping. With trembling fingers, I picked up the top missive, folded over so I couldn't read what was inside. I opened it and read the first words, "Lizzie, my love." Crying out, I dropped the letter, leaned back against the tree and put my face in my hands. Oh, Josh, I thought, why did I go through that light? Why didn't I stay? I was so happy with you. My thoughtless action had put me on a journey I did not wish to be on and had set Josh on another path, one which he had not planned.

I don't know how long I cried at the base of that beautiful tree. The sound of a bird chirping above my head finally penetrated my thoughts and brought me out of my misery. I glanced up to where the bird perched on a limb above my head, thinking it must be the same one that had drawn me to this tree. A cardinal, its plumage bright red, telling me it was a male, peered down at me. Why were the males so glorious and the females so plain, I wondered, thinking this was Josh's favorite bird. Feeling ridiculous, I whispered, "Josh, is that you?" The bird tilted its head at me, chirped again, then flew away.

"Okay," I said to myself, wiping my eyes then picking up the letter. The paper had yellowed and the ink was so faded in spots, I couldn't make out the date it was written as well as some of the letters of the words, but I forced myself to read, telling myself I had to know. I had to put an end to this constant guessing.

"Lizzie, my love, my light, my life. I miss you more with each passing second. I am in agony, I cannot rest, cannot focus, cannot function. Wherever you are, whenever you are, know that I wanted more than anything to follow you through that light. When my fingers touched yours, I was certain I would be with you for all eternity and would have gone through if the bushwhacker had not pulled me back, away from you. I fought him off, Lizzie, I might have killed him, I'm not sure, I was so furious, so frantic to get to you. When I turned back around, the light had disappeared and you and Abbie with it. I searched for that light, ignoring the screams coming from Sarie's cabin, and that has damned me, Lizzie. Damned me to stay because I chose you."

"No," I said, my voice quavering. "No, please." I wiped my eyes and continued reading.

"They assaulted her, Lizzie, I don't know how many. Sarie won't talk about it. If I had gone to her cabin instead of trying to find the light, I could have saved her, should have saved her. When I finally returned, I found her on the floor, bloody and bruised, and almost out of her mind. She had hidden Amanda May in a large trunk upstairs, and when Amanda May heard me, she came downstairs to help with Sarie. But you know her, Lizzie, how strong she is. She dealt with it the way Sarie does, by herself, and eventually by dismissing it from her mind. But when she found out she was with child, Sarie came to me. She wanted to keep the baby but did not want it to be a bastard. You know what would have happened to her if she had, how the mountain people would have treated her, possibly, no, most probably, ostracized her. What could I do, Lizzie, but offer her my name because I had not offered her my protection when I should have? If only I had saved her."

I closed my eyes and leaned against the tree. Of course, I thought, Josh would do that. He was an honorable, noble man, and he would carry the guilt with him for the rest of his life, even though it hadn't been his fault, even though he might not have been able to stop them. I looked at the letter, my eyes burning.

"We married, with the pact between us that we would search for the light together. Sarie mourns Abbie as much as I mourn you, and we both want nothing more than to go through the light and find you both. Oh, Lizzie, I pray constantly that you are trying to find your way back to me. Are you, my love? Will you? Can you forgive me for what I've done?" I noticed there was a PS at the bottom. "I know how much you loved Beauty and Jonah. Rest assured we are taking good care of them and have made plans with Maggie for their care if we should leave. Amanda May and Tommy are living in your cabin, taking good care of your homestead and your animals, hoping you will return. Please tell Abbie Billy and Bob are healthy and well. All my love, Josh."

The letter ended there. I looked down at the next one, picked it up, started to unfold it, then put it back. No, I told myself. Enough. I didn't think I wanted to know what happened. I heard movement nearby and looked up to see Abbie watching me.

"I reckon you found a letter," she said.

I gestured at the packet beside me. "More than one."

"Did you read em?"

"Just the first."

She walked over and sat beside me, taking my hand. "Did you get your answer?"

I shrugged. "One of them. I just read the first."

She gave me a curious look.

"I don't know if I can read anymore, Abbie. It's just too sad."

She stared at the opened letter for a long time. "Can you tell me what he said?"

I shook my head, picked up the letter and gave it to her.

She took a long time reading it. She finally looked up. "By assault, I reckon he means ..."

"They raped her."

Abbie sighed and went back to reading. Finished, she placed the letter tenderly on the ground. "Poor Sarie. All she went through with Pa and now this. No wonder she hates men so."

That got my attention. "You knew what your pa was doing to her?"

"Maggie and I suspected. Then when he disappeared, I figured she couldn't do it anymore so put an end to him so he'd stop. Neither one of us could find fault with her for that, Lizzie. He mistreated her so."

"That's not what happened, Abbie."

Her eyes grew wide. "You know what happened 'tween Sarie and Pa?"

I nodded. "She told me, the day those outliers raped Connie."

"You reckon you can tell me, Lizzie?" When I hesitated, she said, "I ain't as fragile as you all think I am. I'd like to know."

I nodded, thinking, yes, of course, she had never been as fragile as we all thought she was, or maybe wanted her to be. "Sarie said your pa gave her to Constable Jackson in payment for a debt. You know how much she hated Jackson, but what concerned her more was what your pa would do to you and Maggie when she was gone, so she told him no. She said they got into a fierce argument about it and he threatened her with a knife, telling her he'd kill her like he did your mother if she didn't do what he said."

Abbie gasped. "He killed her?" she said, her voice shrill.

"He told Sarie he beat her, then threw her body off a cliff for the bears to eat. She said she lost control of her temper when he said that and killed him, then did the same thing he did to your mother, threw him off a cliff."

Abbie sat back, her lips in a tight line. She finally sighed. "We all thought she ran away and left us behind. Couldn't understand why she'd leave us to the likes of him."

"That's what Sarie told me."

Abbie shook her head. "Don't know why we didn't think otherwise. We all knew how mean and cruel a man he was. We all knew how he'd beat her at the least little thing. But it never occurred to me he'd kill her, Lizzie, never once."

"I'm sorry, Abbie."

When she looked at me, her eyes were hard, her expression grim. "Wish I'd killed him myself, to tell you the truth. I hope he's rotting in hell right alongside Jackson."

I didn't know how to respond to that so simply said, "I'm sure he is."

We sat side by side holding hands for a long time. Abbie finally stirred, her gaze darting to the packet. "You want me to read the next one, Lizzie? I can tell you what it says."

I picked up the letters and handed them to her. "Why don't you read it out loud?"

She looked at the second letter, but something below caught her attention. She laid that one aside and picked up the third and last letter. "It's from Sarie, it's for me." Her eyes filled with tears. "Oh, Lizzie, I don't know what to do."

I tried to smile at her but couldn't. "You read mine and I'll read yours. How's that?"

She nodded, her expression solemn as she picked up Josh's second letter. "My darling Lizzie, I'm leaving this for you along with my first letter and one for Abbie from Sarie in hopes you remember our special tree, in hopes that they survive the years forward. If that's where, no, when you went. Lizzie, we searched countless nights for that light but it avoided us, as if it knew we were looking for it. But I despair that if we were to find the light and come to you, you would hate me for what I've done and would not want to see me. There's something I have to tell you, Lizzie, and the words will not come in a way that will help you understand. So I suppose I'll just say it as simply as I can. I'll begin by telling you that Sarie had her baby, a beautiful little girl who looks just like her. We named her Abigail Elizabeth and she's a sweet, happy, healthy girl who carries none of the darkness of her father, whoever he may be. When Gail was a year old, we celebrated her birthday with Maggie and Randall, who are now proud parents of a boy, by the way, and expecting another child in a few months. When Sarie and I returned home, we were forlorn and sad, wishing you and Abbie were here with us. We did the one thing we shouldn't, drank moonshine Sarie had found hidden in the barn, presumably by her father, and in our drunkenness, turned to each other for comfort. Oh, Lizzie, I am so sorry to tell you that we now have an infant boy and I find myself a man with a family, a man with responsibility, a man who cannot just leave this life for another."

Abbie glanced up at me. "I'm sorry," she whispered, tears in her eyes.

I shook my head, wiping my face. "I was afraid something like that had happened. Go on, finish it, Abbie. I don't know if I can bear much more."

"Lizzie, you will always be my true love but I cannot abandon my life here to go through a light that may not take me to you. Although Sarie would like nothing more than to find Abbie, she has decided she doesn't want to chance taking two babies through a light she isn't sure will take her to her sister. So we've decided to stay here on Brown Mountain, praying you and Abbie will find your way back to us. I pray your forgiveness, I pray your understanding, I pray you will return. My heart aches for you but my love is now torn. My son and daughter need me, Lizzie, and love me with such tenderness it hurts my heart. Please, Lizzie, come back, come back to us, you and Abbie. All my love, Josh."

I closed my eyes, leaning my head back against the tree. Abbie put her hand over mine. "Are you all right, Lizzie?"

I shook my head. "I can't blame him for anything. I'm the one who put us here, I'm the one who was so gal-darned stubborn about finding that damned light and going through it."

"We'll find the light and go back, Lizzie, if that's what you want."

I looked at her and could see how much it cost her to say that. "But that's not what you want and you know it."

She stared at me. "Do you?"

"Yes. No." I wanted to scream. "How can I, Abbie? He's married to her now. Their lives are set in motion. They had … they'll have children, create a life together. I can't just go back and demand he leave her, divorce her for me. It wouldn't be right."

She sighed. "No, it wouldn't. But you know Sarie, she'd do it for you if you asked her."

"And you know Josh, how honorable he is. He wouldn't give up those children for me. He shouldn't." I gave a harsh laugh. "I reckon I'm stuck here, where I don't want to be. It's Brown Mountain 1859 all over again."

"Maybe not. You wanted to get back to 1969 so bad, Lizzie. Maybe you should try to go back there."

"I don't know. Maybe." I squeezed her hand. "But if this is where you want to stay, because of Zach or for whatever reason, I understand, and that's what you should do. You should be happy, you deserve that." I picked up Sarie's letter. "You ready?"

She stared at the letter for a long moment before slowly nodding. "Read it."

To be honest, I don't remember what that letter said. Although I read the words, I wasn't paying attention, my mind instead focused on my situation with Josh. And as long as I'm honest, I might as well say that I hated Sarie at that time, hated her with a passion that surprised me. She had taken my life, my love, bore him the son I thought I would bear. I supposed she loved him, if Sarie could love a man. And she must have been a good wife, a caring one, for Josh to want to stay and raise a family with her. Maybe, my mind whispered. Or maybe it was because Josh was a man of the 19th century, whose honor was a priority with him. He would be more than aware how he would be looked upon if he were to abandon his wife and two children for another woman, one who had disappeared from his life for a time. No, Josh wouldn't do it, even if he wanted to with all his heart.

When I finished, I gave the letter to Abbie, who was crying. "You all right? I asked, feeling guilty for not paying attention to what Sarie had said to her.

She nodded. "She sounds happy, Lizzie." She flinched at that. "I'm sorry, that's not what you need to hear right now."

"No, it's fine, I'm glad she is." But I didn't want that, oh, no, I wanted her just as miserable, just as unhappy as I was.

Abbie sighed. "I know it ain't right, I know it ain't what you wanted, Lizzie, but you got to decide what you want to do, what's best for you, and I'll help you in any way I can."

I tried to smile at her but my lips wouldn't move. My whole body felt rigid, frozen, as if weighted with concrete. "Why don't you go on and meet up with Zach. I'd like to be alone for a bit, re-read these letters, think about this."

She leaned in and kissed my cheek. "I love you, Lizzie, and I want you happy. We'll do whatever it takes."

I looked at her. "Do you realize how much you've changed since we got here? Are you aware?"

She thought about it. "Not really. But I think maybe I've found my place, the way you were always trying to find yours. Mayhap if you give it a chance, the same thing will happen to you." She picked up her letter, rose to her feet, and with a wave, walked away from me.

I sat beneath that tree all that afternoon, reminiscing about Josh and my times with him on the mountain, laughing at some points, crying at others. It occurred to me at one point that I was grieving him and I suppose that's what I was doing. Why do you have to be so damned honorable, Josh? I thought more times than I could count. When the light began to change, I forced myself to my feet. I stared down at the two letters from Josh for a long time then finally bent down, picked them up, folded them, wrapped them in the canvas and leather, and put them back in the tree's hollow. I placed my hand on the tree's wide trunk, patted it as if it were an animal, saying, "I won't be back, old friend," then turned and headed back toward the encampment.

When I walked in the door, Jonah was conferring with several of his troops in the dining area of the cabin. They were bent over a large map he had laid out on the table, speaking in low voices while pointing at different locations. Jonah glanced up when I stepped inside and smiled, the kind of smile that is spontaneous and open, not guarded and wary, as was his usual expression when looking at me. I found myself thinking how handsome and strong and virile he looked, and realized with a start I wasn't for once comparing him to Josh. I didn't smile back, only stared at him as I came to a decision in that instant, and when I saw he understood what I wanted, turned on my heel and left, knowing he would follow me. I led him into the forest, to my cabin, and once the door was closed behind him, I threw myself into his arms and kissed him, my lips grinding against his, my body pressed close.

And later, while he slept, I got up and left that cabin, full of guilt, full of remorse, full of sadness, bidding a final goodbye to Josh.

I don't think I slept more than a couple of hours that night. I couldn't get what had happened in the cabin with Jonah off my mind and this frustrated me more than anything. I wanted to forget it, put it down to my own way of saying goodbye to Josh, but a small part of me knew it was more than that. Much more.

The next morning, I waited until I heard several voices downstairs before rising. After a fast shower, I headed to the kitchen for a quick breakfast. At the bottom of the stairs, I glanced at my watch, telling myself I didn't have much time before clinic hours started, and ran headlong into something hard. Stepping back with an "Oof," I glanced up. When my eyes met Jonah's, I cringed inside. "Sorry," I said, sidling around him, trying not to look at him. "I wasn't watching where I was going."

He reached out and caught my arm. "Hold on a minute."

I couldn't meet his gaze so brought my arm up and studied my watch. "Clinic hours start in about 30 minutes, Jonah. I need to eat, get everything set up." I tugged away from him but he hauled me back. I stared at the floor, the walls, beyond him.

"Look at me, Lizzie," he said in a low voice.

I tried to get away, but he wouldn't release his hold on me. "Really, I don't have time."

"Look at me."

I reluctantly raised my eyes to his. Such beautiful eyes in a beautiful face, I thought.

He cocked his eyebrows, gave me that crooked grin that reminded me of Josh so much. I blinked hard against the nascent tears.

"Where'd you go last night?" he asked, glancing around to make sure no one was listening.

"Home. Here."

He looked uncomfortable. "It's just, I was wondering why you left. Why you didn't stay."

I wrenched out of his grasp. "I don't have time to get into that now, Jonah. I'll talk to you later, all right?" I hurried off down the hallway, cursing to myself when I heard him following me.

I ignored him as I took time to greet Andrea and coo over the babies, lying on their backs in a playpen. I hugged Abbie good morning and promised to go gathering with her that afternoon then grabbed a pastry from the cabinet. Deciding to eat it cold, I left, more than aware that Jonah's eyes had followed me throughout this horrible pretense that everything was normal. It wasn't. It never would be. How could it?

I escaped to the basement with the flimsy excuse that I needed to prepare for my clinic. When I heard the door above close and footsteps descending the stairs, I sighed inwardly. I wanted Jonah to go away, not to speak to me, not to acknowledge what had happened between us in any way.

I kept my eyes on my task, busy laying out supplies, ignoring him when he came to a halt in front of the table and simply stood there, watching me. I didn't need to look at him to know that. He finally sighed, placed his hands on the table, and leaned toward me. I closed my eyes against those hands, remembering how they had felt, how unexpectedly gentle they could be, how they seemed to know my body as if we had been lovers for years. How they had set me on fire.

"Listen," he said, his voice low, "you can ignore me all you want but it won't negate what happened between us last night and you know that."

I breathed deep before meeting his gaze. "I used you."

I saw the fleeting look in his eyes, knew I had hurt him, and felt terrible for that.

"No," he said, softly. "You didn't, Lizzie, although tell yourself that if it helps."

"It's the truth." I looked away from him. "I'm sure Abbie told you about the letters, about Josh and Sarie. It was my way of saying goodbye to him, of letting him go."

"Maybe at first, not during. Not after."

"Jonah, please, let's not make this anything more than it was. It won't happen again, I promise you that. I'm really sorry, I had no right to do that, but it was the only way I knew how to release him."

"His hold on you, you mean."

"It's over, okay, there's nothing more to be said. There's no reason to discuss it, debate it, take it apart and look at it more closely, all right? Let's just agree it happened, it won't happen again, and get on with our lives."

"Kind of hard to do if you're going to be dodging me all the time or ignoring me like you've been doing, Lizzie."

I watched his lips as he spoke, flashbacks flaring through my mine like sparks from a firecracker. How they felt against mine, how they felt on my body, trailing heat, trailing fire. I shook my head to clear these thoughts and tried to smile at him but my mouth wouldn't cooperate. "I won't ignore you, I won't dodge you, we'll just go back to what we were before."

He gave me that crooked grin, but I could see the anger in his eyes. "Friends? Well, we weren't even that, really. But that's what you want, to be friends."

"Yes, friends."

He shook his head. "No. Not after last night."

"It has to be that way."

"Why?" he yelled, slamming his fists on the table.

I jumped, startled. "Because that's the way it is."

"No, I don't accept that." He leaned close to me. "You might have started out with the intention of saying goodbye to him, maybe even pretended I was him, but during, afterward, you were there with me, in the present, Lizzie, and you know it." He gazed at me, his eyes hard, his mouth set in a firm line. "It wasn't his name you called out. It was mine, *mine,* Lizzie, and I claim it."

He turned on his heels and left.

Chapter Eleven

Late Winter 2055

Look Out

Jonah and I entered into an awkward truce after that. We were always civil to one another and tried to act as if nothing had happened between us when in one another's presence, but I sensed Abbie and Andrea suspected otherwise by the looks they gave us or would exchange between themselves. Abbie tried to broach the subject of Jonah a time or two but I always found a reason to escape her company or would steer the conversation in another direction until she cornered me one day in the greenhouse, where I was compounding herbs for medicine. I didn't know what to say when she shared Zachary's news that Jonah had broken up with Clancy. Ignoring my effort to forestall her telling me anything further, she bulled on, saying, "They had a big row, from what Zach told me. Lots of shouting and Clancy accusin him of every evil act under the sun. But he just stood there and took it and when she finally run out of steam walked off without sayin a word." She sighed, watching as I processed this news.

"And why does this concern me?" I said, struggling to keep my expression neutral.

"Lizzie," she said, putting her hand on my arm, "watch out for her. She don't like you and I reckon she'll blame you for this."

That got my attention. "Me? What did I do?"

The look she gave me was part pity, part irritation. "It don't take much to see something happened between the two of you, the way you tip-toe around one another, acting so polite and all, with faces set in stone. But I see the way he looks at you when you're not watching and, yes, the way you look at him. And I ain't the only one."

I shook my head.

She held up her hand. "You can deny it all you want but I see what I see and I know what I know. There's fire between you two." She leaned her shoulder against mine. "It wouldn't be the worst thing in the world if you took up with him."

I glared at her.

She shrugged. "You might think you're betraying Joshua, but you ain't. He ain't here, Lizzie, he ain't even alive now, and he chose Sarie over you, even if it was bein honorable and all. So the way I see it, you deserve to be happy and to do that you're gonna have to quit grievin Josh and let him go."

"Never," I spat at her as I rose to my feet and stomped off.

But she was right, Clancy obviously blamed me for what had happened between her and Jonah. I wanted to tell her it had nothing to do with me, but she so obviously hated me, I knew she wouldn't hear my words. So I tried to stay out of her way as much as possible. She didn't make it easy, and when we would pass would brush against my shoulder hard, as if she wanted to knock me down, or glare at me if we were in the same area together. I tried to ignore her behavior as much as possible but at times it was almost impossible. I then began to worry she might be a bit psycho when I found weird objects made out of twigs and feathers and some kind of animal fur on my pathway or outside the clinic door.

When I told Andrea about this, her eyes grew wide. "She's trying to put a hex on you."

"Who?"

She frowned at me. "You know who."

"You're kidding, right?"

Andrea's look told me she wasn't.

"What is this, the medieval ages? Who puts a hex on someone? That doesn't even make sense."

"She claims she's a wiccan," Andrea said.

I snorted. "More like witch."

Andrea leaned close to me. "Stay clear of her, okay? She's weird, crazy jealous over Jonah. Always has been, even when we were kids. Since he broke up with her, she's even worse than ever."

"I do stay clear of her, Andrea. I don't know why she's singling me out."

Her eyes told me I was being a fool. "Yes, you do." She moved closer to me. "I sense things about people, Lizzie, and she's a real danger to you. She'll hurt you if she gets the chance. You need to be careful." She glanced around. "I need to tell Jonah about this before it gets out of hand." She squeezed my hand and hurried off.

Since being in the house had become so uncomfortable to me, fearing I would meet up with Jonah, I spent my time either hidden in the clinic in the basement treating patients or on the mountain seeing to those too ill or injured to come to me or gathering herbs in temperate weather. Once every two weeks, Abbie, Andrea and I would drive down to Morganton, where Abbie and I saw patients while Andrea relayed Pearl's latest developments to Meredith as she and the other women passed the baby around, fussing over her.

I felt adrift, like I didn't really belong anywhere. I thought about cleaning out my cabin and living there but that seemed to me a way of settling down, of making this my permanent home, so I stayed away. Besides, I knew it would remind me of Jonah and what had happened that night. Evenings the weather permitted, I roamed the mountain searching for the lights and would only return well after dark, eat a quick dinner and climb into bed. Although I wasn't sure what I would do if I encountered the lights, I stubbornly clung to the belief that when the time came, I would make the right decision. I did know one thing, I would not, could not stop the union between Josh and Sarie.

When the days began to lengthen and the temperature grew warmer as spring crept closer, I ventured out more, walking the mountain near the point I had come through. One night, I arrived back home later than usual, well after midnight, irritated that the lights continued to elude me. I despaired it might be as it was when I came through this time, on the anniversary of my first time through the lights. The thought that that would keep me here several more months put me in a foul mood.

As I was crossing the yard, heading toward the house, a shadow appeared out of the stand of trees to the west and began to walk toward me. I halted, then recognizing Jonah, began walking again. He had apparently been on sentry duty as he was dressed all in camouflage and carried a rifle.

"Lizzie," he said, when he reached me, his voice curt and cold.

"Jonah."

"Been out searching for the lights?"

"Yep."

"Take it you didn't find them."

"Nope." I hesitated when I heard loud music coming from the open window.

We glanced at one another then both proceeded onto the porch and inside.

Andrea, Abbie and Zachary were watching what Jonah and Andrea called a video recorded on a small plastic rectangular object they called a flash drive, which plugged into the side of the TV. Although they told me this was an ancient gadget, as was the television, which was large and flat and mounted on the wall, it certainly outdated anything I knew back in the 1960s. I'd never heard of videos or flash drives or even personal computers back then.

I smiled at the screen when Andrea said, "We're watching the video from Woodstock. Isn't that where you were headed when …" Her voice trailed off and she quickly took a sip from the bottle she held in her hand.

Judging the beer bottles littering the coffee table, it was apparent they'd been drinking. I smiled. Tyler Sawyer, one of Jonah's men, had begun brewing beer and it looked like his first batch had passed muster. All seemed very happy, wide grins on their faces and moving their bodies to the music. I looked at Andrea, hoping she hadn't imbibed since she was nursing.

As if reading my thoughts, she held up a bottle. "Non-alcoholic."

I nodded as I removed my backpack and placed it on the floor beside the door. "Where are the babies?"

"Blissfully asleep," Andrea said with a grin.

"Lizzie, I was just thinkin of you," Abbie said. "Remember all them times you, Josh and me would play that music you taught us." She waved her hand at the large TV on the wall. "Just like this."

I stiffened at this memory. Abbie and Josh were both musically inclined and could play several instruments. During my time in 1969, my boyfriend Ben, who had been a rock musician, had taught me how to play the guitar. I wasn't great but passable and had taught Abbie and Josh some of my favorite rock songs. We used to get together on cold evenings just to sing and play. Josh had a beautiful voice and I'd watch him strum his guitar, singing a rock song foreign to him but one he made his own, and think how beautiful he was and what a fantastic rock musician he would have made. Abbie had a voice much like Janis Joplin and I loved to hear her sing. Sometimes Josh and I would slow dance while she sang a folk ballad. How wonderful it had felt to be in his arms, swaying to the music, smiling at the sweet words he whispered in my ear, goosebumps traveling up and down my body. What a beautiful time that had been, I thought fleetingly as I blinked my eyes to hide my tears, thinking to myself, Oh, Josh, how I miss you. I noticed how quiet it had become and glanced at the others, watching me with sympathy in their eyes. All but Jonah, and I didn't look at him long enough to read the expression on his face. I didn't need to.

I forced myself to smile. "Good times, Abbie."

Andrea handed me a beer with a mischievous grin. "Zach says it tastes pretty good for a first batch. Come join us." She grabbed my hand and led me to the couch. I sat, smiling at the video. "Joe Cocker, one of my all-time faves."

"I reckon Dylan's my favorite," Zachary said, putting his arm around Abbie.

"Jonah, don't be a grump, come watch with us," his sister said. "This is one of your favorite parts."

He gave her a smile more grimace than grin but accepted the beer she offered and sank into the recliner. I began to relax as I listened to the music and drank the beer, and eventually found myself wishing I had made it there. The music was fantastic and everyone looked to be having a good time. I then began to wonder what my life would have been like if our van hadn't broken down and I hadn't encountered that light. Would I still be with Ben? Would I be a medical doctor now with my own practice? Would I be happy?

Andrea leaned against me, bringing me out of my thoughts. She smiled when I looked at her.

"Did music ever get any better than this?" I said. "I honestly don't see how it could have."

She gestured toward Jonah. "Ask the master."

He smiled at her. "Not for long. 1960s, '70s, can't beat it."

"I missed the '70s."

"Well, we'll just have to catch you up," Andrea replied.

Abbie and Zachary got up and began to dance. I had taught her some of the dances of my time and watched with amusement as she showed them to Zach, then encouraged Andrea to join them. They were having a grand time, laughing and dancing, while Jonah and I sat like two geriatric chaperones at a school dance. I wanted nothing more than to get up and join them but felt self-conscious with Jonah there.

After several minutes, I felt him staring at me, and when I glanced at him, he raised his eyebrows and gave me that crooked grin which now seemed more his than Josh's. "Want to show them how it's really done?"

I suppose the beer had done its job by that time. I no longer felt awkward around him and the lure of the music was too great to ignore. "Why not?" I stood when he reached out his hand to me.

We joined the others, dancing and laughing, and for the first time since I had come to this century, I lost myself in having fun, in making memories instead of reliving them.

When the video ended, I found myself in Jonah's arms, my eyes closed, swaying to the music. His body felt good against me, warm and comforting, the muscles of his chest, abdomen and thighs hard against mine. I breathed deeply, liking the way he smelled, of sun, woods and gun metal intermingled with his own male scent. Realizing the video had stopped playing, I opened my eyes and stepped back. Without meaning to, I looked into his eyes. He stared at me, his gaze burning into mine with an intensity that was almost tangible. I started to pull away but he held onto me and I found I didn't want to leave the confines of his arms. I glanced around the room. Abbie and Zach sat on the couch, heads together, murmuring to one another. Andrea had disappeared, I supposed to check on the babies, sleeping upstairs.

Without saying a word, Jonah took my hand and led me outside, into the woods, onto the trail, and toward my cabin. I didn't try to stop him. I didn't want to. Neither one of us said anything as we walked, our bodies close to one another, our hands tightly grasped. We didn't need to.

Warmth on my closed eyelids told me the sun was up. I opened my eyes, expecting to be in my bedroom at the house, momentarily disoriented when I recognized my cabin. Was I back? Had I gone back to the 1800s? I rolled onto my side and met a warm, hard body which I immediately knew wasn't Abbie's. I turned my head, my gaze meeting Jonah's sleep-hazed eyes, and squelched my panicked reaction, to jump out of bed and run.

When I moved to get up, he lightly grasped my wrist, saying, "Don't." The expression on his face was one I had never seen before, soft and pleading. "Don't, please," he said. "You don't need to run away."

"Jonah ..."

"Just stay for a bit. That's all I ask."

I turned on my other side to face him. "Jonah, we shouldn't have done this."

He cocked an eyebrow. "No reason not to. We're both adults, of free will and choice."

"But I'm still in love with Josh."

His expression hardened to the stern one he usually wore. "Then you love a ghost."

I started to say something, but he interrupted. "You're chasing a ghost when you chase those lights, Lizzie. You have to know that."

"Jonah, let's not get into this, not now."

"Josh isn't here," he persisted. "He chose not to come after you. Why can't you accept that?"

"He didn't have a choice."

"Yes, he did. He could have chosen to find that light, to find you."

"He's an honorable man, he did what was right."

He propped himself on an elbow. "Honorable? No, not honorable. Romantic, maybe. I'll give him that."

I sat up. "Don't make what he did less than it is."

He scooted to sit, leaning against the headboard, the sheet slipping to reveal his muscled chest and abdomen. My body heated and I forced my gaze away. "Lizzie, if it had been me, if I had been faced with that choice, I would have helped Sarie in any way I could, found a way for her to deal with her pregnancy, but I would not have chosen to stay and marry her. I would have chosen to come after you, to find you, to be with you."

I stared at him. "What are you saying?"

"I'm saying I love you. I've loved you ever since I came down those stairs and found you holding a rifle on me." A smile played along his lips as he closed his eyes. "God, I don't think I've ever seen anything so beautiful, you standing there with a fierce warrior look on your face, sighting down that rifle, ready to shoot anyone who threatened you and those you were protecting." He opened his eyes and gave me an embarrassed smile, smoothing my hair from my face. "Lizzie, if it were me in Josh's situation, the way I feel about you, I wouldn't let you go. I couldn't. And no matter what you claim, I think you have feelings for me, you just don't want to acknowledge them."

I wanted to scream with frustration. He was right, I did have feelings for him, but saying it would make it valid and I didn't want to do that. "What good would it do? I'm leaving here when I find the lights, I'm going back."

He leaned toward me, speaking low. "To him, right? To a man who has abandoned you for another woman, another life."

I lunged out of bed and began to search for my clothes. "I won't listen to this."

"What will you do when you find him? Ask him to divorce Sarie, marry you instead? If he's as damned honorable as you claim, he won't do that and you know it."

I sat down on the bed, put my face in my hands. "I won't do that," I finally said, looking at him. "I can't end you, Zach, Andrea and her baby. I care too much for you all to do that."

"Then why go back?"

"Because I don't know what else to do," I said, tears streaming down my face. "I feel like I don't belong anywhere anymore, either here or 190 years ago. I can go back to 1969 but there's really nothing there for me other than my father who would pressure me to live the life he wants for me and who may not even be alive now. I didn't love Ben, I can't go back to him."

He put his hand on mine. "You don't have to go back for anyone, Lizzie. Stay. Stay here for you or stay with me."

"Oh, Jonah, don't you see? I look at you and I see him. I think about him and see you. It's all so confusing."

"Just give it a chance," he said, squeezing my hand. "Make a life with me. Give us a chance, see where it goes." He shrugged. "Or like I said, stay for yourself, if that's what you want. You're strong, independent, you don't need anyone."

I jerked my t-shirt over my head. "I'll think about it." I looked at him, could see how much I hurt him. "I promise, I'll think about it, Jonah." I couldn't resist reaching out and placing my palm against his stubbled cheek.

I got dressed quickly, watching as he did the same. I turned toward the door then back to Jonah, seated on the edge of the bed pulling on his boots. I kissed him goodbye, my body instantly heating as our lips met. With great reluctance, I pulled away and hurried out the door before I changed my mind and stayed, ignoring him calling after me to wait.

As I hurried along, I contemplated the change in Jonah's demeanor. Before, he had never chosen to show his emotions to me other than that one night when I instigated our being together. But just now, with me, he had allowed his emotions to show on his face, something I had never known him to do before with anyone, other than the love he showed for his sister and brother.

I was near the edge of the forest, the house in sight, when I heard footsteps behind me, bringing me out of my thoughts. Thinking it was Jonah, I turned around, freezing when I saw Clancy. She had a determined look on her face as she raised her arm, and I had just enough time to wonder what she had in her hand before my head exploded and everything went black.

I woke up in a dark place smelling of mold and dirt. Groaning, I put my hand to the side of my head, feeling a large pump knot there. When I moved, my head pounded with each heartbeat and I felt sick to my stomach. I wiped my face with my hand, my forehead and upper lip slick with perspiration. It was too dark to determine if my vision was blurry or double but I knew my symptoms meant I was probably concussed. Gingerly raising up to a sitting position, I slowly rotated my head, looking around, but it was so dark, I couldn't make out any shapes, not even walls. I could see no light filtering through cracks around windows or doors. "Is anyone here?" I said into the void, panic creeping up my spine when no one answered me. I eased back down, fighting nausea, telling myself not to go to sleep, although that's what I wanted to do more than anything to stop that insufferable pain in my head.

Once my stomach settled, I sat back up and put out my hands, feeling around me. Nothing, only air. I ran my fingers along the ground beneath me, feeling rough floor planks. Surmising I must be in a cabin, I tried to stand but felt too woozy so sat back down. I scooted backwards until I finally came up against a wall and leaned there, panting, feeling sick again. Could my brain be bleeding, I wondered wildly, fighting a sense of alarm, knowing what that could mean.

I rested for a bit, trying to remember what had happened. I kept losing focus due to the pain but eventually recalled Clancy's face in front of mine, her arm raised, and figured she had hit me hard enough to jostle my brain and knock me out. How could you be so naïve, I asked myself. Abbie and Andrea had warned me about Clancy but I had wrongly assumed she would eventually calm down and leave me alone. What was she hoping to accomplish, I wondered as I sat there. Keep me here, away from Jonah, until he took her back? Or do something more dire? You need to get out of here before she comes back, my inner voice screamed at me. I nodded to myself, this slight movement causing my head to feel as if it were going to explode. Trying to ignore this, I placed my hands behind my back, against the wall, and slowly edged upward to a standing position. The room spun and bile rose in my throat. I breathed deeply, trying to calm my stomach, my pounding head, as red lights shot across my vision. Losing the fight, I leaned over and threw up, which made my head hurt worse. I lost my balance and toppled to the ground.

I found myself on the floor again when I woke, cursing when I realized I had passed out. "Stay awake," I muttered, sitting up, gasping with the pain. Oh, God, what did she hit me with? How did she get me here? Where was I? I wanted to scream with rage, with fear, with frustration. My body began to tremble and my teeth chattered. In an effort to calm down, I began to breathe deeply, inhaling for four seconds, holding for four, exhaling for four, until I felt more in control. I scooted back until I found the wall again, then slowly gained my feet. When the room quit spinning around me, I began to edge my way along the wall, feeling with my hands as I went. I encountered no furniture, no obstacles, not even a window, only the rough surface of wooden planks. I thought back, trying to remember whose cabin didn't have windows as I shuffled along, moving slowly, stopping constantly to rest. What I would have given for some pain killers, I thought, shutting my eyes against that horrible ache in my head. Trying to distract myself, I began to run scenarios in my mind about how long it would take the others to realize I was missing, how long before they would begin to look for me. Would they even think of Clancy doing something to me or wonder if I had had an accident or just assume I had found the light and went through it? Oh, Abbie, I thought, for once see the fate of someone you care about and come look for me.

I stopped when my hand touched a smooth wooden pane, feeling along the width of it until I encountered a doorknob. Yes, I thought with glee as I turned it, but it wouldn't budge. Assuming it was locked, I fumbled with the knob, searching for the latch, but there was none. What the heck? I shook the door hard but it wouldn't budge. It was as if it had been nailed shut. Tears came to my eyes as I stood there fighting for control for a short while then took a deep breath and began moving along the wall again, searching for a window, some way to escape this place.

When I circled back around to the door, I put my hand on the knob and shook it again. When that didn't work, I kicked at it with my foot but each kick made my head pound harder so I quickly gave up. I slid down the door until I was sitting. I wanted to sleep so badly just to stop my head from hurting. But you might not wake up, I told myself. Would that be so bad, I wondered miserably, praying for a way to escape that horrible pain.

Leaning my head back against the door, I drew my knees up to my chest and focused on breathing, trying to ignore my head, my heaving stomach. It will pass, I kept telling myself, but time crept by and the pain only seemed to intensify. I thought I heard shouting nearby and placed my ear against the door but it was gone as quickly as it had come. I tried yelling as loudly as I could but that made the pain worse so I stopped, closed my eyes and tried to think of some way to manage my discomfiture.

I was dozing when someone opened the door behind me. I fell back, hitting my head on the ground. The pain was dazzling and I momentary lost consciousness. I came to, vaguely aware of someone dragging me inside by my feet then closing the door again, but had no strength to fight them or try to stop them. I rolled onto my side, heaving, but my stomach was empty, I had nothing to expunge. I finally rolled onto my back, putting my hands on each side of my head, moaning.

"Oh, shut up," a female voice said.

I opened my eyes. "Who's there?"

Someone kicked my feet, then Clancy said, "Who do you think?"

"What the ...?" I said, weakly, which infuriated me. I didn't want her to know how much she had hurt me. When I spoke again, I tried to make my voice stronger, more commanding. "Where am I? Where'd you take me?"

"No need to worry about that. You won't be here long. As soon as he gets here with the truck, you'll be gone. For good. It'll be like you never existed."

"He? Who?"

"You'll see," she said in a teasing tone.

"What are you doing, Clancy?"

"Getting rid of the competition," she snarled.

I struggled to sit up. "Competition? For what?"

But I knew the answer even before she said, "Jonah, who else?"

I wanted to laugh, I wanted to cry. I wanted to say, "All this, over a man?" but didn't dare. She turned on a battery-powered lantern, which she held above me. She looked disheveled, like she hadn't slept in days. Her eyes were crazed, furious.

"Look, you want Jonah, you can have him, I told you that already. I have no designs on him, I love—"

"I saw you," she screamed at me. "I saw you come out of your cabin this morning, and when I looked in the window, saw him getting dressed."

Well, shoot. I frantically tried to come up with a plausible reason for Jonah and me being together in the cabin but it hurt too much to think.

"You were with him last night, don't tell me you weren't." She leaned close. "Lucky for me, Jonah didn't have anybody watching you. Guess he figured he'd do that for himself."

If I had only waited for him, I'd be safe, I thought with despair as Clancy kicked at my side. Her aim was off and she barely grazed me with the tip of her boot. I scooted away from her, grateful for this. I didn't need a broken rib on top of a broken skull. "Listen, we were just talking, Clancy. He's helping me with something and we were talking about that."

"You're a lying slut and I don't want to hear it. Now shut your mouth or I'll shut it for you."

"What are you going to do? You can't keep me here forever."

She smirked at me. "Don't intend to. I have someone coming to take you away. You'll never be seen on this mountain again."

"And you think that will get Jonah to love you? Me disappearing?"

"He did before."

"Are you so sure that was love? Or just convenience?" I snarled.

She kicked me in the side and this time her aim was on-target. I gasped, rolling over, away from her, angry at myself for letting her get the best of me.

She jerked me upright by the hair. I screamed in pain as tears sprang to my eyes. She leaned close to my face, so close I could feel her spit as she spoke. "He's mine, he'll always be mine, and I'll make damn sure you don't ever see him again."

I grappled with her, struggling to get out of her grip. She finally released me, shoving me back down, then straightened up at the sound of a motor outside the door. "He's here," she said with glee as she went to the door and threw it open.

The light streaming through the door was so bright, I had to close my eyes against it so didn't actually see who came inside with her but heard the deep bass of a male's voice, one that sounded familiar but I couldn't place.

"How bad'd you hurt her?" he said.

"Don't worry, I made sure to keep her intact, other than a lump on her head and a few bruises."

"You able to get to the other one?"

"She's with her boyfriend. Guess you'll have to wait on her. But for now, this one's yours, take her."

"I reckon I will." Footsteps approached then he yanked me to my feet. I opened my eyes when the man's body blocked the light coming through the door, screaming when Constable Jackson's vile countenance loomed in front of me, grinning like a fiend from the fiery depths of hell.

Chapter Twelve

Late Winter 2055

She's Gone

My heart stopped beating and I screamed again, praying this was a nightmare and I would wake up. And if not, that my aching brain would explode and free me of this dire predicament. Jackson slapped me hard to shut me up. Tears sprang to my eyes and my body shook uncontrollably as I stared at him, my mind refusing to believe who was standing in front of me. "It's not you," I said, trying to convince myself. "It can't be."

Clancy laughed as if delighted by this.

Jackson gave me a wicked smile before grabbing both of my arms and tying my hands together. "It's me all right. I reckon you and me've got some unfinished business to see to, girl." I struggled weakly to get out of his grasp but he easily overpowered me. He glanced over his shoulder at Clancy. "I owe you a debt for this."

She shrugged. "Only payment I want is her off the mountain forever."

"You got it. You'll never see her again." As he marched me through the open door, I couldn't help but notice his pronounced limp. I did that, I thought to myself, glad I had inflicted this type of injury, but this feeling quickly turned to panic when I realized he would pay me back twofold. I lowered my head as he forced me into a rusty, dark-green pickup truck, shoving me in the back, where I fell onto the bench seat. I immediately lunged for the door but he slammed it shut before I could get to it. I turned the handle, trying to open it, but it had some sort of lock engaged and wouldn't budge, even when I tried the pull-up lock on top of the door panel. I scooted back and kicked at the window, making so much noise, I couldn't hear what was being said as he conferred with Clancy outside. Where had Jackson come from, I wondered wildly, and why would he do this for her? Two birds with one stone, my inner voice whispered. He gets me, gets his revenge, while she gets what she wants, me off the mountain and Jonah back in her arms. When he turned away from her to get in the truck, Clancy smiled at me while giving a small wave, as if seeing off an old friend. Jackson started the truck and drove off, ignoring my protests from behind him.

Realizing I was in serious danger, I sat back, considering my dilemma, ignoring the pain in my skull. Surely someone would hear the truck's motor and investigate. Jonah and his group didn't use vehicles on the mountain unless they were leaving or coming back from scavenging and none had been planned that I was aware of. But I knew I couldn't depend on that, I had to get out of this situation or no telling where I'd end up. I was certain of one thing, though. If I didn't, I wouldn't be alive at the end of it.

Ignoring my aching head, I worked at the rope around my wrists, trying to untie it, but it was too tight and wouldn't loosen. I frantically stared at the scenery as Jackson drove down a pitted road, one I had never traveled, well near the bottom of the mountain. Where are the sentries and who taught him to drive a truck. I thought crazily, watching him fight the gear shift. I looked at him in the rust-spotted rear-view mirror, wondering if he'd been on the mountain all along. Of course, he had. That was the only thing that made sense. He wouldn't have known about me otherwise nor been in cahoots with Clancy. If he'd been a stranger, the sentries would have spotted him for a raider.

Think, I told myself, do something. My head hurt so much, I wanted to lay down and go to sleep just to escape the pain but then I thought of something. "I'm gonna be sick," I groaned, lying on my side, hoping I was below his line of sight in the rear-view mirror. I began to rub my wrists against the rope, shredding skin, hoping to get them bloody enough to lubricate my hands so I could slide them out of the knots

He darted a glance at me in the rear-view mirror and when he didn't see me started to turn but hit a pothole, which drew his attention back to the pitted road. "Bet you didn't think you'd see the likes of me again," he said, his voice a growl.

"Something I prayed for every day," I snarled at him.

He chortled. "I prayed too, that one day I'd see you so I could get justice for what you did to me. Liked to died that day Jonah brought you to the greenhouse. It was pure luck you didn't see me before I could hide."

Hoping to distract him by talking, I said, "How long have you been on this mountain?"

"Ever since you pushed me into that light. One of the many things you're gonna pay for."

"So you've been here all this time while I've been here?"

"Never left. I know places to hide they've yet to find. Hid myself away until you left that day, then told the others I was going to be gone for a bit, scavenging."

I vaguely remembered Jonah telling me about some guy named Lem who had a limp. "You're Lem."

"Yep."

"You didn't find another light and go through it?"

"Only saw the light the once when you pushed me into it. Been looking for it, though, hoping to get back to you, see that you paid for what you did to me."

I shook my head with disdain. The center of that light must have been brown, not black. I should have seen that, but it had been dark and I was crazed with the need to get away from the bushwhackers. I should have made certain, nonetheless. I lay my head back with a groan. "How'd you hook up with Clancy?"

"Didn't think I'd ever get a chance to get at you, the way Jonah had you covered all the time. Overheard Clancy threatening to kill you once, so I sought her out, told her I'd do it for her if she could get to you alone."

"I heard you ask her where the other one was. Who'd you mean?"

"Abbie, a-course. I got plans for her too." He glanced over his shoulder at me and gave me an evil grin. "Gonna have fun with you, girl. By the time I'm ready to kill you, you'll be begging me to do it just to put you out of your misery."

"I won't make it easy for you," I said, in as threatening a tone as I could manage.

He laughed. "That's what I'm counting on."

I lay there for a few moments, fighting dizziness and nausea, telling myself to do something and do it now. When the dizziness passed, I sat up and without hesitating put my hands over his head and around his neck, using the rope to squeeze his throat. Jackson's eyes and mouth opened wide and he squawked in alarm as he took one large hand off the wheel to try to remove my garrote. But the rope was taut against his throat and I pulled as tight as I could, watching his face turn red in the rear-view mirror. He surprised me, suddenly jerking his elbow back toward my face, which I barely dodged. I sawed at the rope, surprised at the thought that I'd like to take his damn head off. When the truck started to swerve back and forth on the roadway, I felt a thrill of victory. Placing my feet against the back of the seat, I leaned my weight back, knowing I was probably crushing his trachea, hoping I was. When he took the other hand off the wheel to try to pull the rope away from his neck, the truck veered off the road and into a tree, throwing me forward and over the back of the front bench seat, my rope-bound hands still tangled around his throat. I ended up with my legs in the floorboard, my torso twisted in the seat but managed to turn myself around so I was face to face with him. His chest was against the steering wheel and when he leaned back against the seat, the rope loosened and he began gasping for breath, the redness starting to fade from his complexion. I knew it wouldn't be long before he would be able to overpower me. Raising my hands above his head, freeing my hold on him, I leaned back and kicked him in the chest as hard as I could. He was still weak from lack of oxygen and slow to respond, feebly reaching out to grab me. "Not gonna happen," I said, kicking him in the temple. His eyes rolled up as his head snapped back against the window. It tilted onto his shoulder and I could see blood smeared on the pane. I hoped I'd given him his own concussion.

I started to open the door then hesitated, turned back around and began to search his pockets, breathing a sigh of relief when I found a pocketknife. I sawed at the rope with the knife, my gaze constantly darting toward him, fearful he'd gain consciousness. It seemed to take forever but I finally freed my hands, then checked the glove box, where I discovered a small pistol hidden beneath a large manila envelope and took that. Jackson groaned, startling me. Panicked, I opened the door and half-fell out of the truck, feeling dizzy and weak, the knife and gun spilling out of my hands. I fell to my knees, searching for them among the dead leaves, constantly listening for signs of Jackson moving around in the truck. After I found both, I rose to my feet, tucking the knife in my pocket and the gun in the waistband of my jeans. Knowing I had to get away before he came to, I staggered off into the woods, searching for a place to hide until I felt strong enough to climb the mountain, to get back to safety. To get back to Jonah.

I hadn't gone far when dizziness overtook me. I hid behind a tree, leaning against it, my arms wrapped around the trunk to hold myself up, breathing deeply, black dots dancing in front of my eyes. I heard an infuriated roar behind me and knew it was Jackson and he'd catch me if I didn't get away. I began to run, tripped over a tree root and rolled down into a ravine. I had just enough time to try to cover my body with rotting leaves before unconsciousness took me.

I don't know how long I was out and the sun wasn't bright enough that day to gauge the time. I do remember someone speaking to me softly when I came to, saying, "Lizzie, wake up. You have to wake up now." I opened my eyes, gasping when I spied Joshua leaning over me.

"You're not real, you can't be," I moaned, blinking hard to clear my vision. I looked around frantically, ludicrously wondering if I had died and gone to heaven. But I was still in the ravine, leaves and pine needles and dirt all over me. I opened and closed my eyes several times but Josh remained by my side when I looked again. I scooted back away from this apparition, telling myself I was delusional.

He put his finger to his lips. "Shhh, Jackson's close by, he'll hear you. You need to get up, Lizzie, and follow me. I'll take you somewhere safe."

I clutched my head, telling myself I was having hallucinations until he spoke again. "We have to go now, Lizzie. Hurry." I looked up, watching as Josh walked away from me. When he turned and beckoned, I got up and followed, wildly wondering if he had become my guardian angel. We stayed in the ravine for awhile then Josh led me out of it, up a slight incline. At the top, he stopped, listening.

"Where are we going?" I asked, thinking even if this was a hallucination, it was all I had at the moment.

He leaned close, whispering. "Remember that treehouse we built for the Adams' children?"

I nodded. The Adams were a poor, struggling family with seven rowdy, energetic children. Josh and I had taken a liking to them and helped the family out as much as we could, bringing food and gifts for the children, occasionally taking them to church or on outings to give their beleaguered parents a much-needed break. With their help, Josh, Abbie, Sarie, Amanda May and I had built the Adams children a tree house among the stout limbs of a tall oak tree near their cabin, with the wooden rungs of a ladder nailed to the trunk for easy access. Oh, how they had loved that tree house.

"It's still there?"

He nodded. "I think it's been used in the past for hunting, so it's been maintained. It's safe. He won't see you if you hide there. Follow me but stay quiet."

I watched him walk away from me, wondering if he would fade away like a ghost, but I could see him clearly, so began to follow. I hesitated at a crashing sound nearby, but Josh beckoned me on. I don't know how I made it to that tree, but I was determined, my impetus being that I did not want to lose Josh, I wanted to keep him with me as long as I could.

When he stopped beneath the large oak, he gestured at the ladder rungs, still there, and motioned me up.

"Come with me, please," I said, placing my foot on the first rung.

"I'm right behind you. I know you're woozy, but you have to get up there, Lizzie, and quick. He's not far behind you now."

Loud cursing nearby startled me and I climbed that ladder as fast as I could, fighting dizziness the whole way. When I reached the little house, which now was nothing more than a rough plank floor, I collapsed on my back, closing my eyes against the sight of the leaves at the top of the tree slowing revolving around me. I don't know if I passed out or not, but when I opened my eyes again, I heard Jackson below me, crashing through the brush as he searched, calling me terrible names, threatening me with what he'd do to me when he found me. I lay still, not moving a muscle, my eyes sweeping the area around me, looking for Josh, but he wasn't there. Tears welled but I made myself stop, knowing Jackson might hear me if I made the slightest sound. He was close enough I could hear his heavy breathing. Was he aware of the tree house, I wondered? Did he know we'd built it? Oh, please, don't let him see the ladder, I prayed, please make him go away.

After what seemed an eternity, Jackson moved on, and when I was sure he wasn't close, I sat up. "Josh?" I whispered. Receiving no response, I lay back again, wondering if I'd really seen him or if my subconscious had just conjured up his image as a way to help me get to safety. I must have dozed off, because when I woke, it was beginning to get dark.

I have always been uncomfortable in the dark without any means to light my way, and at night in the forest, it seemed to me that the world would disappear into a black void filled with carnivorous nocturnal animals in search of prey. Although I knew most of the animals were gone now, it didn't help my state of mind as night settled around me, even though a full moon shone above, coating the Earth below in a mellow yellow light. The temperature dropped and I curled up, shivering, wishing I had a heavier jacket to cover me than the one I wore. I debated descending the tree and trying to find my way home—I knew I could from here—but fear kept me in that tree, not only of prowling animals but of Jackson and his cohort Clancy. I drifted off again, and when I woke, Josh was beside me, watching me. "I thought you'd gone," I said, in a low, wondering voice as I smiled with pleasure.

"I'll stay until they find you, until I know you're safe."

"Stay forever, Josh."

He gave me the saddest smile I'd ever seen on his face. "Oh, Lizzie, love, you know I can't."

I began to cry bitter tears. He made comforting sounds but never touched me, and I was fearful of reaching out to him, afraid I'd touch nothing but air or that he would dissipate in front of me like mist and disappear once more. After I got myself under control, I struggled to sit up so that I could face him.

We stared at one another for a long time. "You're so beautiful," I finally said.

His smile was tender and filled with love. "Oh, darlin, you're the most beautiful thing I've ever seen." Something he had said to me many times.

I froze at a rustling sound nearby, listening. After a bit, it went away. When all was quiet again, Josh said, "Lizzie, please tell me you forgive me for staying, for not coming after you. Please tell me you understand why I did what I did."

I wiped at my eyes. "You're the most honorable man I know, Josh. I do understand but that doesn't mean I like it or want to accept it."

"You have no choice, darlin. It's done, it can't be undone."

"Not even if I go back?"

"Not even then. You know that." He looked off into the forest. "You know what that will do if you and I ..."

"I know but I don't know what to do," I said, miserably. "If I go back just to be near you, I don't think I can stand seeing you and Sarie continue on as a family. I can't do that, Josh, it would be too painful."

He shook his head. "God help me, Lizzie, I wish I had found another way but I did what I thought was right without thinking of the consequences or what it would bring about."

"Were you happy, Josh? Did you have a happy life?"

He smiled. "Maybe not as happy as it would have been with you, Lizzie, but happy enough. And I always had that time with you to think back on, to remember."

"I love you so much. It's been so hard letting you go."

"I know, love ..." He looked off. "Someone's coming," he said and disappeared.

"No," I said, loudly, reaching out for him, not caring if anyone heard me.

"Lizzie?" I heard Abbie shout.

"Lizzie, where are you?" Jonah yelled.

For a fraction of a second, I debated not answering, staying in that tree until I died, from the concussion, starvation, dehydration, I didn't care. But then I decided I couldn't give up my life simply because Josh was no longer with me. I wiped my eyes, swallowed hard, and said in a hoarse voice, "Here, I'm here." I cleared my throat and called out as loudly as I could, "Here, Abbie, at the tree house."

Their voices mingled as they made their way toward me. At the base of the tree, Jonah called, "Where are you?"

"Up here." I was so weak I didn't know if I could climb down by myself. I hadn't eaten since the night before, nor had hydration of any kind.

"Stay there, I'll come up," he said.

"Me too," Abbie called out. I listened to their muffled voices as she showed him where the ladder rungs were then both were beside me, speaking over one another, asking if I was all right, asking what happened, asking if they could do anything.

When they wound down, I said, "I think I have a concussion. I don't know if I can get down by myself. I'm still dizzy."

"Concussion?" Abbie touched my face. "What happened? Did you fall, did you get lost?"

"No, Clancy hit me over the head with something, I don't know what, then took me to this cabin and—"

"Wait, what?" Jonah said, his voice pressured, as he helped me sit up.

I leaned back against his chest as I quickly told them what happened. I could feel him growing rigid beneath me, sensed his anger, and was glad for it. I wanted Clancy and Jackson to suffer for what they'd done to me.

When I finished, Jonah handed me a water bottle without saying a word. I drank greedily until he put his hand over mine. "Go slow. You'll get sick if you drink it too fast."

He stared at me as I drank, and when I put the bottle down, said, "You're sure Lem's this Constable Jackson you knew from before?"

"Definitely sure. I'm the reason he's here. I caused him to stumble into the light and shattered his knee trying to get away from him. He wants revenge for that."

Jonah shook his head. "I never suspected he was anything but who he said he was."

I looked around, starting to feel fearful. "He could be anywhere, he could be listening to us now," I said, my voice panicked.

"We didn't see anybody," Abbie said. "We got people all over the mountain lookin for you. Surely he won't hang around."

"Abbie," I said.

She nodded. "I know." She looked at Jonah. "He's dangerous, Jonah. He's mean and cruel and won't just let this go."

"He'll have to face me first." Jonah used his walkie-talkie to alert the others about what had happened. After instructing them to begin a search for Clancy and Jackson, he took my hand. "Let's get you home."

"I can climb down if you can give me something to eat. I haven't had anything since last night."

Abbie opened her backpack and pulled out what Jonah called an energy bar. He cautioned me to eat slowly and it was all I could do not to cram it all into my mouth, I was so hungry. After I devoured that, I handed Abbie the gun I had. "You might need this." I took a deep, calming breath. "Okay, I'm ready. Let's go."

Jonah helped me to my feet, then guided me toward the end of the platform. "I'll go first, then you follow. Abbie can bring up the rear. Let me know when you're ready."

"I'm fine. My head isn't hurting like it was. I think the dizziness is more from dehydration and lack of food at this point."

Jonah descended the ladder first then waited at the bottom of the tree, watching as I came down. When I joined him, he put his arm around my waist and we both waited for Abbie. Once she was on the ground, she put her arm around my waist from the other side. "Let's go home, Lizzie," she said.

I balked.

"What's wrong?" Jonah said.

"What if he's here, waiting?" My voice rose, became almost hysterical. "What if he finds us?"

"He won't," Jonah said. "And if he does, I won't let anything happen to you, I promise you that. You're safe with me."

"With us," Abbie said, a fierce look in her eyes.

We hadn't gone far before we were joined by several of Jonah's soldiers who fell into step alongside us, offering their protection.

As we made our way home, Abbie asked Jonah, "How did y'all come to accept Jackson?"

"I've been wondering the same thing," I said. "Abbie and I are still looked at by some with suspicion, but it seems like he was part of your group. How'd that come to be?"

Jonah shrugged. "One of the sentries found him hobbling around, dazed and confused. Could barely walk because of a busted knee." Abbie and I exchanged a look at that, which Jonah didn't miss. He raised his eyebrows before continuing. "We thought he was a raider at first but he claimed he wasn't. He kept asking who we were, where he was and what had happened to the mountain. We figured he had amnesia and would eventually remember but he claimed he never did. We told him he could stay until his leg healed but somehow he ended up just blending in, I guess, and never left."

Jonah disappeared once I was home, in bed, being fussed over by Abbie and Andrea. I wanted to tell him in all probability Clancy and Jackson wouldn't be on the mountain or would be well-hidden if they were but knew it wouldn't make a difference. Jonah's body seemed to vibrate with anger and his facial expression never wavered from furious and determined, even when he looked at me. After he had gone, when Abbie was bandaging my bloody wrists while Andrea fixed a cup of tea, I whispered, "I saw Josh, Abbie. He led me to safety."

She stopped what she was doing, staring at me. "Was he real or do you reckon you only imagined him, Lizzie?"

I shrugged. "You tell me, you're the one who sees haints, as you call them."

"It's purely strange to me but I ain't seen any since we came here. Ain't had any visions about the future either. Why is that, do you reckon?"

I shook my head. "Maybe the light altered your mind in some way."

"Mayhaps. I'd love to see Sarie and talk to her for a bit but that ain't happened." She reached out, tucked a strand of hair behind my ear. "Maybe one day it'll come back." She picked up a flashlight and shone a beam into each eye then put it down. "Not dilated, that's a good sign, right?"

I nodded.

She sat back, studying me. "What'd Josh say?"

"It doesn't matter. He was just an illusion, he couldn't have been real. Probably a way my subconscious was trying to motivate me to get to safety." I took her hand. "I think I decided a long time ago I'm not going back to Josh, but this only helped make it more solid, I guess. I wouldn't do anything to jeopardize Jonah's, Andrea's, Joseph's and Zach's existence."

She breathed deeply and I could see the relief on her face.

"You really love him, don't you?"

She smiled at me. "Never knew such a feeling existed till I met Zach. I reckon we're meant to be together." She cocked her head at me. "You said once as how he was my you didn't know how many times great-nephew. Do you think ... does that count now?"

I smiled, squeezing her hand. "No, it doesn't. That bloodline's been filtered more than enough."

She nodded. "I never thanked you for pushing me into that light, but I will now. I reckon I've found my place in life, where

I'm meant to be, who I'm meant to be with, what I'm meant to do."

I leaned forward, kissed her cheek. "I'm happy for you, Abbie."

She studied me for a moment. "What do you think you're gonna do? Go back to 1969, stay here ...?

I shook my head. "Maybe stay here. I don't know yet."

She frowned at me.

"What?"

"You got a man here who looks to be in love with you, Lizzie, just as much as Josh was. Why, you should have seen how worried he was when you disappeared. Andrea tried tellin him you might have found your light and gone through, but he refused to believe that, he kept insisting somethin had happened to you and we had to find you. And I'm glad he did."

"Oh, me too." I looked toward the door. "What do you think he'll do?"

She followed my gaze. "You mean if he finds them?"

"Yes."

"I don't know but I hope he kills em."

At my look, she went on. "I don't know what their rules are here for such a situation. Make them leave, at best, I'd say. If it was up to me, I'd do something harsher, make sure they couldn't hurt you again."

"Jackson wants you too, Abbie. I'm scared for you."

She shrugged. "Hope he finds me. I'll deal with him, make sure he can't hurt either one of us ever again."

"You're such a bad-ass," I teased.

"They tried to hurt my best friend. I won't forget that, won't forgive it neither. Even though we're not blood, you're my sister, Lizzie. You're family and I mean to see you safe."

"Me too you," I whispered.

I passed a restless night, being woken every couple of hours by either Abbie or Andrea, who would ask me who I was, where I was, what day it was. "Don't ask me who the president is," I said to Andrea just before dawn, "'cause I have no idea."

"Neither do I," she said.

By morning, my head didn't hurt as dreadfully as it had the day before. I lay in bed for a time, thinking about Josh, wondering if he had been a hallucination or not. I suspected he probably had been but didn't want to believe that. In any event, I looked upward and whispered, "Thank you, Josh," just in case.

When I heard voices downstairs, I got up and took a hot shower. I found that moving about slowly and with care managed the pain well enough to function so made my way down the stairs, holding on to the railing, stepping gingerly. At the bottom, I met up with Jonah, who appeared to be headed upstairs. He still wore the clothes he had on the day before and his hair was disheveled, his eyes bloodshot. Dark-blond whiskers covered his cheeks and upper lip, giving him a rakish look. My pulse quickened as I stared at him, thinking how awfully strong and powerful and gorgeous he looked.

His smile was a forced one, more grimace than actual smile, one that disappeared quickly. "I was just coming to see if you wanted breakfast."

I nodded. My head throbbed, and I put my hands on either side of my skull, as if to hold it steady. Seeing his look of concern, I dropped them, giving him back my own fake smile. "Don't have much of an appetite but I think a cup of coffee will do me good."

His gaze raked over me. "How are you feeling?"

"My head still hurts but not like it was. Vision's a little blurry and my balance is iffy."

"That sounds bad."

"Could be worse. I'd say I probably have a grade 3 concussion."

He frowned. "Is it serious?"

"It can be, but I don't think there's any internal bleeding. My brain just got jostled around is all. I'll be fine in a few days."

He took my arm and with great care began to lead me toward the kitchen.

"I'm fine, Jonah," I said, trying to reclaim my arm. "I think I can walk to the kitchen by myself."

"And risk falling, maybe making your injury worse than it is if you hit your head," he growled. "Quit being so stubborn and let me help you."

I didn't reply to this, merely went along with him, wondering at his bad mood, pretty sure it had something to do with Clancy and Jackson.

Abbie, Zachary and Andrea were at the table, conversing in low voices. When they saw me, they stopped talking, each greeting me with fake enthusiasm. I smiled at them before bending down to kiss Joseph and Pearl, each in identical highchairs, oatmeal smeared all over their faces.

"Are you feeling better, Lizzie?" Abbie asked with a concerned look which told me I apparently didn't look much better. "Here, sit down. I'll get you some coffee or make tea if you'd rather have that."

"Coffee's fine, thanks," I said as Jonah pulled out a chair and helped lower me into it.

"Thank you, Jonah." I glanced around at the others while I settled, noting the way they acted, as if they were hiding something. I sighed. "Okay, what's wrong?"

All looked at Jonah.

I started to shake my head with frustration but the slightest movement caused too much pain so I stopped almost immediately, wincing. "Just tell me, okay? I can see something's going on. What is it?"

"They're gone," Abbie said, placing a steaming cup of coffee in front of me.

I didn't need to ask who she meant. "Well, I'm not surprised by that." I poured milk into the cup and added sugar, deliberately not looking at them as I stirred.

"We don't know where they are," Jonah said, sounding flustered. "I've been all over this mountain, there's no sign of either one of them."

I wanted to laugh with derision. "As for Jackson, he told me he'd been hiding since he first saw me until he found a chance to grab Abbie and me. He's probably still on the mountain somewhere."

"We'll find him," Jonah said. "Everyone's on alert."

"No one saw him before when he was hiding out, Jonah."

He shook his head. "I should have figured something wasn't right when he was gone so long. I thought maybe he'd joined another community or gotten hurt or possibly killed somewhere. Never occurred to me he was right here." He looked at me, a determined expression on his face. "He won't get away with it. Neither will Clancy. If they're here, we'll find them."

"After what Clancy did, do you think she'd just hang around, waiting for you all to confront her about it?" I said.

He rubbed his hand over his face, his beard making a rasping sound. "No, but as of now, there's no telling where they are or what they might do."

"Hopefully go somewhere else." I eyed a piece of sour dough toast, wondering if I could keep that down. When no one said anything, I looked up. "What?"

"It's just, you ain't acting too concerned," Abbie said. "They could come back, try to hurt you again, Lizzie."

Oh, if only she knew how hard I was shaking inside, I thought. But I was determined not to give into the hysterics simmering inside me like bubbles in a carbonated drink, dangerously ready to overflow. "Us, Abbie. He wants you too." I watched as Zachary reached out and grabbed Abbie's hand in his. I picked up the piece of toast, but my hand was shaking so badly, I put it back down and hid my clenched fists beneath the table. "As for Jackson, you know he won't give up. Not that easily. But surely Clancy's not so stupid that she'll try it again." None of them seemed convinced by that. "Look, she went after me because of Jonah, which, if you ask me, is just plain idiotic. Surely she'll realize that."

"She won't give up," Andrea said. "She'll be back."

"And get caught if she does."

"Lizzie, I warned you about her before. She's nuts when it comes to Jonah, she always has been. You're not the first woman she's felt threatened by."

"Has she done this before, kidnapped and hurt someone?"

"Well, no, but she's been verbally abusive enough and acted crazy enough they got the message and backed off before things went any further."

"What are you saying? That I instigated this, that I caused this to happen?"

"No, that's not what she's saying," Jonah hastily put in. He turned to Andrea. "This is all my fault, don't think anything else."

"Were you aware she was like this?" I asked, wondering how he could not have been.

He shook his head. "I've known she's been unstable for a long time but chose to ignore it for the most part. It just seemed easier that way, not having to deal with her craziness on top of all I deal with here." He looked away and I was surprised to see his face reddening. "I used her and I shouldn't have. That was wrong. It wasn't until you … until I realized I had feelings for you that I knew I had to get her out of my life for good. I botched it up when I told her I didn't want to see her anymore. I should have been more considerate, more caring with my words."

"Or not," I said.

"What does that mean?"

"She's nuts, Jonah. I don't think you could have said anything that would have made a difference with her. The way she sees it, I took you away from her, and if she takes me out of the equation, you'll go back to her."

"I reckon Lizzie's right," Abbie said. "Women like Clancy don't seem to understand there's more to life than having a man." She put her hand over mine. "I'm worried for you, Lizzie."

"I'll be fine, Abbie." Although I said it with conviction, I didn't mean it. It concerned me that Clancy had found at least one cohort to help her, my very own nemesis from almost 200 years in the past, a man who wanted to kill me. I still couldn't wrap my mind around that. Goosebumps broke out along my arms. "I pray Jackson doesn't come back. I got the better of him and you know how he is, Abbie. He won't be thinking too kindly toward me because of that. He'll be more determined than ever to get at me."

"He'll have a hard time of it," Zachary said. "We've alerted everyone on the mountain to be on the lookout for him and Clancy, and if he has any sense, he'll realize that and move on. But you need to stay with someone at all times, Lizzie, just to be safe." He squeezed Abbie's hand. "You too, Abbie. Don't go gallivanting around by yourself, always make sure you're with someone."

Abbie nodded, her expression solemn.

"I'll try," I said, "but if anyone gets sick or injured and needs my help, I'll have to go, whether someone's with me or not."

"Someone will be with you at all times," Jonah said with finality. He looked at me, dropping the stern mask he usually wore on his face, letting me see how concerned he was. "I'll make sure of it."

"This is crazy. So now aside from having to look out for and fear raiders on the mountain, we have to contend with a crazy woman and demented man seeking revenge." I looked around at the others but no one responded. I shoved away from the table. All this was making me sick. "I think I'll go lie down."

"Alert someone if you want to go outside," Jonah called after me.

I nodded as I walked away.

Chapter Thirteen

Late Winter – Spring 2055

Ring of Fire

Although Jonah and his soldiers searched the mountain countless times, there were no signs of Jackson or Clancy. When Meredith paid us a visit one afternoon to visit her niece, she told us her sentries had seen a dark-headed man with a serious limp passing through the outskirts of Morganton. Although the others seemed relieved at this bit of news, I wasn't. I didn't think Jackson would just give in, not if he was still the cruel, determined man he'd been back in the 1800s, and nothing in the way he had acted toward me convinced me otherwise.

Jonah kept his word. I didn't go anywhere without someone following me. Most times it was Abbie, always armed, with Zachary by her side. The more I talked to Zach, the more I understood why Abbie had developed feelings for him. He was sweet and gentle but with a realistic, logical bend that told me why Jonah considered his brother's opinions above all others. When Jonah wasn't occupied with other duties on the mountain and offered to accompany me, I would make excuses not to be alone with him. Although I tried to keep a distance from him, it grew more difficult each time I saw him.

Winter bid its final goodbye by gracing us with a foot of snow on the mountain, but the very next day, spring heralded its arrival with sunny skies and warm weather which quickly melted winter's last gift. The deciduous trees began to bud, wildflowers popped their heads up inquisitively, and the mountain quickly dropped its dull winter colors in favor of the bright, colorful ones of spring.

One sunny afternoon, Jonah showed up unexpectedly while Abbie and I were making our clinical rounds on the mountain, being shadowed by two of Jonah's soldiers. We had just left Hazel's house, dropping off a salve for her rheumatism, when Jonah stepped onto the path in front of us. I startled, stepping back with a small squeak and grabbing Abbie's hand to pull her away.

Abbie, who didn't seemed phased at all by his sudden appearance, simply smiled and said, "Hey, Jonah."

"Abbie, Lizzie." He grinned at me as he held up a backpack. "I brought lunch."

Abbie smiled at someone beyond him. I looked around Jonah and spied Zachary walking toward us.

Abbie glanced at me then back to Jonah. "Well, if'n y'all don't mind and if Lizzie can spare me for a bit, I figure I'll eat with Zach."

I watched the way they interacted, my suspicions rising with each word and look that this was a setup. "Actually, I'm fine to go on by myself, Abbie." I smiled at Jonah. "Thanks, but I'm not really hungry right now. I'll get something when I get back."

His smile vanished as he said in a curt tone, "You're not going off by yourself."

I tilted my head at the two soldiers behind me. "I'm not alone."

Jonah must have given some sort of signal I didn't see because the two men glanced at me and with a nod at Jonah turned around and walked off.

"Where are they going?" I asked.

"Lunch break," Jonah said.

"I'll see you later, Lizzie," Abbie said without even looking at me as she took Zachary's hand, stepped into the trees and vanished.

I folded my arms. "This seems planned."

Jonah smiled at me. "Nope, an impromptu meeting is all this is."

"With lunch in hand? I don't think so."

"Okay, you caught me. I haven't been able to spend time with you since Clancy's and Jackson's stunt and thought I'd help you on your rounds this afternoon."

"You know that's probably not a good idea, Jonah. Not if Clancy's still on the mountain and sees us."

"Maybe that will draw her out." He glanced around as if expecting Clancy to step out of the forest at any moment.

"So I'm bait?" My voice rose with anxiety.

"No, Lizzie, you're not." He stepped closer and lowered his voice. "I would never do that to you. I just want to be with you, that's all. Just to talk, nothing else. Make sure you're getting through this all right, see where your mind's at."

"In regards to going back?"

"That's up to you. How many times do I have to tell you that? I was talking about any trauma you may be feeling over Clancy's and Jackson's idiotic plot to remove you from the mountain." He frowned as if unhappy with his words. "Look, let's just have some lunch, relax for a few minutes, then I'll accompany you as you check on your other patients." At my expression, he held up his hands. "I'm not asking anything in return, just an afternoon with you. You don't even have to talk to me if you don't want to." He let the mask drop from his face and I had to look away before I succumbed to the same emotions his expression revealed.

"Lunch, then rounds," I said, starting down the path.

"I know the perfect place." He caught my hand in his and steered me off the path and into the forest.

I tried to tug my hand back but he wouldn't let go, so I quickly gave up. "Where are we going?"

He grinned at me. "My favorite place on the mountain. It's not far. I think you'll like it."

He led me to an outcropping of rocks overlooking the mountain vista. I sat on a flat-stoned one, near the cliff's edge, struck by the beauty of the mountains marching across the earth, one after the other, as if no flat terra firma existed. "Was it this colorful last spring?" I asked, noticing the deep fuscia of blooming redbuds and the crisp white flowers of dogwoods amidst varying shades of green foliage. Nearby were a clump of daylilies, their yellow blooms waving in the air, nicely complementing a large patch of wild purple crocus.

Jonah shook his head. "It's coming back," he said, his eyes filled with wonder, looking out over the mountains. He turned and smiled at me.

Glancing up at Jonah, I could not help answering his grin with my own. "It's beautiful. And look, no beigy-looking sky today. You're right, Jonah, it is clearing." I tilted my head back and stared at the sky, a brilliant shade of blue, no dirty air to mar its beauty, with fluffy white clouds riding the air currents. The sun was warm and comforting, and a light breeze caressed my face, twining through my hair. I breathed deeply, noting the air today didn't have that peculiar ashy smell it usually bore. A perfect day, I thought to myself, smiling with delight.

He dropped the backpack then sat beside me, staring out at the scenery. "I love it here," he said, his voice low. "Reminds me that there may still be a God up there looking over us, that there may still be hope."

"Yes," I said, in a quiet voice. "Hope. I pray for that."

"Me too."

We sat in silence for a long while, enjoying the view, then Jonah stirred and said, "Let's eat."

I watched as he unpacked peanut butter and jelly sandwiches, carrots, celery, and small apple tarts Abbie had made from his backpack. When a twig snapped behind me, I jerked around, my gaze roaming the forest. "Does Clancy know about this place?"

Jonah hesitated then looked behind us, waiting in silence, as still as a predator. When nothing revealed itself, no further noise was made, he turned back to me. "I don't know. I never brought her here. She could have found it on her own, I guess."

"Why not?"

He gave me a curious look.

"Why didn't you bring her here?"

"Never wanted to. You're the first." He glanced away, acting embarrassed. "I always felt this was my place, I didn't want to share it with anyone." When he looked at me, the longing in his eyes was so intense, I felt drawn to him. "Not until you."

"Jonah," I began.

"I know, we're only here to eat lunch. Here."

I took the sandwich he held out to me, along with a lightweight jar, made out of some material I didn't recognize, filled with water. I settled back with the sandwich, eyeing the jar. "Tell me about this time, my future. I know about the internet, cell phones, ebooks and all that. Microwaves were just becoming popular when I left but they're so much more advanced than they were. I've been meaning to ask about cars since you all don't have any modern ones. How have they advanced?"

"Well, for one, they can drive themselves now."

"What?"

He grinned at my reaction. "When they still functioned, before the asteroid strike, they had backup cameras so you could see what was behind you, the car's computer could talk to the driver, steer them away from other cars when they were too close, even brake and parallel park for them. Or just drive the car itself. Best of all, they all had GPS."

"GPS?"

"It's a navigational system using signals from orbiting satellites. People used it for directions from one place to another. All you'd have to do was tell it where you wanted to go and it'd get you there." He shrugged. "We can't use it now, of course, with all the air interference from the asteroid fallout. But one day, maybe."

"Good Lord," I said, in awe. "Is there a reason you all don't use the newer cars on the mountain? I've noticed your cars and trucks are all from my time and a little beyond."

"Because those aren't electronic like the newer ones are, powered by computers and fueled by batteries."

"Meaning no gas."

"Right."

"So what, you'd just plug them in and charge them up?"

"Basically, yes." He picked up his water and drank, then turned to me with a mysterious grin. "And we had drones," he said as if it were something magical.

"Drones?"

"Tiny flying aircraft controlled remotely. They were used to deliver packages, take pictures from above, track criminals, find lost people or animals, even to drop bombs."

I tried to picture it but couldn't imagine it. "Drop bombs where?"

"Middle East mostly."

"That never got resolved?"

"No." He shrugged. "It may be by now, but not the last I heard."

I picked up a bag of carrots and began to munch on one, my mind turning to my own interests. "How about medicine? How has it advanced?"

"We had just gotten to the point where most organs were replaceable with mechanical ones. Most diagnoses were made with blood tests and terminal diseases were treated with stem cells. Even the paralyzed could walk after stem cell treatment. Of course, it was so expensive that not many were able to benefit but eventually it would have been affordable. Or so the medical field claimed."

"Dang." I shook my head. "Maybe this time isn't so bad after all." I gestured around us. "I mean, after this works its way out of the atmosphere or wherever it will go."

"It really wasn't, not before. But since, it's been pretty brutal." He caught my look. "Of course, not as brutal as where … when you came from but still …"

"Oh, Jonah, you don't know how much this time reminds me of how it was almost 200 years ago. It's a lot like it was then except, of course, you have generators and windmills and solar panels for power."

"And solar panels are iffy at best."

"But won't be one day."

"Right."

"What about space travel? Man first walked on the moon right before I left in 1969. Has anything happened since?"

"We have an international space station floating around up there. Astronauts would go up, spend time on it doing experiments, space walks and such. They were even beginning to allow visitors who weren't astronauts." He glanced upwards. "They have interplanetary stations on the moon and were building a community on Mars before the asteroid strike. I have no idea how that's faring now."

"Mars? The red planet? You're kidding." I thought about that for a bit. "Maybe there's hope for Earth after all."

"Had to do something. We've been killing the planet for a good while now. Pollution caused global warming, the polar caps were melting, a lot of animals were going extinct, the oceans were filled with plastic, the world was overpopulated with not enough food and water for everyone."

That sobered me, causing me to again berate myself for pushing Abbie and me into this time.

Jonah caught my expression. "It's not all so dire, Lizzie, and it's getting better. We'll have all that back one day, and more. Look, it's a beautiful day, let's finish our lunch. Here, have one of Abbie's apple tarts."

He handed me the tart and I bit into it, moaning with delight. "That's so good. I have to give it to Abbie, she's almost as good a cook as Maggie is ... was."

"Her sister?"

I nodded.

He reached out, touched the corner of my mouth with his finger. "You have a bit of apple," he said, putting his finger in his mouth.

Before I realized what I was doing, I leaned over and kissed him.

He immediately responded, pulling me to him, his mouth covering mine with urgency and need. I hesitated for a fraction of a second, if that, but could not resist the longing I felt for him and quickly gave myself over to my feelings as my body reacted to his, fire racing along my veins, every nerve ending relaying sensations of heat, pleasure, want, need, yearning. Such yearning, I wanted to scream with it, rake my nails down his back, bite him, wound him, *own* him. I lost myself in those sensations until a sharp pebble beneath me scraped against my back, refocusing my attention. I drew away, glancing around.

Jonah sighed. "You're right. Now's not a good time. Maybe later."

I smiled, thinking, yes, later, as I lay back on the rock, closing my eyes, feeling the warm sun beaming down on my upturned face. When Jonah lay down beside me, I reached out and took his hand in mine, glancing over at him. He had his eyes closed and I took that chance to stare at him, comparing the way I had felt with Josh to the way I felt with him. When he opened his eyes, I glanced away, but he had seen.

"You're thinking of him."

"No."

"Lizzie, one thing we don't do is lie to one another. Don't start now."

I turned back to him. "More like comparing," I admitted.

"Because we look so much alike."

"No, not that." I moved to pull away from him but he wouldn't let my hand go. "About how I feel when I'm with you and how I felt with him. It's different."

"We're two different people, I would hope so."

How could I tell him what I felt for him was more primitive than what I felt for Josh, more physical, more demanding? With Josh came comfort, security, safety and warm contentment. With Jonah came uncertainty, conflict, danger and heat, such heat I thought I'd melt. I couldn't tell him any of these things so instead said, "I don't think about him when I look at you anymore, Jonah. I see you, I feel you."

He leaned forward, kissed me lightly. "That's a start, I guess."

I pulled back. "We really shouldn't be doing this."

He put his finger over my mouth. "We should. You wanted to, didn't you?"

"And that's the problem."

"No, it's not. You only want it to be."

"Jonah."

"Admit it, you have feelings for me, Lizzie." He lowered his voice to a whisper. "Just this once, tell me."

I cupped his cheek in my palm. "I do, Jonah, I can't deny it, but what if I decide to go back?" At his look, I said, "I'm not talking about going back to the 1800s. I think I decided I wouldn't do that a long time ago, I just wasn't ready to admit it to myself."

He sat up, took my hand. "Don't decide that for my sake."

"How can I not? Or Zachary's or Andrea's or baby Joseph's?" I turned his hand over, running my finger lightly over the lifeline of his palm. "I haven't decided about going back to the 20th century."

He grinned. "Maybe I'll go with you." He hesitated. "If things are better here."

I stared at him, contemplating his words. "Did I tell you what Pokni told me? What Amanda May said her great-grandmother, who was a time traveler from the future, told her?"

He looked away, considering. "I remember you said something to Abbie about a war within America."

"Yes, that's what Amanda May's great-grandmother told her, that another country would invade America and there would be a war. She was a guerrilla fighter who stumbled into a light and went back so she didn't know the outcome."

"Did she say when the war started?"

"All Amanda May told me was she came from over 200 years in the future. Her great-grandmother was on Brown Mountain in the 1800s, long enough to get married and have children, grandchildren and great-grandchildren. How many years would that be?"

He shook his head. "I don't know. Maybe, what, 60 years?"

"So it could be anytime. It could be now. What if that's what's coming? You said America is in a weakened state."

He put his thumb on my lips, tracing the outline. "If war is coming, Lizzie, there's nothing we can do to stop it. Besides, we're pretty isolated here. Maybe it won't come to us."

"Maybe, but you can start getting ready for it, just in case it happens. Right?"

He considered this. "I don't see that we can do much more than we are now except try to find more arms, store more food, make ourselves more self-sufficient." He turned his gaze on me. "You can help, Lizzie," he said, his voice low. "You can be part of it."

I looked up into his eyes, which were as beautiful as Josh's had been but no longer reminded me of him. "I think I'm beginning to love you."

"I love you too." He put my hand to his lips, kissed my fingers. "I don't say that lightly. Other than you, the only other two women I've ever told I loved are my sister and my mom." He leaned forward and kissed me tenderly, almost chastely, then drew back, his gaze locked with mine. "I'm on fire for you, Lizzie," he whispered. "Every cell, every nerve ending, every inch of me. I can't stand to look at you sometimes, I burn so."

We both jumped at a crashing sound headed right toward us. And when a huge elk stepped out of the forest and onto the outcropping of rocks, he was as startled at seeing us as we were him. Jonah and I stared in awe at the buck while he considered us for a moment, then with a snort and shake of his head, turned around and went back into the woods.

"What a blessing," Jonah said.

"He was so beautiful," I answered, in awe. I smiled at Jonah. "I think he might have been an omen."

He smiled at that. "The world's returning to us, at last." He got to his feet, held out his hand and helped me stand. "And it's more beautiful with you in it, Lizzie."

I stepped toward him, watching in shock as a red blossom appeared on his chest and he crumpled to the ground at my feet. "Jonah," I screamed, crouching beside him.

Someone grabbed me and pushed me away from him, toward the cliff edge. I stumbled to my knees and just managed to stop myself from going over, staring down at that vast empty space below, ending in tall trees on the forest floor at least a hundred feet down. I scooted away from the edge, watching Clancy, who stood over Jonah, glaring at me with a crazed look in her eyes. She looked like she'd been living in the woods. Leaf bits and twigs clung to her dirt-stained clothes, and her hair, usually so beautifully straight and thick, was tangled and wild around her face. I cringed away when I saw she held a gun in her hand.

She smirked when she noticed that. "I warned you. If I can't have him, no one can," she said as if speaking about the weather.

I looked at Jonah, lying inert on the rock, blood pooling beneath his back. "What have you done?" I screamed.

She waved the gun at Jonah. "What does it look like? Apparently you weren't going to leave, get away from here, like I wanted you to, and I won't have him with the likes of you." She spared a glance at Jonah. "Or anyone else for that matter."

"So you just kill him?" I spat at her.

She shrugged. "I was actually aiming for you."

"You're a crazy psychopath, Clancy." I wiped at the tears running down my face.

"Crazy about him, maybe," she said matter-of-factly. She waved the gun at me. "Don't blame me. You wouldn't listen so this is all your fault. Now, get up."

"So you can kill me too?" I snarled. "You won't get away with it. The others will know it was you, they'll come after you hot and furious."

She smiled. "Not if I throw your bodies off that cliff behind you. You'll just disappear and they'll never know what happened to the two of you."

Just like Abbie's father did to her mother, I thought wildly, and he got away with it until he confessed to Sarie. I crouched, furtively glancing around me, trying to find something to use as a weapon. But there were no broken limbs or large pieces of rock at hand.

"Get up," Clancy shouted.

Why in the world did she want me standing, I wondered, deciding I wasn't going to make it easy for her. "You get over here and make me."

Her face grew red, I could practically see spittle flying out of her mouth as she yelled, "Do what I told you and get up."

"Don't hide behind that gun like a coward," I put emphasis on that last word. "Get over here and kill me yourself, not like some defenseless little girl," snarling this last.

When Jonah moved slightly, moaning, Clancy glanced away from me to him. I took that moment to hurl myself at her, knocking her to the ground. She screamed with rage as I landed on top of her, locking my hands around the hand holding the gun, trying to take it away from her. I don't know how long we fought over that gun. It seemed hours but was probably only seconds, maybe no more than a minute. Even though she was strong, much stronger than she looked, I came from Brown Mountain in the 1800s, where I performed physical chores in all kinds of weather, so she was unable to overpower me. She cursed at me as we struggled, managing to roll me over so I was on my back and she was over me. We were close to the cliff edge and my adrenaline level rose considerably when I realized we could both easily go over and fall to our deaths. Her gun arm hovered in the air over us as she tried to force it down so she could shoot. Realizing I couldn't keep her arm up forever, I drew back my right hand and shoved the base of my palm into her windpipe. She began to falter as she fought to breathe. I hit her again, between the neck and shoulder blade, hoping to cause her to lose control of that arm. She lurched to the side, and when she did, I pushed her off me. She landed right beside me, near the brink, so I turned on my side and kicked her as hard as I could and watched in horror as she rolled away from me and over the cliff edge. She never made a sound as she fell.

I ignored her, turning my attention to Jonah as I crawled to him, my eyes scanning his body as I drew near and put my hands on him. His carotid pulse was there, his heart still beating in his chest. I ripped his shirt open, breathing a sigh of relief when I realized the wound wasn't near the heart, the bullet having exited the upper level of his chest near his right shoulder. I put my head on his chest, listening to his breathing, fearing it had penetrated a lung.

I lightly slapped his face. "Jonah, can you hear me?"

He moaned again. Although he had lost blood, it didn't look like enough to cause him to lose consciousness. I palpated his head, checking for a wound, and found blood on the back of his scalp. He must have hit his head when he fell, I decided. I unsnapped the sheath holding his knife then used it to rip the bottom of his t-shirt into strips. They worked well as a bandage for the bullet wound, which I hoped would staunch the flow of blood, as well as one for the back of his head. Was Jackson nearby, I kept wondering, my gaze darting all around us, fighting the urge to take flight and get out of there. But I couldn't. I needed to get Jonah to safety, but how? Then I remembered the walkie-talkie he always carried.

He didn't have it clipped to his belt, like he normally would. I tucked the knife into my belt then looked around for his backpack, which lay where he had placed it after removing our lunch. Grateful it hadn't gone over the cliff, I crawled over to it and snatched it up. Usually in situations like this, a calm would come over me and I would be able to perform any activity with quick dexterity, but my fingers wouldn't cooperate. I fumbled with the zipper, talking to myself all the while, telling myself to calm down, it would be all right. I finally got it unzipped and began throwing out items, finally turning it upside down and shaking it. The walkie-talkie wasn't there.

I crawled back to Jonah and lightly slapped his face. "Where's the walkie-talkie, Jonah?" I said, becoming concerned he hadn't gained consciousness yet. "Where is it?" I screamed.

He opened his eyes. "What happened?"

"Clancy shot you and you hit your head when you fell. Did you bring the walkie-talkie?"

He turned his head, scanning the area around us. "Where is she?" He tried to sit up. "I've got to get you away from here, Lizzie."

I pushed him back down. "She's gone, don't worry about it. Just tell me where the walkie-talkie is. I can't get you down this mountain by myself."

"I don't know." He groaned as he tried to sit up again. "I don't remember. It has to be here, somewhere."

Okay, I told myself, check around, maybe it fell off his belt or the backpack. I crawled around that site, running my hands over the rough surface of the rocks, even though I could see it wasn't there. A movement in the brush nearby caught my attention. A cardinal sat on top of one of the bushes, watching me. I stared at it for a moment, thinking, no way, this couldn't be, as I crept closer to it, and there, at the base of the bush, hidden by greenery, was the walkie-talkie. "Thank you, Josh," I said. It seemed to me as if the bird nodded its head then took flight. I keyed in the signal on the walkie-talkie, sighing with relief when Zachary answered. The connection was weak and I could barely hear him on the other end so kept repeating we needed help and where we were. When we lost the connection entirely, I threw the walkie-talkie down in frustration, praying he had gotten enough information to come find us.

As we waited for Zachary to come, I helped Jonah sit up, leaning him back against a rock face as far away from the cliff's edge as I could get him. I kept looking around us, wild with panic, fearful Jackson would show up at any moment. I found the gun I had tucked in my backpack and removed the one Jonah wore in his shoulder holster. I handed his gun to him and kept mine in my hand but still didn't feel adequately protected. My gaze darting all around us, I told Jonah what had happened after I gave him a couple of sips of water.

His eyes widened as I relayed the conflict between Clancy and me. Afterward, he glanced at the edge of the cliff. "She fell? You're sure?"

"She didn't fall, I kicked her off," I said, tears coming to my eyes. "I killed her, Jonah."

"Hey," he said, pulling me close. "Hey, you were defending yourself, defending us. It's not your fault."

"Yes, it is." I turned away from him. "I don't know if I can live with this."

"Lizzie, what do you think she would have done if you hadn't kicked her away from you? She already told you she planned to send us both over the edge. You know what that means."

I nodded. I knew all right, but God help me, I didn't want this burden.

He looked around. "Was she alone? Do you know?"

I shook my head. "She didn't have anyone with her. She looked like she'd been living in the woods. I don't think she ever left."

He nodded.

I put my hand on his arm. "I need to go … to go see, to make sure."

His gaze drifted to the edge of the cliff. "You're sure you're up to it?"

"I have to."

"I'll go with you."

"No, you stay here. You're still bleeding, you don't need to make it worse."

I walked over to the edge, then knelt down and started to peek over the side but felt like I would lose my balance that close to the rim so lay on my stomach and inched closer until my head cleared the rock. The foliage below appeared undisturbed. I couldn't see any indication Clancy had gone into the trees at all. There were no broken limbs, no ripped pieces of her clothing clinging to branches. No indication anything of mass had fallen through the trees.

I turned my head, saying to Jonah over my shoulder, "I don't see a thing. It doesn't look like she fell at all."

"It's pretty far down plus it's so dense down there, you might not be able to. Lizzie, come back over here. It's making me nervous you being so close to the …" His eyes widened just as someone grabbed my hair.

I screamed in agony as my head was jerked back. I tried to push myself away from the edge, watching in horror as a hand with bloody, ripped fingernails came over the cliff's rim and grabbed the rock edge next to me, like a demon climbing out of hades. A face appeared just below mine, her eyes crazy, her black hair tangled and wild about her face. I could hear Jonah behind me, scrabbling to get to me as Clancy steadily and slowly pulled me over the edge while I struggled to get away from her. Jonah grabbed my legs from behind and I felt like I was being pulled in two as she twined her fingers through my hair, securing her hold on me, while she still held onto the rock with her other hand, slowly inching her way up the rock shelf and onto the surface, using me as leverage to hoist herself over. I fought her hold on me with one hand while holding onto the edge of the rock with the other, terrified she'd pull me off. Jonah had hold of my hips now, slowing inching his way over my body. When Clancy saw him, she screamed with rage, moving her hand away from my hair to the back of my neck, clutching me with all her strength and pulling. I slid forward, the side of my neck and upper chest scraping the rock surface. Jonah's hands were suddenly gone as he shifted his weight off me, temporarily leaving me at her mercy while he put his hands over hers, to try to loosen her hold on me. "Jonah," I screamed with desperation as the upper half of my torso went over the cliff. I was staring down now, at the trees so far below they looked like a miniature forest playset. Would I die before I hit, I wondered wildly, or would the trees spear me, tear me apart? My hand still clutching the edge of the rock began to slide away and I screamed again, trying to jerk away from her hold, then felt her release me suddenly as I began to fall.

Just as my knees went over the edge, Jonah grabbed me and hauled me back. My belly scraped against the rock, and I could feel blood seeping through the burning, broken skin, but I barely noticed as I rolled over onto my back once I cleared the edge, reaching for him. I clung to him, almost hysterical with relief, glancing wildly around for Clancy. "Where is she? Where'd she go?"

"I don't know," he answered, clutching me tightly against him. "She must have fallen after she lost her hold on you."

"Are you sure? She didn't before."

"I don't know, Lizzie." He drew back away from me. "Go over to those bushes while I look over and make sure."

"No," I screamed, grasping his arm. "She might grab you."

"I'll be fine," he said. But he didn't look fine. His face was pale, sweat beading his forehead, running in rivulets down his cheeks. His eyes looked weak and I feared he was about to pass out.

"We'll both go closer to the trees," I said, urging him with me. "We'll wait for Zachary and the others. They can look over for us, make sure she's gone."

We moved over to a large rock at the edge of the forest and sat, holding one another, our eyes never leaving that cliff edge, waiting for Clancy's face to suddenly appear over it as she made her way back to us.

When we heard movement nearby, we froze, our eyes shifting to the forest. "What if it's Jackson?" I whispered, snatching up my gun, hearing Jonah do the same. Just as I brought it up to aim, Zachary and Abbie stepped out of the forest. When they saw us, both rushed over, asking questions over one another about our wellbeing and what had happened.

"Stop asking so many questions and I'll tell you," I said, overriding their voices, making a shushing motion with my hands. "Clancy came back, she came up from below." I couldn't keep my gaze from going back to the rim of the cliff. "I need someone to check and make sure she isn't still down there. Please, she's tried to kill us twice."

Zachary and Abbie both looked at the edge of the cliff.

"She came up from below, you said?" Zachary asked, giving me a confused look.

Abbie put her hand on my arm. "What happened, Lizzie?" Her eyes traveled over my bleeding neck, my torn and tattered shirt spotted with blood.

I realized they weren't aware of what had occurred between Clancy and us. When I spoke, words tumbled over one another as I tried to convey my urgent need to make sure she had truly fallen. "She found us up here and shot Jonah then tried to kill me, and when I kicked her, she went over the edge. I thought she had fallen but she came back up and tried to pull me over. Hurry, Zach, go check, make sure she isn't down there, on her way back. She's crazy strong, she would have thrown me off if Jonah hadn't gotten her off me."

Zachary glanced around. "What about Jackson? Did you see any sign of him?"

I shook my head. "Surely if he was here and wanted to harm us, he would have done it before y'all came."

He rose to his feet and began to walk that way. "Wait! Abbie, go with him, hold onto him. She almost pulled me off the edge earlier."

Abbie nodded as she quickly joined Zachary. He lay down on his stomach, with Abbie beside him, holding onto the waistband of his pants. I didn't know if she'd be strong enough to hold him, so I joined them, kneeling on his other side, holding on to his belt. Zachary inched his head over and looked for a long time.

"What do you see? Is she down there?"

He shook his head. "I can see where she must have landed the first time. There's a ledge right beneath this one, jutting out far enough it could have stopped her fall. She's not there, though."

"Are you sure?" My voice was shrill. "She might be coming back, right now!"

"Lizzie," Abbie said, "why don't you go back with Jonah? We'll make sure she ain't nearby."

"I won't let go of Zachary, not while he's looking," I said stubbornly.

Zachary made a sound in his throat.

"What? Is she there? Do you see her?"

"I think I see where she went through the trees." He glanced over his shoulder at Abbie. "Grab my binoculars. They're in my backpack. I'll be able to see better."

As she rose to her feet and left us, I glanced back at Jonah, sitting against the rock, his eyes slitted. "Are you all right?"

He opened them fully but it didn't seem as if they were focused. "I'm good. Y'all be careful."

When Abbie returned with the binoculars, Zachary took them from her, then turned his attention to the forest floor. After several seconds, he said, "She's down there. I can see where she went through the trees." He scooted back until he was well away from the rim, then stood up. "I'll notify our sentries in that area to go have a look, make sure she hasn't gotten away.

"Away?" I asked, stunned. "That's at least a hundred foot drop, Zachary. Surely she wouldn't."

"No, she wouldn't, but after what you've been through, I think you need to know for sure, Lizzie."

He was right. I had to know.

While Zachary and Abbie saw to Jonah, debating with him whether he was well enough to walk on his own or if they should get additional help to carry him down the mountain, I gathered everything I had emptied from the backpack and repacked it. I took Jonah's gun and tucked it into the back of my pants, along with my own, vowing to myself I wouldn't go anywhere without one on my body now. I kept glancing at the cliff's edge, expecting to see Clancy come over that rocky rim like a devil from the bowels of hell. Finally, I rejoined the others, my eyes raking over Jonah, checking to see if his eyes were dilated, taking his pulse, counting his breaths. Only then did I give my okay for him to try to walk, warning him if he felt too weak at any point to let us know. We could always call for someone to bring a travois to take him down. But Jonah stubbornly refused that, saying he was fine, just a bit weak. I knew better. He had been bleeding since he'd been shot and had endured that scuffle with Clancy while trying to keep me from going over the cliff, which I knew had weakened him even further.

As we made our way down the mountain, me on Jonah's right, his arm around my shoulder, Zachary on the left, Abbie bringing up the rear, I kept glancing around us, fearful of attack from Jackson. My adrenaline level was elevated, my breathing rapid, close to hyperventilating. I kept telling myself to calm down but couldn't quite manage it.

When Zachary's walkie-talkie beeped, I startled, almost falling to my knees. "Sorry," I said to Jonah. We stopped so Zachary could answer and I listened as one of the sentries told him they had located Clancy's body beneath the cliff.

"Is she dead?" I asked. I had to hear it.

The sentry on the other end said, "She's dead all right. Doubt anyone could survive that fall."

"Good," I said, more to myself than the others.

"What do you want to do with the body?" the sentry said.

"Burn it," I said, before I could stop myself. When the others looked at me, I said, "Sorry, I didn't mean that."

"Bury it," Jonah said. "Unmarked grave. After what she did, she doesn't deserve an honorarium of any sort."

By this time, he was close to passing out. His pallor concerned me, so I suggested we get someone to come help us carry him the rest of the way.

"No," Jonah said, frowning at me. "We're close, I can make it. Let's pick up the pace a bit."

"Jonah, you're still losing blood and we need to get it stopped. I'm worried for you."

"I'm fine, Lizzie," he said, without looking at me. "Let's go. I want to go home."

I don't know how we managed to get Jonah to the house, but through sheer stubbornness on his part, we made it. Once there, I had Zachary and Abbie place him on the table, much as we had done with Zachary, then turn him on his side so I could check the entrance and exit wounds of the bullet, amazed that it didn't appear to have done any major damage. I was more concerned at the loss of blood than anything else and had Andrea make sugared water and give it to him.

"I'd give anything for an IV bag," I muttered as I washed the wounds, palpating around them. "I didn't see the bullet, Jonah. Did you?"

He shook his head. "You think it's still in there?"

"No, can't be. There's an exit wound."

"You gonna try that weird glue you used on me?" Zachary said, watching with interest.

"Probably. I need to debride the wounds first There are small pieces of material in there from his shirt."

He leaned forward squinting. "Looks like a small caliber wound," he told Jonah. "You're lucky she didn't use one of a higher caliber."

Jonah grunted. "Hurts like hell, though."

"I also wish we had an anesthetic," I said. "This is gonna hurt, Jonah."

"Do what you have to do then let me die," he moaned.

"Baby," I said, trying for levity.

"Men," Abbie said, joining in. "Can't stand pain of any sort."

Andrea laughed. "I'd like to see them go through the pain of childbirth."

"Okay, I get it," Jonah said, his voice weak. He closed his eyes. "Just get it over with."

It wasn't pleasant for him or me, but I finally had the entrance and exit wounds as clean as I thought I could get them. After dousing them with rubbing alcohol we found in Morganton, ignoring his muffled curses and screams, and treating his head and chest wounds with a calendula ointment Abbie and I had made, which would work well as an antibacterial and anti-inflammatory, I bandaged both, warning him to lie as still as possible. He ignored this, moving to the couch, issuing orders into the walkie-talkie and talking to those who came to see about him. Meredith had shared with us pain tabs she had found at an abandoned clinic in Morganton, but Jonah chose not to take them, claiming they'd make him sleepy and he wasn't ready to sleep just yet. When I urged him to go upstairs to his bedroom and lie down, he refused, insisting on resting on the couch. He wanted to wait for reports from his soldiers who were searching for evidence Jackson might have been on the mountain with Clancy.

I refused Abbie's efforts to treat my own injuries, telling her I'd sit up with Jonah that night in order to monitor his temperature. Although I didn't voice it, my greatest fear was that he'd develop an infection from the gunshot wound. He finally gave in and took a pain tab, and while he slept, I found myself watching him, thinking how much he resembled Josh but glad that he no longer reminded me of him. At one point, he opened his eyes and caught me staring at him. He tried to sit up, but I urged him back down, insisting he drink sugared water.

"I'm fine," he told me in a cranky tone.

It had become more than evident that he didn't like people fussing over him, but I told him that was too bad, he had me until he was out of danger. As I checked the bandages, I asked, "Are you hurting anywhere? Do you need me to get you anything?"

"I'm fine, Lizzie," he said in a harsher tone.

"Sure you are," I replied, giving him a sardonic smile.

He frowned at that, his gaze locking on mine, and I watched as his expression softened. He reached out, lightly touched the scrapes on the side of my neck. "You need to see to that."

"Abbie will later. It's fine for now, don't worry about it." I put my hand over his. "Thank you, Jonah. If you hadn't helped me, she would have pulled me off that cliff."

"I was terrified she would."

"Me too."

"I don't think I've ever been so scared in all my life."

"Me either, frankly." I couldn't stop the shudder that went through my body.

"I'll never be able to repay you for all you've done for me, protecting Andrea and her baby from the raiders, saving Zach's life, dealing with Clancy, keeping me from bleeding out. And they've all been my doing."

I put my fingertips on his lips. "Hush, now, you know that's not true. Besides, you saved my life. I think that's payment for anything you might owe, which you don't."

He looked at me for a long moment. When he spoke, his voice was soft, caring. "I promise, I'll always protect you, look after you, love you with all my being."

"And I you." When I realized what I said, I sat up straighter, stiffening.

He caught that and I could tell it hurt him. "You mean until you leave."

"Maybe. I don't know." I sighed, picking up his hand in mine. "It's just, it's so different, Jonah."

"Different than it was with him? I hope so."

"Josh and I were more similar, is what I'm saying. You and I, we clash, we don't always agree, we argue, we hurt one another."

"I think that's called passion, Lizzie."

I almost laughed at that. "Passion? I was thinking more along the lines of incompatibility."

He frowned. "You can tell yourself that but you know that's not what you think. When we're together, it's me you're with, right? Not him, not even in your head."

I shook my head.

"Or your heart."

I jerked my head up at that. "That's not fair."

"Maybe not, but I think you have this romanticized, idealistic version of Josh, and maybe he was like you say, but I'm not, I'll never be, that's not who I am. I'm not a romantic, I can't afford to be at this time in my life, and I can't offer you that. I'm pragmatic, a realist, someone who loves you more than I've ever loved anyone, but I'm me and I want you to see me, not him."

"I do, now." I looked into his eyes. "What you said when you were talking about how you feel, about being on fire. It's the same for me. This thing between us, it's … scorching. I'm afraid it will burn itself out one day and we'll be looking at one another, wondering what happened."

He smiled at me. "Or not."

I grudgingly smiled back. "Or not."

He put his hand on the back of my neck, drawing me close. "One thing I can promise you is I'll never leave you, never abandon you for someone else, something else, no matter what the reason, even if it's ignoble to do so."

We were leaning toward one another, our heads close together when the front door opened, startling me. I drew back away from him in a jerky motion. Abbie and Zachary stood there looking uncomfortable as if they knew they had interrupted something important.

"What'd you find?" Jonah asked, pushing himself up onto his elbows.

Zachary stepped into the room, speaking in a low voice. "I've checked with all the sentries, we've been all over the mountain, no one's seen anything or anyone out of the ordinary. She must have been alone. Jackson's not here."

Jonah nodded.

"We can keep lookin if you want," Abbie offered.

He shook his head. "If he's here, he's well-hidden and all we can do is wait."

"Then we'll wait," Zachary said, taking Abbie's hand and leading her into the kitchen.

I looked back at Jonah, who was watching me. "I'll get you some more water," I said, picking up his cup. The look he gave me sent a pang through my heart. Why do I keep hurting him, I wondered, as I followed Abbie and Zachary into the kitchen.

Chapter Fourteen

Spring 2055

Raise Your Hand

Jonah healed amazingly fast which I think was due more to his stubbornness about not letting anyone help him than anything else. I would sit with him at times while he rested, and in order to distract him from the pain of healing would ask about how his world had been before the asteroid strike hit the Midwest. Before, when I had inquired about his parents, he always told me they were dead and left it at that. Now, he talked about how they died at the hands of raiders in the early years of the chaos that followed the asteroid strike, leaving Jonah responsible for his sister and brother at an early age. Although his words about his parents' deaths were clipped and curt, I knew him well enough by now to see how much he still grieved them.

At his urging, I began to talk about both my lives, the one from the 20th century and the one from the 19th. He asked a lot of questions but never about Josh. Although I had given up on ever seeing Josh again, I was thankful for this. I didn't want to revisit old memories or feelings.

He told me a bit of the history of America from the time I left in 1969, about how America had pulled out of the Vietnam War after massive protests and failed promises, and its continual involvement in conflicts within the Middle East. He talked about the civil rights and feminist movements and how each affected our country and continued to be fought decades later, how the political system had become so corrupt through greed and the influence of special interests, how global warming had affected the world. Counterbalancing this, he told me more about the advance of medicine and technology before the asteroid strike.

The more we talked, the more I came to like this Jonah, who didn't feel the need to be so serious and stern and commanding, who had a sense of humor when he allowed his true self to show through. A man who loved his family and friends fiercely and would die for them, a man committed to keeping his people safe.

After Jonah recovered, we began to spend a lot of time together under the guise that I needed a bodyguard in case Jackson might still be on the mountain. I suspected the others knew the real truth, that we liked being with one another, but I wasn't ready to openly acknowledge that fact. Although Jackson hadn't been spotted on the mountain since he had kidnapped me, his words that he knew places to hide all over the mountain the others weren't aware of stayed with me. I felt safer with Jonah than anyone else and was grateful to have him beside me, both of us armed with more than one weapon and always alert. If Jackson came after me, I intended to stop him for good and knew Jonah felt the same.

My search for the Brown Mountain lights diminished considerably. I told myself it would be a waste of time and effort until my anniversary date in August but that wasn't the real reason. I was caught up in my relationship with Jonah, in the physical chemistry we shared between us. I knew I was in what my mother would have called the honeymoon phase and that this would eventually pass. At times, I wondered what our relationship would evolve into if I remained here. Would we develop a deep care and respect for one another or be at odds over even the least little thing as we had at first? It wouldn't have been that way with Josh, my inner voice would whisper, but I had learned by then to squelch that voice.

Time moved on, as it always does, but now it seemed to fly by, my days filled with treating my patients, gathering and compounding herbs, and going on long horseback rides with

Jonah when time allowed. My nights passed in a heated passion I shared with Jonah that I feared might consume me. Although I continued to vacillate between going back to the 20th century or remaining in the 21st, I found myself accepting this time more and more, and at times, usually while with Jonah, I would decide this was where I wanted to be. But away from him, the doubts would creep in and I would begin to wonder again where I should be, where I needed to be. But I had finally come to one decision, that as long as I was on the mountain, I might as well return to my old homestead, one I had loved dearly back in the 1800s. There were many repairs to be made, and between Jonah and me, we managed to tackle most with ease.

One night, alone at the cabin, Jonah pressed a small, ribbon-bound box in my hand. My heart began to hammer as I stared at it. As if sensing my anxiety, he put his hand over mine. "It isn't an engagement ring or anything," he growled.

I tried smiling at him but couldn't. "I—I didn't think it was."

He tilted his head at me.

"Okay, I wondered."

"Open it."

I untied the ribbon and opened the box. Inside lay a thin silver bracelet, the tiny links connected to an infinity symbol. "It's beautiful," I said, drawing it out and holding it up.

He smiled. "Belonged to my great-grandmother, given to her by my great-grandfather the weekend of Woodstock."

"Oh, Jonah, it's lovely." I put it on my wrist, admiring the dainty links of the chain, the silver infinity symbol. "I'll never take it off," I said, kissing him.

He pulled me to him roughly as he kissed back. "Don't," he whispered.

"What?"

"Don't say something you don't mean."

"I wouldn't. Not to you."

He drew back. "Even if you go back? You'll still wear it."

Oh, Jonah, why do you have to ruin the moment, I thought. "Even then," I said, not missing the sadness in his eyes. I knew I had disappointed him. When he turned from me, I caught his arm. "I don't think about it so much anymore,"

I said. "It's not as important to me now as it was. That's all I can give you right now."

He nodded.

"Is it enough?"

He stared at me for a long moment before saying, "For now."

As spring beckoned with a teasing hand toward summer, Jonah and I began to spend most nights at my cabin. I toyed with the idea of asking him to move in with me but could never decide. When Abbie pointed out he was actually already doing that, I strongly denied it although it was true. But I was glad he stayed. I wanted him there, wrapped in his arms when I would wake screaming, seeing Clancy climbing over that cliff edge, pulling me over with her.

When the weather turned and the nights warmed, I occasionally would accompany Jonah when he made his nightly rounds or would check in with the sentries on duty, telling myself I could look for the lights along the way. But I had lost my intense yearning to chase after them, so much so that most nights, I didn't think about them.

But that changed one evening as Jonah and I were returning home late from visiting Evelyn and her baby Chloe. We walked along slowly, holding hands, enjoying the weather and one another, speaking in low voices. The night was filled with the promise of summer and the sky had cleared enough that we could see a full moon hanging above, casting the earth below in creamy shades of ivory. I wasn't watching where I was going and tripped, falling to the ground, pulling him down with me. He laughed when he landed beside me, rolling me over on top of him. We wrestled with one another until our eyes met, then we were kissing. We did that a lot these days when we were alone.

"How far is it to my cabin?" I whispered.

"Not far."

"Let's go. Now," I said, giddy with anticipation.

He rose, pulled me up, and we began to run. We had just passed Sarie's old cabin when I saw a bright light up ahead. What the? I thought, stopping at once. Jonah tugged on my hand, trying to urge me forward with him, but I stayed still, dropping my hand from his. He turned and looked at me then followed my gaze.

He cursed under his breath. "Is it?"

I nodded. I couldn't speak as I watched the light move toward me as if it had honed in on me and was coming to meet me.

"Over there," Jonah said, pointing to the west.

I looked that way and there was another light coming straight for us.

"It's not been a year yet," I whispered. "I thought I'd have more time." My eyes met Jonah's. I could see pain, desperation, anger in his. I turned back, my gaze going back and forth between the two lights.

They arrived at the same time, and both hovered right in front of me, as if waiting for me to make my decision. I studied them for some time, Jonah quiet beside me. I nodded, saying to him without looking at him, "The one on the right is my light back to 1969, the one on the left will take me back to the 1800s, back to ..."

He didn't touch me, didn't reply, only stood there, waiting.

I glanced at him. "I don't know what to do."

"Stay," he said with such intensity my heart ached.

I realized with a sense of finality that what I chose would decide my fate for the rest of my life. To go back to my father, who had loved me and I knew must still grieve me if he were still alive, but who I doubted would believe I'd been traveling through time; to return to Josh, who I thought had been the love of my life but who now shared his life with another, one I dare not interrupt because of the love I now bore Jonah, Andrea, Zachary and Joseph; or to stay with Jonah, whom I felt more connected to than anyone, to face what lay ahead which could only be war and more hardship. It has to be more than that, my inner voice whispered. Decide where you'll be happy, where you'll do the most good.

I stepped toward the light from the 1800s, could feel it drawing me into it, but then my attention was drawn to the light from the 1900s. Without realizing what I was doing, my right hand rose and I reached toward both lights, one then the other, knowing the danger if I touched either one. When Jonah took my left hand, his own warm and solid, I looked back at him.

"Make sure, Lizzie, make sure what you want."

Grasping his hand, I turned back to the lights.

Coming Next:

Book 5 of the *Brown Mountain Lights* series, to be released in 2020. Did Lizzie choose to stay with Jonah or return to Josh in the 1800s or go back to her own time in the 20th century? And will her decision be one she will come to regret? We hope you'll continue to share Lizzie's journey as she seeks to find her place, purpose and time in the world.

Acknowledgements

We usually have a plethora of folks and resources to thank, but since we chose to take Lizzie into the future and not the past, thus eliminating the genre of historical fiction, that list has dwindled considerably. We do want to thank the following for their help in the production of this book:

Our brilliant book cover photographer and designer Kimberly Maxwell, for producing another beautiful cover.

Our beta reader Sherry Cannon for her "eagle eyes" in proofing the manuscript and offering much-appreciated feedback.

And a special thanks to our beloved readers, who (and we know we say this a lot but it is so true) are inspiring to us in so many ways. We can never express enough how much we truly appreciate you all and how blessed we are to share this journey with you.

About the Authors

CC Tillery is the pseudonym of two sisters, both authors, who came together to write the story of their great-aunt Bessie in the *Appalachian Journey* series, at the conclusion of which they continued writing Appalachian historical fiction with the *Brown Mountain Lights* series.

One C is for Cyndi Tillery Hodges, a multi-published, award-winning romance/fantasy author who writes under the name Caitlyn Hunter.

The other C is for Christy Tillery French, a multi-published, award-winning author whose books cross several genres.

To find out more about their work or for more information on their joint writings, please visit their website at https://cctillery.com or their page at Facebook: https://www.facebook.com/cctillery or contact them at cctillery@yahoo.com.

Books by CC Tillery:

Appalachian Journey series:

Whistling Woman
Moonfixer
Beloved Woman
Wise Woman

Brown Mountain Lights series:

Through the Brown Mountain Lights
Seeking the Brown Mountain Lights
Into the Brown Mountain Lights
Chasing the Brown Mountain Lights